Never Yours

S Hall-Wood

For my patient family

(Trigger warnings are in the Author notes for those that might need them.)

Copyright © 2024 S Hall-Wood

All rights reserved.

ISBN:
ISBN-13: 9798344430782

CHAPTER ONE
Lily of the Valley

The Morning Post, May 21st 1845: Is the declining morality of our fashionable circles to blame? London's elegant homes were thrown into a state of the utmost excitement with the sudden disappearance of a young lady from beneath the roof of her guardian, who resides in the most aristocratic part of the beautiful city of our sovereign.

I stuffed the torn article back into my beaded reticule and huddled closer to my sister, Harriette as grey swirls left a cold, damp layer on my skin.

Fellow debutante and friend, Sybil Parker, was the young lady whose morals the paper had questioned. The article had cast a shadow over what should have been a highlight of the evening, and her crowning glory. Her engagement was to be announced. Yet the ball was about to proceed without her. The unseasonable gloom of the weather soured the night further, as we waited, shivering.

"Jane, stop slouching." My mother tapped her toes on the pavement. "You will see. There is still a chance to save the season."

"Should we really be dancing when Sybil is missing?" I asked.

"Sybil would want you to enjoy yourself." She paused as if unsure whether to continue. "She has brought enough shame already. I see no need to delay your marriage opportunities further."

"We don't know what happened to her."

My mother tutted. "My girl, I have seen enough young ladies make foolish decisions in my time to know an elopement when I see one."

"But the article said there were drops of blood in her room, and what about Charlotte last season?"

Harriette squeezed my arm in warning.

"That's enough." My mother snapped. "We have our own family to think of. These girls should know better, and I won't talk about them any longer." She stamped her feet louder. "Where has that carriage got to?"

A breeze filtered through the crescent and the street lights cast an eerie glow. As the shadows of the park shifted, the bushes grew teeth and glowing eyes one moment and soft leaves the next. A figure stepped forward into the light and as his tall hat tilted, I caught his eye. He focused his glare as he studied me. He spread his legs and planted his feet before he charged. His steps grew louder as he picked up the pace, and the movement caused his long coat to spread like wings behind him. His mouth widened to reveal a grin full of sharp white teeth.

As I took a panicked breath and reached for my mother, our carriage pulled in front of us, cutting the man off from his quarry. My father emerged from the front door, his head haloed in light from the arc of glass panes.

"Jane, you're white as a sheet. Let's get you in the carriage." He pulled on the leather handle, and the door swung open.

"Did you see him?" I addressed everyone as I climbed in, my eyebrows knitted together.

"Who?" my father questioned.

"Harriette, you must have seen him," I said, pointing out of the carriage window to where the man stood.

As swiftly as he had arrived, he turned to approach a couple who had appeared through the gloom. The lady's red shoes were a pinpoint of colour in the swirling grey fog. A glint of silver caught my eye. The aggressor's jacket had a small representation of a female with bird wings pinned to it. The couple drew near, and the lady clutched her black cloak tighter across her chest. Her husband straightened his back, drawing himself up to full height. With linked arms, they took a wide arc around the intimidating obstacle.

Fog rode the tide up the Thames, making ghost ships of the carriages that hurried their passengers home. Figures appeared in the lamplight of the crescent as our carriage moved down the street. Their clammy skin in an orange gaslight glow as they promised paradise for the cost of a meal. The further into the square mile you travelled, the more it comes alive by moonlight, wages spent, gambled, or stolen. Yet even here, on the respectable fringes, existed an undercurrent pursuant of their business.

I retreated into the safety of the dark interior of the coach as it lurched forward. I lost sight of the man, and the couple walked on, so I settled back into the warm hug of the carriage. One of the two downy ostrich feathers in my hair came loose and brushed against my cheek. Safe with my family, I stifled a giggle as a thought occurred to me. Being introduced to society was like being a duck. All graceful curves and so many feathers on top, paddling for all your worth against the current.

I reached up and adjusted the feather while considering the many rules to follow. Watch your manners. Refrain from showing who you are more fond of or dancing too much with one person. Back straight. Shoulders back. Mouth closed. All the while yearning to be the belle of the ball.

To be noticed by the most eligible gentlemen is a challenging task for anyone. My desire to be with someone my age bubbled under the surface of all the conversations with my mother. Someone with whom I could share the adventure of marriage. At eighteen, I had few choices in life, but I had made this one wish very clear to my mother. I had impressed on her the importance of this detail.

The carriage jolted me from my musings. We alighted in front of a grand townhouse in Belgravia. As we entered the ball, I waved my fan in front of my face as my mouth stretched wide in a yawn. My mother let her arm slip from my father's as she veered off toward a group of whispering friends.

I walked beside my father, his back straight and head held high. His dark hair was cut short, and his black moustache tickled at the corners of his mouth. Every day, he wore a double-breasted waistcoat with his watch chain strung across the front, and a starched white shirt was beneath. Today, he also had on his frock coat with medals pinned to his chest. They replaced the usual leather bag and the familiar clink of bottles and stethoscopes.

I watched as he caught sight of my mother, and his gaze followed her journey. Her dress had so many ruffles it could have been mistaken for the cake which graced the table behind her. It even had the same delicate pink shade. A mother-of-pearl comb held back her red waves of hair. She came towards us and smiled a soft, patient smile. Looking at her brought the memory of her warm arms wrapped around me in a hug. Her face now rounded along with her body, the weight of children having changed her forever.

"Back in a moment, my dear." She clutched my father's hand before she disappeared amongst the ladies. My mother and the other ladies appeared as if they were floating, gliding around the room, their feet hidden beneath long dresses.

Then, crowds of gentlemen joined them. A sea of black ebbed in and out between the frothing ruffles and ivory skirts. They gathered in the middle of a rainbow of married couples. It made me quite dizzy.

Circling the ballroom were the sharks. The older, greying gentlemen were often looking for second wives after the first had died.

The gossips' huddled to discuss the case of one poor woman. Her husband had committed her to an asylum. I lingered close enough to overhear their conversation. They left out no detail. Hushed tones fell as they spoke of the shrieking and wailing. The alienist and his assistants had dragged her from her home as she protested her sanity.

They tutted and whispered, "All for the want of a new wife."

As I passed, they stopped their conversation and turned to watch me. My cheeks grew pink as their eyes bored into me. I wondered if perhaps I had forgotten part of my outfit and checked my reflection in the glass of a picture frame as I passed. Dropping my eyes from theirs to the ground, I continued on.

The room shone, its polished parquet floor reflecting the light of chandeliers, which hung in painted heavens. The plaster work framed murals of cherubs, dainty among fluffy white clouds. They threatened to pierce our hearts with tiny arrows, and a clear blue sky promised a future free of worries. A long table appeared between the bodies, heavy with food and tall glasses of blood-red wine.

I blended in with the other debutantes with black ribbon details on my cuffs. I only stood out because of my red hair piled high, revealing my long neck, decorated with only a black ribbon choker. My fair skin showed further as my dress straps sat on my arms, exposing my shoulders and the curve of my breasts. Whale bone strapping held me fast from there to my hips. The effect combined demure innocence with a subtle suggestion of what was reserved for a husband's eyes only.

The hand of my eldest sister guided me through the throng. Harriette had taken it upon herself to be my chaperone in the world of courtship. She separated and distracted the unsuitable, while allowing the acceptable gentlemen to fill my dance card.

Across the room and above the nodding heads, a man approached. His head appeared above the small crowd that surrounded us. He strode over, full of confidence, his arm knocked into Harriette, hard enough to send her spinning out of his path and into the arms of an older gentleman. I watched as the other gentleman steadied her and then waltzed her around the room. This caused a ripple of whispered disapproval, which soon dissipated. The gathered guests did not want to insult their host.

The stranger looked down at me. Dark hair flopped across his right eye as he bent his head towards me. No longer gangly or held back by the nerves of youth, his skin was clear, and he sported a clean, practised shave. He appeared to be older than would have been my choice.

"James," he announced, "James Bell. I believe you have been introduced to my mother." He gestured towards the stern-looking grey-haired lady who appeared at his side.

She nodded towards me, and her tiara glinted in the

candlelight. I recognised her from earlier that week, at tea. What had once been blonde curls were pinned tight to her head, with a hat, decorated with black plumes, balanced on top. Her eyes struck me. Turned down at the corners, with lines that continued to her high cheekbones, etched in time. Her mouth, with lips pursed, thin and pale, did the same, as if she hadn't smiled in years. I gave a small curtsy in her direction, but did not speak.

James continued, "This is my brother's house." Seeming to forget his manners entirely, he pointed at the gentlemen with a firm hold of my sister. "We are hosting the finest and most talked about ball of the season. How do you like it?"

A hush had fallen on the room and I felt all eyes upon us. I opened my mouth to answer, but he interrupted me before I could speak.

"Our parents have agreed to a match and the wedding plans are being completed. You will honour the dance requests already on your card. After tonight, your dance card will be mine only." He saw the puzzled look on my face and finished, "We must get to know each other after all." His tone grew lighter now, but his smile remained empty, and his eyes gave no hint of fondness.

"I thought you were engaged to Sybil. Shouldn't we wait to see if she comes home?" I said.

His face blanched, and he turned sharply and left. Although I imagined I caught glimpses of him through the crowd, I didn't speak to him for the rest of the evening.

Unable to find Harriette, I hurried through the throng towards my mother. Catching her arm as she stepped towards a huddle of women, I swiftly placed myself between her and the group.

"Mother, what have you done?"

"Keep your voice down," she said through gritted teeth,

all the while keeping a smile plastered across her face.

"But you promised me to him. Why? He's nothing like I imagined, and so soon after Sybil's disappearance. It's not right." I dropped my hand from her arm and checked around us for anyone who might have overheard.

"I will not talk about this here." She deftly stepped around me, keeping up the appearance of a jovial conversation before joining the group of women.

I caught the attention of Mary, who had been my friend for as long as I could remember. Our fathers' estates backed onto each other. We met riding one summer's day and have met every day since, rain or shine.

We escaped Harriette's gaze as she extracted herself from her dance partner. Harriette pushed through the women, making her way towards my mother. Her face creased, and her march was determined.

"There's going to be trouble," I told my mousy-haired friend as we found a corner to discuss my news.

Shoulder to shoulder, we squeezed behind some long curtains, finding a larger space than expected. The thick damask material muffled the conversation. The cool air from the window behind wafted through, a relief as we sat on the window seat.

"What's happened?" Mary said, seeing my worried expression.

"See that man?" I peeked past the curtain, pointing out James. "Oh, Mary, I didn't think it would all go so fast. It appears we are to be wed." A tear glistened at the corner of my eye.

"Jane, you are lucky. I haven't found anyone yet. Isn't that James Bell?" she reassured me, rubbing my arm.

"Yes, although I had not talked to him until a few moments ago."

"Did you know Sybil Parker was meant to marry him? She had her eye on him forever." She clasped her hands over her mouth. "Did you see the paper this morning?"

"My mother has been trying to convince me she ran off with some ne'er-do-well. I'm not convinced," I rubbed at my wrist and sighed. "James isn't exactly what I had hoped for. The scandal of it." My shoulders were low, and I held my arms across my stomach.

"He won't inherit the houses. His older brother is indeed in line for those, but he will have an income," she added in the futile hope that it would buoy my mood.

I gave a small shrug of my shoulders. "I suppose that's one thing. At least I can stay at Wendsom Hall. Isn't he a little old to not be married yet?"

"He has been travelling and working for the family business, I believe. Come on, I promised to dance with Lord Hill." Her nose wrinkled in disgust.

We discussed each dance partner's merits and less desirable qualities. I caught her making faces over the shoulder of a grey-haired man, and I did the same. Discreetly poking tongues out. I grimaced at the musty smell of one gentleman's jacket. By the time the dance reached the halfway point, it was all we could do to keep from falling about laughing. We huddled in the dark corner once more with drinks in hand, gossiping, when a shape moved into view. Realising we hadn't pulled the curtain shut, we sank back further. We feared being caught at any moment, as our cheeks were now pink from exertion and the contraband wine.

A gentleman joined the first, his hair cut short as fashion dictated. His clothes were not familiar; the silks of his coat were ornate and decorated with delicate patterns of coiled creatures mixed between flowers. I did not recognise them from any materials we had seen in the many dress shops we had visited. Then the first shape stepped further into view, tall with broad shoulders and pale as a ghost. His long dark hair was tied back and still it reached the middle of his back. A silver pin on his lapel, the figure of a woman with arms outstretched and bird wings extended from her back, owls at her feet, caught the candlelight as he turned to his companion.

They were deep in conversation, but I couldn't make it out. I shuffled forward as quietly as possible, hiding behind the curtain. I leaned close to listen, and the warm, earthy scent of musk and floral jasmine filled the air.

"Luther, I told you it's in hand." The second shape addressed the first.

"It's hard to believe I haven't seen you in a hundred years. Your letters do not fill me with confidence." Luther folded his arms across his chest as he observed the room before them.

"Don't exaggerate. It can't be more than ninety." The man shifted from one foot to the other.

"Your sense of time never was much good, Chen. Your head is always buried in your work. Do you even recall what century we are in?"

The second man continued, dismissing Luther's joke at his expense with a wave of his hand. "The twins were sent. It won't be a problem any longer."

"Not an end I would like to meet. Having them as the mistress of your fate. I shudder to think." Luther made a shuddering move under his long coat.

"Sabrett found them, didn't he?" Chen asked.

"I believe so. In a cave high in the mountains of Greece. The girl didn't even know what was happening," Luther chuckled. "I believe he is back in London, although I haven't seen him yet."

"I don't understand why Zane imagined he could get away with it," Chen replied.

"He always was a pompous ass," Luther laughed, and as he did, a glint of light flashed across brilliant white teeth.

I slowed my breathing, aware of how one slip would mean being discovered, one mistake, and they would hear me. My heartbeat thumped hard in my chest.

"But to try to be the embodiment of a prophecy, that's just crazy," Chen shook his head.

"He sired too many and lost his wits. He must have imagined he could also sire a dhampir," Luther shrugged.

"Now, with your permission, can I continue my work? I have heard of another witch, a sun holder not far from here." Chen brushed at his clothing, removing some invisible lint. He paused for a moment, taking in the room before him. "What are you doing here, anyway? It seems like an unlikely place to meet."

"There are rumours the Egyptians are planning a rendezvous close by. I thought I would grab a snack on my way to inform them of this new threat." Both men laughed, and with that, they departed.

Mary gasped, taking deep breaths in, filling her lungs once more. "Jane, what were you thinking?"

"You know me, nosy," I said, tapping the fleshy protrusion. I shivered, feeling a sudden chill.

"I hope it was worth it," she replied.

Extraditing ourselves from our hiding place, we made our way back to our families as they made ready to leave. Our parents stood together, discussing my news. Harriette had her back to my mother, and my mother had a huge grin spread across her face. She looked far too pleased with herself.

As we waited for our carriage, a black buggy, pulled by a single black mare drew up in front of us. The tall, dark-haired gentleman brushed past me and climbed in. Close behind him trailed a young lady. She drifted up the stairs as if in a dream.

He closed the door, pushing the folds of her ivory dress further into the gloom. Catching my eyes on him, he bowed his head towards me, smiling. The hairs on the back of my neck stood on end, and a shiver ran through me. Two points of white shone against the red of his lips and the silver of his pin. These were the only points of reference as he disappeared into the dark of the carriage.

I caught up with my mother at lunch the next day, determined to confront her on her choice of husband. I flung the door open and marched up to her. She did not take her eyes from the letter she held, although her eyelids flickered as I grew near. She locked her feet around the legs of her chair.

"Why did you choose him? And without asking me." I rubbed at the hollow at the bottom of my neck.

"Jane, I'm very busy. We can talk later!" She closed her eyes for a moment.

"Busy. Too busy to discuss my future husband with me?" I huffed.

"Don't be dramatic. He has a good income, and his family is very well-connected. I'm surprised. You should be thanking me." She sat up straight and placed the letter on the table.

"He's rude and arrogant. Look how he treated Harriette. Not to mention already being engaged to Sybil," I replied, placing my hands on my hips.

"Harriette had quite enough to say for herself. You do not need to speak on her behalf. Sybil has only herself to blame as you well know." She had turned her body to me, but her feet remained wrapped around the chair legs.

"The scandal. Mother it's too soon, everyone was whispering. I don't want to marry him. He's too old," I whined as if I were a child once more and not getting the pet I wanted.

"I suppose it is best that I die first. If your father were to go, bless his soul, I would not know what to do or where I would live. Would you have me left to the mercy of some stranger?" My mother fretted.

And with that one speech, she put an end to the conversation and any say I had in my marriage.

Harriette would be leaving to rejoin her husband soon, and I was the youngest of seven sisters, all of whom had estates of their own to manage. My father would be forced to leave Wendsom Hall to some distant cousin if I could not find a husband to take it on. Otherwise, my future, and that of all who lived and worked there, was uncertain. I could not rely on a cousin to care for my well-being. In all likelihood, the estate would be sold, putting many good people out of work.

My shoulders slumped under the weight of duty, and my stomach tied itself in knots thinking about it. As my stomach churned, I was unable to contemplate eating, instead I returned to my room.

The season felt like an age and I longed to return to the country. The sights and sounds of the city were intoxicating but overwhelming. I had always been more at home amongst the fields and woodland of my youth. Apart from the endless dances, there remained very little to hold my interest. I had a privileged life with tutors and the freedom of our country estate. I spent many happy days in the long grass, devouring books, or the walled gardens, chasing butterflies. But lessons also interrupted my days, drawn out instructions on being the perfect wife and hosting the perfect gatherings. These lessons held no interest to me.

The city house represented the end of childhood. Some short excursions for shopping were the only other reason we ever came here. The house was kept for fathers business and our entry into society. Here, there were no such diversions; most days were spent lounging and eating cake. Our only other distraction was shopping for dresses. That afternoon, we had an appointment with a dressmaker in the city, intending to find gowns for the night's theatre visit.

The carriage moved through the busy streets, bumping along the cobbled roads until we came to a stop.

"That's as far as I can go," the coachman shouted, as the horses' hooves pawed at the stones below.

"What is happening? We haven't reached our destination yet," my mother shouted, still seated inside the carriage. Her head poked through the window, looking up at the driver.

"The street is blocked. I can't see from here, but I can go no further. Alight here, Madame!"

My mother huffed, and we stepped out onto the pavement. She brushed her skirts down and begrudgingly handed the coachman some coins.

"Come, girls. We are losing the light, and Madame Whitacker only had this one appointment left." She glared at the coachman before striding forward.

In truth, it was a matter of minutes before we arrived, but with each step, my mother grew more agitated. Harriette took her arm. They were talking among themselves when a peeler stepped in front of them, holding his hand aloft.

"That's as far as you go, ladies!" The constable stood, legs splayed and shoulders back.

"Oh Jane, what is the meaning of this?" My mother

refused to look at the man.

His tall hat, with its shiny silver badge, did nothing to impress his authority on her.

"Sorry, Sir. What might the trouble be?" I asked, stepping around my mother and sister to better understand.

"I'm sorry, Madame, but no one can proceed." He nodded in greeting, which made the hat wobble unsteadily on his head.

His accent had an Irish lilt, but from what county I could not say. My experiences were limited. I had never travelled beyond London, which lay only a days train journey from our estate. I had only heard the accent amongst the bustle of the city streets, but it was nevertheless recognisable.

"Surely you could let us through. We only have to reach that very shop." I gestured to a small building with large bay windows that curved out onto the pavement.

"There's been a murder," was his whispered reply.

Harriette gasped and put her gloved hand over her mouth, while my mother suddenly decided the man was worth her time.

"What do you mean? Who?" she said, spinning around to face him.

"I shouldn't be telling you this, but I wouldn't want you young ladies out alone in the city on a night such as this. A man and his wife were found in an alley, just over there." He nodded in the direction of the dress shop we were due at.

I peered in the direction of the shop and a small crowd of peelers had gathered at the gap between the buildings.

"What do you mean … found?" My mother's voice trembled.

"White as sheets they are, slumped on the ground, still holding hands. Terrible sight, I tell you." He leaned in towards us. "It makes you wonder why the husband did not protect his wife." Leaning back again, he continued, "Apologies, but no one will be going any further today."

The crowd parted briefly, and I caught a glimpse of a lady's foot in the lamplight, her red shoe half hanging from her toes. Her long black cloak lay in pools around her.

"I think I've seen her before," I mumbled under my breath, remembering the couple from the previous night. "Harriette, I— "

We turned to leave, and I only took a few steps before colliding straight into a gentleman's shoulder. The strength of the man sent me crashing against the window of a baker's shop.

The glass shuddered, and a loaf fell from its perch, dropping onto the sill below. The man turned briefly, but enough for me to take in his long grey jacket and a silver pin attached to the lapel. It caught my attention because of its strange figure, the very same from the evening before.

"Oi you, watch where you're going!" The peeler shouted at the man.

The stranger's blond hair covered his face. He did not stop to check if I was harmed. Instead, he headed straight for the peelers.

"Are you alright, Jane?" Harriette fussed.

"A little bruised pride, that is all." I looked for the man again. He and the peeler were turning the corner and vanished into the alley.

On our return to our city home, we went straight up to change for the night's entertainment. My head ached after every ball, and I was tired of being paraded like a prize cow. I straightened the plumes that stuck out from my hair. Turning to the side, my hands on my stomach, breathing in, I tried my hardest to look slimmer. Tonight's excursion took us to the theatre, where we would meet Mary and her family, minus new dresses. We were safe at least from the killer loose in the city.

A theatre trip meant no less pomp and ceremony, for we would see and be seen once again. I couldn't help but compare myself to all the other girls. The corsets pulled their tiny waists even smaller. My friend Mary grew so slim we had joked that she might disappear if she turned to the side. But as Harris girls, my sisters and I were born with fiery hair, temper, and a body to back it up. My breasts, I was convinced, might be my saving grace; pushed up by ball gowns, they helped to take away from my hips.

"Childbearing hips," my mother chided from the door. "Believe me, my darling, the mothers will all be on the lookout for women who have the hips to bear children. We all have the same; why do you think your sisters all found such good matches?" She had walked into the room and caught my grimace as I examined myself.

I guessed she decided it was best to try to repair some of the damage from last night's catastrophe. She had proved that childbearing hips were a family trait, as had my aunts. They had such large broods that we found meeting in the same place difficult.

Our carriage had arrived and my father's voice grew loud, demanding we all attend him. We were ushered out into the dark streets. Not hesitating too long in the gloom, the shadows had no chance to make their move tonight. We went straight from the door into the safety of the horse-drawn transport, the curtains pulled tight against the creatures beyond. The newspapers on my father's breakfast table this morning had shouted the news of the murder in the city. He had taken special care tonight to ensure no risks would be taken.

Our theatre box sat close to the stage, where Mary and I leaned on the cushioned side, our heads on our hands. We watched the actresses in all their glamour. The sweet scent of Mary's corsage of nodding white bells drifted up into my nostrils.

The actors and actresses had it all. Their admirers waited at the theatre door, hoping to catch sight of their favourites. They were their own masters and mistresses, earning a wage they could spend as they wished.

Seeing my adoration, my mother leaned forward, taking the opportunity to extol the virtues of marriage as the way a true lady could be free.

"A husband will provide you with everything you could wish for. Look how much they have to expose themselves to get the attention of other ladies' husbands. You will have James' love with none of this indecency."

I trusted her. My parents' example was a happy one. At least once married, I could become the country squire's wife, with children at my knee, just like my mother before me. We had such happy times, and my father doted on her. Now older, that's all any of us wanted for ourselves. As I watched, a calm settled over me, and I glowed, a pure white aura floating up around me.

Our box appeared illuminated, and in the audience below, heads began to turn. They searched for the source of the light. A warm feeling built in the pit of my stomach. My whole future was opening up before me. I sat up abruptly, as the cushion I rested my hand and head on started to smoulder. Tiny red embers and a thin line of smoke drifted towards me. The velvet singed at its edges. The smell of the hair stuffing filled my nostrils, extinguishing the floral scent. My legs stung, even through the thick skirts. My mother's palm found its target, shaking me from my reverie and snuffing out the light and embers along with it.

CHAPTER TWO
Lavender

My future mother-in-law stood before me, clutching a black box with an engraved gilt border. She presented me with the container, holding on to it a little longer than necessary. I opened the lid; its hinges creaked stiff and resistant against my fingers.

Within lay a silver tiara that glinted with sapphires in the June morning light. The jewels were made more eye-catching by the black velvet lining, on which it sat.

"My husband's mother handed it down." Her hands still raised, and her elbows pinned to her side as if she would take it back at any moment. "It's tradition for all Bell brides to wear it."

"Thank you." I beamed, desperate to use this to connect with her. It slipped neatly into place over the white lace veil and train. "How do you think it looks?" I said turning from side to side.

"It looks fragile. I remember presenting it to Eliza, James' brothers' wife, at their wedding. She looked beautiful." For a moment her stern expression changed. It revealed another personality below the mask. Then as if remembering herself, the wistful expression returned to its hard stare. "Take care not to let it slip. I will collect it after the ceremony." Her black skirts rustled as she walked down the corridor.

I joined my six bridesmaids, all wearing white veils with flower crowns. Gypsophila softened the frame of their faces. The noise of their laughter and chatter filled the room as they discussed the day to come and told tales of their weddings. As sisters, we had our rivalries, jealousy, and childhood memories. But this was set aside, as adults, we could be easier with each other.

Every lady in the room had one feature, the same as the rest. It stood out to anyone who had met us. We all had long auburn hair with a slight curl. Our father had questioned it many times, commenting that not one of us had inherited his dark hair. My mother would laugh, saying he was aware when they married. This was how it would be.

Her family always had large broods, all sporting wild red hair. She was the seventh child of all girls, although not all the sisters had survived until adulthood. Mother had put the hair colour down to some rumoured and distant Scottish ancestry. Now with seven children of her own her red hair was fading to grey.

A new understanding had formed between us sisters as women with our own lives. There no longer existed the pressure for Harriette to lead the way. Her responsibility of being the first to marry was now complete. She had married at sixteen, to make way for the rest of us. With children of her own and a devoted husband, she was relaxed and amiable. Harriette's little girls ran around the room. Their coloured sashes flicked the air behind them.

Elizabeth, the second oldest, was bossy and stern; she

had taken it upon herself to keep us all in line. Often, we feared her punishment more than our parents. I empathised with her little ones.

"Elizabeth," Harriette called, gesturing to a small boy in the centre of the room. "You have a future zoologist on your hands, I see."

Elizabeth and Sarah's sons played on the rug with frogs captured in the garden. The green-skinned creatures used their long legs to escape the clutches of the boys. The gentle hands recapture and return them to the rug.

"I blame Sarah entirely. Ralph is a bad influence on Edward," Elizabeth complained.

Ralph's blonde hair and Edwards's brown hair looked out of place, each favouring their father. And so, the family eagerly awaited the arrival of daughters for the two women, placing bets on hair colour. Speculation grew rife on whether they would be the ones to break the cycle.

Sarah was quiet and had been in no hurry to get married, to the great annoyance of Alice. But once she did, she found a good match.

Alice, the prettiest of us all. Everyone knew she would never struggle to find a suitor, and the many proposals had come thick and fast. She had dreamt of her wedding since we were children.

Her favourite game had included turning our meadow into a makeshift church aisle. The wildflowers, both her bouquet and the guests. At the centre, the giant oak tree is a stand-in clergyman and her husband, the favourite toy or pet of the day. She would dance all the way home and pester our mother for stories of their wedding day. Everyone loved Alice.

Margaret had always been sickly and pale, even now, a ghost of a girl made worse by being heavily pregnant. She was supported by Elizabeth, who had always been her best friend and remained so.

We had lost Clara the year before. She had taken to her sickbed and never emerged. My mother had worn black right up until my coming out. It should have been her season, not mine and I felt her loss even now.

I was the youngest and last to marry. A surprise child. Later in years than my mother would have liked. The pregnancy and my birth had been hard on her.

All at once, in a flurry of lace and silk, the time came to leave for the little chapel at the edge of the village. We would walk the gravel drive that led from the house to the austere building. Our low heels crunched through the stones. White chrysanthemums, white roses and Gypsophila bounced as I clutched the bouquet.

"Don't sulk, Jane; the flowers are beautiful." Elizabeth strode past.

"I wasn't sulking, I objected.

"Ignore her; she's had a long journey, that's all. She's tired," Elizabeth's husband consoled me as he went to join her.

The flowers were not my preferred choice, chosen by my family they spoke of purity, innocence, virtue and chastity. They had all agreed this was a suitable message to send on your wedding day.

I would have preferred yellow carnations, yarrow and lilies. My family made it clear to me that, with a message of disdain, magic, fertility and death, my choices were not appropriate. The language of flowers was a complicated one.

The little grey flint chapel dated back to the first house that had stood on these grounds.

We had recently built ours after the first one had crumbled beyond recognition. My father's money had saved the estate, adding to the footprint of the first house. He also added the glasshouses and orangery, which sparkled in the sunlight.

He had employed Duncan Tucker of Tottenham, as all the big houses had done. But he had commissioned a special design for our hot house. It provided pineapples and all sorts of amazing produce. Some of which would grace the wedding meal.

My grandparents had long since passed and lay at rest in the chapel grounds. Next to their grave lay my grandmother's parents. As I approached, I could see their headstones peaking above the long grasses. Wild daisies waved in the summer breeze. Some of the wedding flowers were placed on top of each one of the lichen-covered grey stones. This only served to make the flowers' white seem brighter.

The Chapel had no steeple, unlike those grand city buildings. It was considerably smaller. However, there was a bell tower, and the pealing bell rang out, echoing against the trees behind.

The rest of the wedding party gathered at the front of the building. My mother and father stood on one side of the gate with smiles plastered across their faces.

A tear fell on my father's cheek. He brushed it aside and straightened his shirt so as not to seem affected by the affair. My heart quickened when my mother held her handkerchief over her mouth, trying to cover a gasp. I hoped of pride and not relief at her last child marrying.

My husband-to-be and his best man looked resplendent in claret frock coats. Matching grey striped trousers and black top hats finished the look. His parents stood behind him, and neither smiled. Their arms were locked at their sides, and their faces tensed as I approached. The intimidating sight made me stumble.

His mother's visage was made all the more severe by the black dress pinned tight at the collar by a diamond brooch. Anyone passing might mistake his family for a funeral party. The two groups stood on either side of the gate as different as night and day.

It was the first time I was conscious of my nerves about the wedding. My heart fluttered in my chest as the implications dawned on me. Our giggling, chattering group stopped at the gates. James reached forward, his lips pursed; he clasped my wrists and held me there.

My smile faded, and my hands shook as he gazed at me from my toes to the tiara in my hair. His gaze lingered, and I grew increasingly aware of all eyes upon me. Finally, his mouth turned up a fraction at the corners as if I had passed some test. He proceeded forward, taking me with him.

We moved through the tall, arched wooden door into the stone porch. Goosebumps appeared on my bare arms. The many candles released a sweet beeswax scent that joined the musty, cool air. It was as though the warmth of the summer sun could not penetrate these walls.

The high ceiling and hard pews had never held much sway over me. I looked longingly through the windows each time I visited. My whole body was itching to get out into the wilds again. I could feel it now. My bones were wrong, uncomfortable, almost writhing inside my skin.

I continued half on tiptoes as James, standing a whole foot taller than me, kept my arm in his. That confident stride was once more evident, as if he was unaware of the height difference.

I hadn't studied him as much as I should have. I'm not sure I would have recognised him if he had passed me in the street. He had a handsome face with the kind of chiselled jaw

I'm sure was attractive to most girls. His nose was neither crooked nor large. But he seemed to lack something. I didn't feel like I should swoon or be repulsed. I suppose that was in itself a good thing.

The old clergyman was the same man who baptised me. Grey and stooped, he stood, his weight half supported by his fingers. The knuckles were white as his digits tightly clutch the altar.

His short white hair was flecked with black, a remnant of the younger man. It had a wave that made it look as though it swooped back behind his ears. His long beard was the same colour. Bushy and parted in the middle like it had grown out from his moustache around his lips. His bushy eyebrows were out of control above the kind face. His robes were long and white with sleeves that billowed out. He wore a long black stole around his neck that hung to his knees, decorated with a simple silver cross on each side.

"We are gathered here today to celebrate this holy union," He began.

I must admit to letting my attention wander, therefore I cannot say what was said. When it came my turn to speak, a sharp pain squeezed in my side. Upon seeing my glazed expression Harriette, who stood behind me, had pinched my skin through the silk dress. How she found it through all the corsets, I will never know. Stifling the exclamation of pain and blushing, I spoke the words.

Thinking my flushed cheeks were because of him, James grinned in a way I thought was a little smug. Showing my distaste at his presumption, my face contorted in anger. This all but made him fall about laughing. The hairs on the back of my neck stood on end. Mocked as if I were a child once more and some village bully had imagined me weak.

The anger built in the pit of my stomach. My skin

prickled beneath the surface like a thousand nettles had stung me. The prickling tingle feeling built to an unbearable crescendo. As I feared I could bear it no more, the room faded.

The image of the Chapel disappeared in a mist, and my knees gave way. I grabbed at the altar for support. The stone was cold as ice on my skin, my fingers pressed hard against it. A hot flash swept across the stone. My fingers slipped from the surface as it grew too hot to touch, and I fell to the floor.

Harriette reached out and stepped forward as I tumbled backwards. At that exact moment, the clergyman pulled both his hands away from the altar, staring at them. As I fell, his eyes lifted to mine in accusation, and then he dropped to his knees.

When my eyes opened, the room spun, and a sharp pain arced across the back of my head. My hand went to the spot. Gently feeling where the pain originated I found a wet patch of hair. Bringing my fingers forward again to look at them I saw the fresh red blood that covered them. James stood over me. He looked down at me whilst his parents stood at his side comforting him in lowered tones.

"An omen. I told your mother you should not marry her," his father whispered close to his ear, but he let it be loud enough for me to hear.

My mother helped me to my feet, and I heard a commotion from the other side of the altar. Turning towards the sound, I caught sight of my father pushing on the chest of the clergyman. A sickening cracking sound, like dry twigs, reverberated around the walls. His hands pushed against the old man's ribs. His movements were violent and shocking as he brought the old man back to this world and away from his maker.

My sisters huddled in a corner, whispering words I could

not hear. At the sound of the crack, Elizabeth ran from the room. I reached for James' hand, looking for answers from my new husband, but found only air. He turned and made his way to the door.

My mother's voice cut across my disappointment. "He will grow to love you, my sweet. Who could resist such a girl?"

"Mother, what happened?" My legs shook beneath my dress.

"No one is sure, but it seems you fainted. Rector Baker, it appears, has had a heart attack. It is good for him that your father is here. Goodness knows what would happen if one of the village doctors got to him." She took my face in her hands, looking concerned. "You should rest. It's fortunate at least that he pronounced you man and wife before collapsing."

I wasn't convinced, my new husband seemed unconcerned about my state. I steadied myself, and my mother helped me sit on a wooden pew. I tried to reconcile what had occurred.

"I remembered feeling angry, and I had let that consume me. Then everything went black." I held my hands up to look at them; they quivered.

She lifted her hand to feel my head. "Well, no wonder you're burning up. Come, let's get you some air."

We found the bench in the vestibule and rested for a while. My father appeared; the rector's arm was over his shoulders. Harriette's husband stood on the other side, helping support him.

"We will help the rector home," my father said. "I have sent for Dr Long."

"Will he be alright?" I asked.

"The old man's heart was fragile. The shock of seeing your fall must have triggered his attack." He looked at me, his face full of concern. "How are you feeling now?"

"I will be fine, father. My head and pride hurt, that's all." I rubbed at my arm.

Something niggled at the edge of my mind, but my head thumped too much to entertain any other notions.

The light faded, and the sky streaked silver as the moon touched the clouds.

The distant tinkling sound of laughter echoed off the trees as we crossed the gardens. I could see light from the windows as the dining room glowed brightly. We found James and his family seated at the table, their plates full and the wedding feast had grown cold.

His father blushed upon seeing us. He sat back, taking his hands from the steepled position on the table to rub his thighs. "We didn't see the point in waiting, as we had no idea how long you would be. James ordered the feast to start."

James sat with his fingers interlaced behind his head as he observed our party. He had already claimed his home and was bossing the staff around before our vows had seen a night through. My head pounded and my stomach churned. All I wanted was some light refreshment and sleep. I sat opposite my husband, who had seated himself at the head of the table. My father, who had by now returned, joined my mother at the side of the table opposite James' parents. A tightness gripped my chest, and tears sprang to the corners of my eyes. I was unaccustomed to seeing my father relegated to a place other than the head of the table.

My sisters and their husbands sat chatting and giggling, the children now in bed. The candlelight was softer and easier on my eyes, and I managed to eat some of the cold feast that lay before me. Wine flowed, and my husband filled and refilled his own glass.

"To your health." Harriette's husband stood and raised his glass, first in James' direction and then in mine.

I smiled and nodded my head towards him. My mother's cheeks were coloured, and her eyes dulled by the late hour and a glass of sherry. I could not feel their joy at the union, but I had heard this was common in the early days. I took a little wine, but I have never been keen on the feeling of losing control of my faculties. Especially as now my headache was easing.

As a group, we rose, deciding it was time to turn in. Harriette's husband took her by the hand and grasped her waist with his other. He danced her to the stairs, spinning and gliding across the floor. She giggled and planted light kisses on his cheek. My parents, arm in arm, followed. Pride spread across their faces as they watched their eldest daughter leave the room. The rest of my sisters, along with their husbands, formed a troop. They marched into the hall in a natural order. The clinking of plates joined yawning and the rustle of skirts as the table behind us was cleared.

The families gathered at the bottom of the stairs, insisting James and I continue first. My sisters barely disguised mocking glances, whispering again as I went past.

"Good luck," Margaret said, in a low voice.

"See you in the morning. Sarah smirked as her elbow knocked against Margaret's. Once more, they started to giggle.

I took my bouquet, and leaving the cold stone floor of the hall, I climbed the solid wooden staircase. As our families waved and whooped, my husband took my hand, and for the first time, I was aware of the warmth of his skin. There was a roughness to his palm as it grated against mine. I was surprised to discover, they felt as if they had been used for physical work. This was not something I hadn't expected from him.

I sent the flowers wheeling through the air. They passed the paintings of my forebears, who cast a critical eye as they went. Stray petals landed on the array of ancient swords, too dull to cut them. There were no unmarried women to catch them, but tradition dictated this must happen. The bouquet landed on the hard floor with a soft thud.

James' grip squashed my fingers against each other as he led me toward our bedroom. The corridor was dotted with many candles giving a sensation of unfamiliarity. It was as if I had never seen these paintings before or walked on these floors. The corridor stretched out before us appearing like it would go on forever. Our feet flattened the soft carpet below, and our shadows cast giants of ourselves across the walls.

Now that we were to be heads of the household, I would no longer be in my childhood room. Instead, the maids had dressed in the master bedroom in the finest linen. My mother's dresser was decorated with vases of flowers; it groaned under the weight of them. Yet more bloomed on every surface of what had once been my parents' room. Candlelight gleamed off the floor-to-ceiling mirror that stood on one wall, while the paintings looked like dreamy other worlds reflected there.

The four-poster bed was hung with heavy purple velvet curtains tied at the corners. I ran my fingers across the smooth surface of crisp and clean white sheets. Bess waited to help me with my corsets and dress. James went through a side door to a dressing room he would use. Bess helped me remove the dress over my sore head. Then brushed my hair to remove the dried blood.

"There, that should feel a little better," she said, as she smoothed my tangled locks.

"Thank you, Bess. It does."

I used some creams that were on my dressing table, and afterwards, I smelled like the flowers in the room. I stretched out my muscles, my arms reaching over my shoulders and up into the air as I allowed a yawn to escape. We had started the day's preparations before the sun had risen, and much had happened. Bess collected my clothes and left as I lay on the bed, curled up on my side, letting my eyes flutter closed.

There was weight against my chest and I felt the crisp sheets on my back. The acrid smell of stale smoke and wine filled my nostrils, and I choked on the nauseating fumes. Struggling against the weight and disorientation, my breathing grew shallow and fast. My stomach muscles clenched.

"Stay still, silly girl," James slurred.

"What are you doing?" I said, every muscle in my body tensed.

"What do you think? It's our wedding night."

"But my head." I reached toward it, rubbing my forehead.

"You should get used to this. You're mine now, and I will do as I wish!"

His hands clumsily ripped at my nightdress. I swung my arm across my chest, clasping my shoulder. He grabbed my arm, wrenched it to my side, and pulled my breast out.

He moulded it in his hand as if sizing up what he had bought at the market. His fingers squeezed, and his fingernails left a semi-circle of deep imprints.

He pulled the nightdress up and I had the urge to shake it free, to gasp for breath as the material folds covered my face. I wriggled, trying to free my hands, he grabbed my wrists, leaving me unable to cover my modesty.

"Please!" I said, at which point he uncovered my face. He stared into my eyes, the light of the only remaining candle still burning beside the bed.

His eyes stayed fixed on mine; the candle wax dripped, marking the passing of time. I squirmed, trying to free my hands to cover my breasts. My skin crawled, dirty, as if his gaze had left a greasy smear wherever it had travelled.

Finally, he spoke. "Neither of us wanted this marriage, but now it's happened I will make the most of my situation. I suggest you do the same!"

At this, he pushed my legs apart with his knees, and then there was a sharp pain. I turned my head and buried it in the folds of my nightdress.

His weight once again was on my chest, pushing the breath from me as he moved back and forth. With each movement, pain pierced me, and tears ran down my cheeks, but I made no noise. I would not cry out.

When he finished, he grunted in a way I instinctively knew was over. He rolled off me and lay for a moment before falling asleep. A low rumbling noise began, and a deep guttural snore followed, the sort of noise only made possible by drink.

I rolled on my side, drawing my knees up, cuddling them, and watched the flickering candle. All I could smell was smoke and wine, and once again, a loud drumming filled my head. I had only a few conversations with my mother about what I was expected to do as a wife. Harriette had tried to warn me earlier that day.

"Are you prepared?" Harriette had said.

"I'm not sure. You haven't seen my necklace anywhere, have you?" I glanced around the dressing table, looking for my emerald.

"No." She laughed 'for tonight." She picked up my necklace and stood to fasten it behind my neck.

"I haven't thought further than getting to the chapel." I touched the emerald and straightened it.

"Oh, sweet girl, do you know what happens at night between a husband and wife?" She took my shoulders in her warm hands.

"A little mother has told me that there are duties I will have to perform and that my husband will instruct me." I watched her reflection in the mirror.

"Her pre-wedding speech hasn't changed." She sighed, her shoulders dropping.

We had been interrupted before she could continue, leaving me none the wiser.

My shoulders shook, and a whisper tickled across my ear, waking me.

"You were dead to the world, Miss. I mean Madame." She bent close, looking into my eyes.

"Bess, the room is spinning." I reached up to rub my hands across my neck, massaging it.

"I'm not surprised," she said, as she helped me to my feet. "Don't worry; I will dispose of the sheets and bedclothes. His mother has insisted on inspecting them first."

I looked down to discover her meaning. My pillow, nightdress, and bedding were punctuated in red spots. They glistened in places and flaked in others. My head must have bled during the night, and I can guess the reason for the rest, but it looked a frightful sight. Bess went to remove the sheets when the dressing room door opened. James stood in the doorway. His tall boots and long jacket told me he intended to go hunting.

"What are you doing, girl?" He demanded, holding his riding crop, the end resting in his palm.

"Sorry, sir, I was going to put fresh linen on the bed." She curtseyed.

"No need. Wait in the corridor." He pointed with the crop

towards the door.

"Your mother is waiting," Bess replied, still holding her position.

James glared at Bess until she scuttled from the room, leaving us alone once more.

"Before you get dressed, we need to put a baby in you." He turned and placed the crop on my dressing table.

"I wonder if I might get cleaned up first?" I pulled at my soiled clothing.

"No need for that, but take that rag off." He pointed at my nightgown.

Nervous, I slipped it to the floor, covering myself with my hands and arms as best I could.

"No, let's not be silly; you're not a girl anymore; show me what I have."

He slumped in a chair, his elbows resting on the arms and his hands clasped in front of his lips as he crossed his legs.

My arms faltered as I moved them. Keeping one arm stretched across my stomach, my fingers digging into my skin. My shoulders were drawn up to my ears.

"From now on, you will show me your body when I want you to. If you put on weight, and you're not pregnant, I will tell the cook to give you less at meals."

I reached down for my nightdress, lifting it to cover myself once more.

"I didn't say to do that, did I? I am your husband now, and your mother must have told you I would instruct you." He looked at me but didn't wait for an answer. "Yes? Drop it until I tell you to pick it up!"

"No. James, I'm tired and in pain. We can try for a baby tonight. My Parents are expecting to see us this morning." I pleaded.

"What did you say to me?" He stood.

Reaching forward, he grabbed my arm and twisted it until I could no longer stand up or hold on to the nightdress. Collapsing to the floor, the pain shot through my arm.

"I'm sorry. Please, you're hurting me."

He threw my arm away from him as if unsure how he had come by it, disgusted at the touch of my skin. Looking at me again, he sneered and walked towards the door.

"Tonight then, but don't disobey me again." He waggled his finger at me.

The sound of the door closing meant I could move again. As I tried to walk, I winced in pain. Realising that I had torn as he had roughly taken his pleasure. Bess came back in as James left and produced a small bottle from her apron.

"Lavender oil Madame. My mum swore by it after childbirth, and when I married, she told me of its soothing properties. Add a few drops to your bath."

Her black curls pinned neatly to the side of her head, and the rest pulled into a tight bun. I had only ever seen her in her maid's uniform of a black dress with a white apron. She had full lips and a small nose that turned up at the end. When I heard her laugh, she sounded like a bird twittering in the bushes. Shy and quiet, she was a thin girl who stood only five feet tall, shorter than me and almost as short as her mother.

I thanked her and made my way to the tub to clean up and soothe the aches and pains. Shades of purple, blue, and green appeared through the swirling water. My wrists and thighs are more colourful now than my wedding flowers had been.

The long skirts would hide my legs, but my wrists would need extra jewellery for a few days while I healed. Memories of the last time I received such bruises, climbing trees as a child, now like a distant dream.

Once I had dressed, I made my way down to find my family. The salty savoury smell of bacon drifted into the hall. I could not face the knowing looks and join in the jokes at my expense, making light of the night before. I made my way out of the back door through the servant's corridors.

I shielded my eyes as the bright light and heat of the day swept across the gardens in a shimmering haze. As I walked, dragging my feet, the toes of my soft white shoes scuffed green with grass stains. I took my time with every movement calculated so as not to cause myself pain.

The tall, deep shade of the yew hedges in the formal gardens surrounded me and hid me from a view of the house. This part of the garden only contained hedges of green in every hue. The pond at the centre reflected the colour of the hedges and added its own in the algae and plants that grew there.

My shoulders relaxed and dropped. I straightened and I took large breaths of clean air scented by the pine trees of the woodlands beyond.

Talented gardeners shaped the hedges. They spend many months of the year taming them into intricate detail. Working in small teams on rickety ladders with sharp scissors. Cutting and shaping until nature bent to their whim.

I found a lichen-covered wooden bench sitting next to a small stone fountain. I perched on the edge, staring into the water droplets. A few goldfish swam below the surface, and dragonflies flitted between lily pads.

As the sun arced across the sky, I made plans. I would contrive to ensure I had plenty of time, away from my new husband, on the estate. I would spend only the necessary amount of time in his company. From observing my parents' relationship, the days were my mother's own. In the evenings, my father would join her.

I did not want to become the source of village gossip. I did not wish to have the doctor visit regularly to treat the wounds. Absent-mindedly, I rubbed at my wrists. The warmth of the friction released the floral fragrance of the lavender oil. The folk remedy had helped. But how would I get enough of it without raising suspicions?

I needed to learn more secrets to healing wounds caused in those necessary moments. I was astonished at how my mother and sisters had managed without me noticing their bruises. How could they continue to smile at their husbands after such attacks? I reflected on my conversation with Harriette and considered asking why she hadn't mentioned the pain.

If I could find things around the house that could be put to use, I might spare myself some of the embarrassment. I would not bother my parents with this. They considered all their children were now settled. I had no way to change my situation, even if they knew. It made no sense to trouble them.

I would cling to the things that made me happy to get me through the years. Maybe I would get used to it, or would he tire of me? Choking back tears, I vowed never to cry in front of him or reveal my shame. It crossed my mind that if I were to produce a child, he might become softer. Perhaps, if I followed instructions, I could make him happy. I feared he would never love me, even if I did what he wanted.

The fleece-like clouds reflected on the water's surface made me feel lighter. It was as though I could let my cares float off with them into the blue.

As he had bluntly put it, I would have to make the best of my situation. What other choice did I have?

I walked back to the house, skirting around the edge of

the gardens. The cool shade from the trees pooled on the lawn, making the grass crisp underfoot. The path before me swept around the corner. Following it, my head swam.

Rounding the bend, a large brown mound appeared to block my path. Individual strands of hair in shades of black and tan stuck out at awkward angles. The door to the house now stood in full view, and my mind made up, I hitched up my skirts. The shape blocked the path, causing me to have to step over it. As I did, a putrid wind blew, and I clutched my sleeve to my nose and mouth. A small lump rose in my throat, and I struggled to control my stomach.

Half straddling the legs and hooves of the creature, its face came into view. Large brown eyes revealed, pulled far back in fearful features. The thin, pure white edges shone brightly. The brown gaze, unblinking, held flies that walked across its jelly surface. Majestic antlers dug ruts into the earth as its neck had twisted up. The writhing bodies of freshly hatched maggots crawled through two holes in its throat.

CHAPTER THREE
Geraniums

"Morning Bess. How are the preparations going?"

"Morning Madame. I believe everything is in hand. I'm waiting for the butcher to deliver this afternoon, and then we should have a store full." She carried a small wicker basket hanging on one arm. It bounced against her hip as I approached. Nestled inside were eggs in varying shades.

"It will be wonderful to have company again." I clasped my hands together.

"I'm sure everything will be ready in time," she said, as she passed me.

The house was resplendent, decked in miniature sheaves of wheat tied with red ribbon. They leant against the pillars or the door and we tied them to the stairs. The mouthwatering smell of warm, fresh loaves drifted through the house. They were baked in shapes that celebrated the ingredients used to create them.

Cobnuts from the woods were still green with their soft husk frayed like little skirts. Apples sat with flowers decorating the table, ready for the harvest supper. Each season held its charm for me and this one shone in the orange and red hues of the squashes and fruits.

I grabbed an apple on my way past the table. Crunching into its flesh, both sweet and tart, the juice ran from the corner of my mouth. We were expecting guests to spend the shorter autumn days in celebration.

We would hold feasts and balls, inviting the people of the village for the Lord of the Harvest meal. It had been a tradition since before the new house had been house built, and I enjoyed planning every detail. Our friends and families would travel by coach, and extra grooms had been brought in from the village. For the most part, my husband had left this area to me. I interviewed each one and took those who were farm labourers. Knowing that work in the fields would be meagre after harvest and through the winter. The open stretches of land lay bare under the freezing sky. I made sure to hire from the village to help support the families there. The queue had stretched into the stable yard.

We were brought up rubbing shoulders with the village children, and I knew most of them by name. This only made it harder to turn away those who were not needed. I was determined not to break with tradition and would deploy locally while I ran the house.

In my letters to Harriette, I had made sure to check I was doing the right thing. Having no family living close by meant I had to ask months before the events were to take place. Her replies, although sometimes brief, always held good advice.

Jane,

Be sure to provide clean clothes for each new hire and have their old ones laundered and mended. Mother started this tradition and the staff have always been loyal. Make sure to employ people from the village and only strangers when no one else is available or suitable.

Your Loving Sister
Harriette

As she had been head of her household for some years, her advice would be good and based on experience.

James had returned the previous evening, his horse dirty and tired from the long journey. He had taken to dividing his time between the house and his smaller apartments. We kept these rooms for his business trips and social occasions I could not extract myself from.

He was home now, though. The regular morning and evening ritual of trying to make an heir to his fortune continued. The weeks passed and with each day, his anger at my failure in this task became more obvious. He stormed around the house.

I came down the stairs to find him lashing out at a rug that had got the better of his feet. Tripping him and sending him across the hall floor. He kicked at it, still lying on his side.

"What are you laughing at? Do you think this is funny?" he screamed at me.

"I'm sorry. It's something I would normally do." I travelled a few more of the steps towards him, reaching out my hand as I went. "Here, let me help you up."

As I reached him, Bess came through the front door. James leapt to his feet, his face beetroot red. He charged towards her.

"What do you think you are doing using the front door? Insolent girl." He raised his hand, ready to strike her.

Guessing what was about to unfold, I dived forward, placing myself between them.

"Bess, leave!" I shouted.

She turned around and rushed through the open door. As

I swivelled to face James once again. He slapped me hard across the face, leaving red welts where his fingers landed. The shock of the blow took my breath and I reached up to touch the hot skin.

This was the first time I would have to hide a visible mark of his anger from the rest of the household.

"Don't do that again. I will discipline as I see fit." He raised his arms, exasperated. "Why are you doing this? Give me a child. That's your only job in this marriage. It's me who has to face the world and my parents with the shame of your barren belly."

The next day, he sent word to the kitchen to restrict my meals. He made sure to instruct the removal of all cream or butter and increase my red meat. He prodded at my stomach, taking the skin between his thumb and forefinger, pinching and pulling at it.

"What did I say? If you got fat, I would have to control your eating. You have left me no choice."

When this didn't work, he instructed the kitchen to remove the red meat. The butter and cream did not return. My plate became more sparse with each new attempt to control my weight.

Observing the apple core in my hand and juice running down my fingers, a twinge of fear crept through me. Midmouthful, I found an empty vase and hid the core; the sweetness turning to ashes in my mouth. Spitting what was left of it into the void, no longer hungry. I vowed to return to remove it later, ensuring that no one would see it.

Another two weeks passed and my monthlies returned as usual. A week's peace ensued, as he would not touch me while I bled. As soon as it stopped, he started again. This time, when he had finished, I rose to bathe. A sharp jab sent me falling to my knees as his hand shoved into the centre of my back.

"This is your plan, isn't it? Wash away my seed before it can take root. You harlot." Rising to tower over me, he spat in my hair, the wet foam sticking the strands to my cheek. "That's a strumpet's trickery."

"I want to clean up before dinner." I cowered at his feet, not wanting to look into his face. He may take that as rebellion.

"No, you will not bathe again until I tell you that you can!" He left me and went to his dressing room.

The sun rose and set and each time I asked to bathe, he would refuse. I hated every minute. My skin grew moist with the sweat of the day and exertion of the night. Brown streaks appeared, evidence of rain showers or sweat running down my arms and face. My hair was a tangled mat. At every opportunity, he would complain about the smell. Even drawing the attention of the stable boys to it. Laughing as they squirmed at the exchange. Their pitying looks made me feel sick to my stomach.

Coming to our room one night, he pushed me away as I went to undo his trousers.

"You stink. You disgust me, you filthy whore."

He took the wash jug from the nightstand. Holding it above me, he sneered as he tipped it over my head and body. The cold water sprung goosebumps to life on every inch of me. My teeth chattered together as he took my dress and scrubbed me with it. He rubbed hard and the rough, raw silk fabric scratched into my skin.

It left red marks, much like some animal's claws had etched deep.

"No wonder you can't have my child. Your poison. Now you're clean, I might be able to touch you."

My eyes stung as salty tears threatened to mingle with

the cold water. The bed sheets squelched when I lay down. The dressing room door slammed behind him as he left me to sleep alone in the wet bed. While he went to his room.

What he didn't know was that the pain of the scrubbing and the cold of the water were a blessed relief. My skin was now cleaner than it had been since our wedding day. Free of his touch, as well as the dirt that had built up there.

I pulled a sheet over my shivering body and I slept fitfully, naked in the puddle. My ribs glistened. The water droplets ran across the surface of my skin. It collected in pools in the dips between each rib.

The carefree, happy young girl, full of life, was no more. Each creak of the house or bang of a stable door sent my heart skipping out of my chest. My hair lacked life and lay lank and dull. My skin broke out with the stress and the dark circles around my eyes grew darker every day. I no longer recognised the reflection in the mirror. I kept the tone of my letters to family, as normal as I could, refusing to be the child that failed in her marriage.

I spent most of my time in the walls of the home I grew up in. Haunting the corridors, I floated between my bed, the sitting room, and the dining room.

After months of repeating the same day, in a never-ending monotony, my supply of lavender oil was running low. This and the first day of sunshine in a week led me outdoors. As a child, I was not permitted to be alone anywhere outside of the gardens. Our estate was so much more than the walls that surrounded it.

I walked out of the front door onto the gravel drive and carried on walking. The warmth of the sun on my skin drew me forward, leading me to follow it. I stayed out of the shadows and kept walking only where the sun shone. Putting one foot in front of the other and allowing the warmth to ease my aching muscles.

A breeze gently moved some strands of hair and brought with it the smell of the pine trees. Like the pot of gold at the end of a rainbow, a red brick barn appeared before me.

I blinked into the sunlight as if in a daze, looking around me at where I had ended up. It stood on the edge of the coach houses and stable yard. It had a low arched doorway that faced the woods instead of the busy courtyard behind. A black tiled roof sloped in all four directions, and there were small openings high in the walls for doves. Wings beat as a few fluttered out. Startled at my presence, sending small white feathers floating down like snow.

An abandoned place I doubted James even knew existed as he spent little time outside other than to hunt. It was a neglected place, and the inside was dark and full of spiders. I brushed the cobwebs from the entrance as my eyes grew accustomed to the light. The floor was thick with dirt as I stepped up onto it. The cool of the walls surrounding me, enclosing me like arms, welcoming me home.

My fingers tingled like a thousand tiny pins pricked at them. Urging me forward. The feeling grew more intense the further I went. I found an upturned wooden bucket, sat, looked out towards the trees and listened.

The birds sang, and flocks of crows took to the wing at the unearthly sound of a fox barking. The leaves rustled as the wind moved through them, and the doves above me returned. They settled back into their places, cooing. My heartbeat calmed, and my breathing was no longer shallow.

The track outside was rough, and the grass grew tall, taking back what was once well-travelled. Despite the side entrance gate to the stable next door, it had become a forgotten place. No human walked this way. A thin smile cracked across my face, something that hadn't happened since my wedding day.

Returning each day, I spent my time clearing out the floor, which was caked with bird droppings. I stole tools from the gardeners' shed, sneaking them out through the woods, making sure I was not seen. I made small, inexperienced dents with a pickaxe in the thick muck.

I shovelled it into my little bucket. I took it into the woods and emptied it out of sight. My hands grew rough, and blisters replaced the smooth skin. My clothes took on a sweet, sickly smell of rotting bird droppings and straw. Sweat marks appeared on what were once white blouses and long skirts. I snuck through the back door, but Bess must have noticed. My mind was made up to inform her of my plans and enlist her help to conceal my endeavours. I also needed her help with the next phase of my plan. As she brought me a dress for dinner, I took the opportunity to do so.

"I need your help, Bess, but I will understand if you can't." I braced my hands on the dressing table, steadying my nerves.

"Of course, Madame. You know I will do anything I can." She continued to prepare the dress to slip over my head.

"I know your job is important, and I wouldn't want you to risk anything for me."

She froze, "You're worrying me, Madame."

"Sorry, Bess, I don't want to be a burden; it's just I'm sure you've noticed my clothing." I rose and touched her arm in an attempt to reassure her.

"It has been different lately," she said slowly, choosing her words.

"Well, I have been cleaning a little barn out." I continued

rubbing my forearm.

"Oh, Madame, I will ask one of the stable boys to do it for you. I apologise if it is dirty," she replied, getting the dress ready once more.

"No, no, this is my secret. Please don't ask them." I begged. "I want to experiment with making more lavender oil myself. I don't want anyone to know I'm using as much as I am." I knew the risk I took entrusting her.

"Oh, but my mother makes it. I'm sure she won't tell anyone," she replied in a singsong voice.

"She does?"

"Oh yes, she makes things for everyone in the village." Her voice rose an octave, and she sounded proud.

I considered my next question for a while as she reached up and slipped the dress over my head.

"Would she teach me?" I ventured.

"But Madame, you don't want to get your hands dirty with things like that. Besides, there is a stigma that goes with those arts." Her voice is less confident now.

"Bess, I have nothing else to occupy my time, and it's driving me to insanity. If I don't have something to do soon, I don't know what will happen." I pleaded.

It was her turn to be deep in thought. Taking my necklace and fastening it. She traced her fingers over the bruising visible below the collar of my dress.

"I will ask her." Bess agreed.

"Thank you so much. Remember our secret!" I placed my forefinger on my lips.

Two days later, I stood at the entrance to the barn. Nervously tapping my toes, my hand grasped the rough wood door frame. Bess had arranged for her mother to visit. A low cart appeared in the distance, bouncing over the large stones on the rough track. Bess and her mother pulled it along, and as they approached, glass clinked against more glass. It sounds musical in the breeze. They reached me huffing and puffing, and a sudden pang of guilt washed over me, asking her to come all this way.

"I'm sorry. Can I help?" I said.

"No, mistress, it's no trouble," the old lady said.

Bess panted.

"My mother, Madame." The grey-haired lady to her right did a short clumsy curtsy.

"No need for that," I said. "Thank you for helping me and for keeping my secret." My arms were open wide in welcome.

"We women have to help each other." Her voice was hoarse.

Standing only four feet six inches, she was already the most petite person I knew, and then age had bent her further. She had a hump at the top of her shoulders from sitting hunched in front of the fire at her work. Her fingers were rough and calloused. She treated the sick and delivered many babies, but also worked on the land next to her husband. Her long grey hair rolled into a bun, and the faint smell of roses emanated. Deep creases etched into her face from the weather and age.

"May I get you some water?" I offered.

"Thank you, mistress." The old woman lent to one side.

I poured water from a bottle I had stashed in the building behind us. We all drank, pausing before the work began to allow the women to rest. Once they had quenched their thirst, we threw aside the tarp and unpacked the little cart.

Glass jars and vials, small lidded pans and herbs were all packed with care.

We took them into the building where Bess's husband

constructed rough tables and shelves. He had found logs from the woods for the legs. He used discarded boards, peppered with holes left by the woodworm, for the tops.

A death-watch beetle tapped out a tune along with the hammering as nails held plank against plank.

Bess's mother listened intently to the drumming of the beetle and, after a short while, hissed, "Be gone." Under her breath. She said, "Can't have him hanging around. He is a portent of death."

Bess had been my only friend and confidant. Months of hearing the torture I had to endure and watching me pick myself up and continue. Had forced her hand. She had promised me help and had enlisted her family. With little recourse for a woman in my position, I had to be happy with whatever help was available. We organised the delicate, precious things into areas. With jars of herbs lining the shelves and the tools to process them on the table. A small fire burnt in the newly built hearth near the door, with a rough chimney poking through the wall. The smell of wood smoke filled the air.

Lenora's voice was no less horse after the drink. We rested, the cart now empty, and talked.

"Bess tells me your husband is a cruel man." Lenora pulled no punches.

My cheeks grew pink, and I stuttered, lowering my eyes to examine the floor.

"He wants a child." That was all I could manage.

"My first husband had been a violent man. Before he died in a farming accident, drunk as usual, he had regularly beaten me," Lenora continued.

"One night, he stumbled in from drinking and went for me. He grabbed a sack that hung near the fire and tried to strangle me with it. My voice has never quite recovered." She rubbed at the loose skin on her throat as if to soothe it.

"This would not be the last time he would try to kill her." Bess continued squeezing her mother's leg reassuringly. The skirt wrinkled under the pressure.

"Despite my rescuer turning him black and blue," she chuckled. "He had not learned his lesson. My second husband was my rescuer. I knew him as a kind man the moment he burst through our door upon hearing my screams. We married soon after my first husband's death. As you can imagine, this has caused some scandal in the village."

"Of course, I've heard murmurs, but never the entire story."

"My first marriage taught me the need for folk medicine, and I learned to distil my remedies for my injuries." She looked with love and affection at her daughter, who was leaning towards her. "Bess tells me you want me to teach you."

"Yes, very much!" I wanted her to know how desperately I needed this.

"Do you realise this is a terrible scandal in itself? If anyone found out I was teaching you to practise these arts, you would risk everything."

"What about you?" I replied.

"I'm used to scandal and have less to lose" She dismissed my concerns with a wave of her hand.

"You say I have much to lose, but I feel like I have already lost everything, and if I don't do this, I will lose myself next." I leant forward, clasping my hands together.

She stared into my eyes as if she were looking deep into my soul

"So be it; we had better get to work." She concluded.

I had access to a garden full of promising plants and

herbs to treat all that ailed me. Before now, I had no way of knowing how and what to use. I had put all my spare time into my studies, finding some useful material in the library, but nothing could beat the hands-on experience of a wise woman.

The smoke and scents of the simmering herbs drifted into the trees, then dissipated there. The delicate, sweet smell of lavender mixed with the heady wood smoke. We spent every spare moment in my barn as I made notes on Lenora's teaching.

The building's shade was welcome on a summer day. I longed to stroll through the garden, collecting specimens to distil into oils. The coming winter meant we had to use dried herbs more and more. We would run out if we weren't careful to use them sparingly. But it also brought with it new plants to use.

My clothes smelled of wood smoke and herbs, more than even Bess could hide. The three of us hid spare clothes in our barn, allowing us to change when we arrived. While we worked, we hung our everyday clothes among the tree branches. The breeze kept them pine-fresh.

In the past, women had been burnt for less than we were now doing. The danger both scared and thrilled me. Of course, this meant we had to be careful, but it gave me a new lease on life.

Autumnal plants and flowers decorated the house. The bunches and blooms had been one excuse I had used to collect specimens. I touched the leaves that adorned the staircase as if they were aware of my heart and mind.

"What are you doing?" James demanded.

"I didn't see you there," I said, clutching my hand to my chest.

"The guests will be arriving soon, and you're

daydreaming," James accused.

"Sorry," I had said sorry a lot more in the last four months than I had ever said before.

"Get changed; you look like you've been dragged through the woods."

The chill winds had blown dry leaves into the trim of my dress.

"Of course, James."

I climbed the stairs to change for the guest's imminent arrival, and a wave of nausea washed over me. The smell of the kitchen preparing our meal rose through the house. The oily scent of fish made my stomach heave, and I ran to our room. Finding the large wash bowl, I retched, the contents of my stomach emptying on the blue and white pattern.

I sat on my seat at my dressing table, holding my belly. I couldn't remember feeling this sick in many years. Memories of a childhood illness were the only reference. Bess came through the door, preparing to help me dress for dinner.

"Are you quite well, mistress?" she asked, looking at the bowl's contents and covering it with a towel.

"I suppose it must be something I ate," I replied

"But you haven't eaten today. We have been busy all day, remember?"

My cheeks flushed with guilt at the thought of the apple I had eaten earlier. I couldn't think of any illness spreading through the village at the moment. Then I remembered how my sisters complained of sickness when they were expecting.

"Bess, I think I may be with child."

"Mistress", she gasped, throwing her hands in the air. "This is wonderful news."

My brow furrowed. "I don't want to tell—"

James burst in. "Whatever is that noise, girl?" he shouted at Bess, who shrank into a deep curtsy and cowered before him.

"Sir," she said.

I interrupted, reluctant, needing to protect Bess. I could not hide the truth as I had wished, and I had no other excuse to fall back on.

"Leave her alone, James. She is only celebrating. I believe I am with child."

The first genuine smile I had ever seen from him crept across his face. He positively lit up, and it took me by complete surprise. I even questioned if I had been mistaken about him. He knelt before me, taking my hand. I pulled it back in an instinctive reaction to his touch. He took it again, and this time, I let him but sat leaning as far from him as my chair would allow.

"I never imagined you were capable. You cannot know how happy I am."

I sat in silence, not knowing if this was a congratulation or condemnation.

"We will announce it this evening."

"No. Please, James, it's bad luck." I clasped his hand with both of mine.

"Don't be ridiculous. How can you make me hide this news? I won't hear of it." He shook my hands free and stood.

I knew not to push him further. I would have to accept his will again. My sides still hurt from the previous night's marital obligations. I needed to bathe and treat the bruises before dressing.

Bess still held the curtsy, and as James left, she could finally stand. She supported herself on a table as she breathed a sigh of relief.

"I'm sorry, Bess. Are you alright?"

"I'm the one who's sorry. I didn't know the master was close." Her hands quivered.

"No need; he would have found out soon enough." I sat her down until her nerves settled.

"I will draw a bath." She stood, her legs now steady.

A tall, dark wooden cupboard stood in the corner of the room. By moving aside some clothing that hung within, I revealed many tiny bottles of oils. I picked each one up and turned it over in my hands to read the tiny looped writing. I chose one labelled geranium.

I emerged from my room dressed for dinner in crimson silk. A glittering ruby necklace caught the candlelight. I tried my best to glide down the stairs in what should have been a grand entrance. Instead, my foot caught a wrinkle in the carpet, and I tripped halfway down. I reached for the thick, polished banister. My small hand could not reach around it, but I grasped it enough to steady myself. The front door stood open as James greeted his parents.

The hall rang with the chatter of a group of James' friends. Recently arrived, they congregated there.

Silence fell; James, rolling his eyes at me and, as if putting on a mask, turned to the throng, all smiles and announced.

"Don't mind, Jane, she is not herself these days. I have the best news."

His mother looked as if she might burst with excitement. Doing a little hop up and down.

"James, it can't be. Are you going to have a son?" She spread her arms as if to hug him and changed her mind. Her husband's nose wrinkled, and she withdrew her hands to her sides.

Don't mind me, I thought; *I am only a vessel of his greatness.*

"Indeed, Mother." He puffed out his chest, and all at once, he was being clapped on the back by all gathered below.

"And about time, too." She shot me a look of frustration.

"Come, all of you. We will celebrate a bountiful harvest in style this year."

James led the crowd through the dining room, and I stood alone, ready to greet my family. They arrived in a wagon train, one following the other, crunching up the gravel drive.

They all flung their arms around me once I had told them my news. I struggled for breath in the huddle, wincing at the pain of their hands on the bruises below my clothes.

After they congratulated me, in the warm way I knew my family would, the weight lifted from me.

"You smell of geraniums!" my mother said.

"Something to help with the sickness," I lied, feeling the bruises again as her hand brushed my sides.

I did not tell her that this was the second of the oils I had learned to distil. I also omitted its healing benefits, including its anti-inflammatory and antiseptic properties, which soothed my raw skin.

The party was boisterous, with James and his family and friends at one end of the table and my family and I at the other. I avoided the fish and covered my nose with a handkerchief as it was dished out. Dry wine and sweet sherry were passed around with generosity in a true celebration. The cloud over me lifted, and a sensation, as though this could be the start of happier times, replaced it.

The warmth of the fire cast a soft yellow light over the gathering. Our news could be a new beginning for us, one we desperately needed, or at least I did. I gazed at James, seeing him in a new light as he looked like the weight of the world had lifted from his shoulders. He caught me looking and even raised his glass in a cheer, which I returned with a smile.

Noticing, my mother whispered, "See, how could he not love a girl like you?" She clasped my hand in hers.

Never yours

I blushed and looked back towards James.

He was leaning in close to one of his friends' wives, who was talking in a low tone. Leaning back again, he laughed and turned to another friend while she gushed.

"Oh, ever the perfectionist, James." Her hand brushed his arm.

The party moved through to the sitting room, and some ladies started to play the piano. I had never mastered it and was amazed at the speed at which their fingers danced across the keys. They were graceful. Something I had never been.

Of course, my clumsiness made it easier to explain away the bruises, even when they had crept out from the line of my clothes. Chokers and other jewellery were useful, but a fall or trip succeeded in helping the lies along.

These ladies and their husbands kept their principal houses in London. With all their city ways, they made me feel small, a country fool. I couldn't sew or play music, and my painting proved a blasphemy against any god that cared to look upon it.

My talents with herbs and healing oils could not be shared. I had to be content with the pitying looks I received from our guests. They talked of the new fashions, the balls and the dinners. It appeared they all attended the city with my husband.

"I don't remember any invites," I told James when he came in earshot.

"We both know those aren't your sort of thing, my dear," he said, patting my leg.

"Maybe I should join you in the city more?" I said, brushing my hand on his arm.

"Why would you do that? Anyway, you will need to stay confined to the house now that you are carrying my child.

Why take any risks when you are happy here?" He clasped both my hands in his before releasing them.

My body rocked with the sting of rejection. I still hoped it would only be a matter of time for a new understanding between us to grow, and I shrugged it off as a misunderstanding. James moved away and went to stand with the lady he had the ear of at dinner. Jewelled clips held her blonde hair up, and it revealed a long neck and a beautiful necklace. It had caught James' eyes. His fingers ran across the jewels as he admired them.

The lady's husband wandered up to them. James dropped his hand from the jewellery and into his cigarette case. He offered one to the gentleman. To my surprise, the gentleman didn't seem to be surprised by this encounter. Instead, he spoke with both laughter and drinking.

Harriette left my mother's side and joined me.

"How are you feeling? You look tired," she said.

"The sickness is using all my energy. How did you find it?" I asked.

"Horrible. With each one, it seems to be different. The smell of frying was the worst; steer clear of that. You're looking slender. Are you eating properly?" Her face creased with concern.

"Of course. It must be the sickness." I lied, gripping the arm of the chair.

"Your letters have been fewer. You must keep writing. I want to know everything about how your little stranger is doing." She touched my dress above my belly. "Promise me, and I will join you when it's time." She took my hand in hers and looked me in the eye, and I prayed she wouldn't notice my rough skin against her soft palms.

"Oh, Harriette, that would mean the world to me. I'm scared—of the lying-in, I mean." A tear appeared in the corner of my eye.

"No need. I will help you through it." She kissed my forehead, her hand light on the back of my neck.

James appeared at my side, taking my hand as we led everyone up the stairs. We all parted company for our bedrooms. As we approached ours, we stopped at the door, and I went to turn the handle. Swinging the door open, I stepped through into the candlelight of the room beyond. I stopped abruptly as his hand dropped from mine.

He stood in the gap, framed as if he were a painting of a country squire, and I examined his face for clues.

"I will stay in my bedroom, and from now on, I will sleep there."

"Why?" I asked.

"You will need your rest now that you're doing your duty to the marriage."

"But I thought — I don't know — maybe we could be happy now." I stuttered, stepping towards him.

"Oh, poor Jane." He lifted his hand to my face, brushing my cheek.

I resisted the urge to back away, closing my eyes, half expecting to be struck. My breathing quickened.

"I wouldn't want to risk the child." His words were carefully chosen, but his tone lacked emotion. With that, he turned and walked to the next door down the hall. My stomach lurched; I had been a fool again, and we could never be happy.

Bess waited inside, and she loosened the corsets that held me. In no mood for conversation, I feigned sleepiness. My clothes were now shed, and I was more comfortable in my nightdress. I laid my hand on the slight bump that protruded below my navel. My gaunt frame proved unable to hide the growing child.

I held my arms around me in the hug I so wanted from my husband. I stood and made my way into James' dressing room. I searched the room for clues as to how I could reach the man I was chained to for the rest of my life.

If a child wasn't to be the key, what would? I ran my fingers across the dinner jacket that hung on the back of his chair. The midnight blue velvet, soft under my fingertips, caught in the rough calluses. I slid open a drawer, not knowing what I hoped to find within. Running my hand along the smooth, dark wood surface of his dressing table as I walked. I approached the door to his room.

A faint light glowed under the bottom of the solid wooden door. I stepped closer, wondering if James was asleep already on the other side. I pressed my ear against the door. The smell of wood polish and the sandalwood of his aftershave mingled. I couldn't hear anything from inside.

If I could convince him that we could be happy, perhaps he would listen this time. I could promise that I would do my best to make him happy. I turned the cold metal handle as quietly as I could, fearing his reaction to my intrusion. I held my breath in case even that made too much noise.

The door swung open. In the flickering candlelight light beyond, the bed's outline appeared. I stepped through the door, my bare feet muted on the wooden floorboards.

"James," I whispered, afraid of what would happen if I woke him. I also knew I could not stop now; I had come too far.

The bed creaked, and the sheets moved.

"James," I spoke a little louder.

He sat up quicker than I expected, and I stepped back towards the door. The sheets were thrown back to reveal the muscles of his chest glistening with sweat. Below him lay his friend's pretty blonde wife.

Her face flushed, and her hair fell free over the side of the bed. I gasped and took another small step back. She looked happy—that's what struck me the most. A smile spread across her face. She wasn't bruised, pinned, or crying. He was smiling, too. As he looked at me, he smiled more.

His mouth opened wide in a laugh that penetrated my chest. It cut deep, as if he had aimed a knife there. I backed away until I reached the door.

"Close it on your way out, dear."

The next morning, rising early, I waited in the hall outside James' door. I paced back and forth, unsure how I would start the conversation. Rubbing my palms together, trying to soothe my nerves, I jumped when finally his door swung open. Looking past him, the room stood empty as he left his bedchamber.

"James!" I said, a little louder than intended.

"Yes, Jane. Why on earth are you lurking in the corridor?"

"I need to talk to you about your — um — visitor." I ventured.

"No, you don't!" His reply was firm.

"No, James, I do!" I surprised even myself.

"Keep your voice down!" he said, grabbing my elbow and moving me back towards my room.

Once through the door, he released me again

"I want to know why you would do that. Especially in our home."

He laughed.

"Our home is it? I think you will find that in the eyes of the law. This is my home, and you are my wife."

"As your wife, don't I deserve some respect in our home?" I reached out towards him.

"All you see are my possessions. You own nothing, not even the dress you stand up in. As it's my home, I will do as I please." He stepped back and stood with his hands on his hips.

I gasped, taken aback. My family home, and myself, were reduced in his estimation to mere belongings.

He dropped his arms to his side once more. "I'm a man, Jane. I know you are a sheltered child, but men have needs. Now that you cannot fulfil those needs, I will take care of them, somewhere else."

"What about her husband's needs?" I pushed.

"Oh, his needs were being met by another member of our party. We have quite the understanding."

He stepped forward and pushed my hair from my face.

"Don't worry, darling," the words left me cold. "When you are once again able, I will return to your bed." He turned and left.

I was sick to my stomach, both hating his rejection and repulsed by his touch. Stuck in an impossible situation and spiralling, I curled up on the bed, clutching my stomach.

How could a child flourish in such a house? If I had a son, would he become like his father? I spent all day in the same position, thinking about how I could survive this life. Before I figured I had it worked out. I had taken my time and hoped for love and tenderness to grow, doing my best to live with his cruelty until that time.

My new hope that a child would stitch us together, making us a family, shattered. No longer convinced that maybe fatherhood would make him tender. I now had to stop living in hope, or I would drive myself insane.

I had certain freedoms that other wives did not. His preference for the city afforded me a part-time life resembling the one I yearned for. I loved my barn and the company of the two women who had taught me so much.

A child would be my blessing alone, somebody I could love and who would love me in return. My hands found their way to the slight bump. This is where I would put my energy. I sat up, feeling light-headed with hunger. The day had passed without me; before I knew it, the time had come to dress for dinner. Unable to face the party, I made my excuses through Bess. It proved easy, as pregnancy gave me more leeway for my absence.

Instead, I had supper in my room and curled on the window seat. I sat with my knees bent and leaning my head against the cold glass with my arms wrapped around my legs. I watched the sunset under the cloudy sky. The rain tapped on the glass, beckoning me to go out into the night and the garden, but I wouldn't go tonight. Tomorrow, I would plan alternative places to be happy on the grounds of the estate. Although wonderful, my barn still didn't fill the hole inside me.

The glasshouses were the perfect place to grow more of the herbs and plants we needed. I would ask the gardeners to teach me a little. Many ladies of great houses were learning this new skill. It wouldn't seem out of place for me to start. I played with the bread and cheese Bess had found for me, tearing bits off and chewing absentmindedly. Geraniums and lavender would be my first choices, followed by perhaps Bergamot.

The title 'Lord of the Harvest' was bestowed upon Bess's husband, Jack. His job was to bring the last sheaf to the big barn where he would lay it out. Bales of hay sat close to the timber walls. A modest feast of meats and ale, bread and cheese, fruits and preserves, was spread on the rough table.

Once the last sheaf was in the barn, Jack would

pronounce the harvest over, and the celebration would begin. Lords and ladies would mix with commoners, dancing to the instruments played. Everyone would drink the same ale and wine and toast the end of the farming year.

Jack's short brown hair was trimmed neatly for the event, and his small moustache was clipped to match. His arms were muscular, and his shoulders were broad. He stood head and shoulders above Bess and her mother. He held her waist with large, rough hands that looked as if he could break her.

Jack took my hand, and James took Bess, not noticing her reluctant grimace. As tradition dictated, we danced the first dance swirling around the big fire. Over the flames, the meat sizzled gently. The smoke and smells drifted out across the chill autumn air. The moon rose high and full, shining on the party as it spilt into the yard.

My parents joined us, light of foot despite their age. The remaining revellers picked their partners, and we made a merry band. Once the dance finished, I bowed out, sitting on the hay bale near the barn door, quite out of breath.

Bess joined Jack, and as she smiled up into his sun-worn face, I saw what love looked like. My heart ached, yearning for someone to look at me with such adoration. I searched for James in the crowd and watched him talking with my father. His head tilted to one side, listening intently to what my father was saying. He chuckled and touched my father's arm. I struggled to reconcile the two sides of his personality. *How could someone so loved by his friends and so respected be so cruel?*

My thoughts turned to my friend Mary, noticeably absent because of illness. Her new fiance had asked her not to travel until she had regained her strength. I resolved then to ask James if I could visit her before she travelled down for the Christmas holiday. I was aware he would be away again soon, and I could travel back with her in time to prepare everything.

My family packed, and chaos ensued as they prepared to travel. Bags and chests piled high in the hall, waiting for the carriages to be brought to the front. My sisters' husbands laughed and joked while they helped load their belongings. It would have been far too much for them to manage on their own. A family our size knew how to help ourselves, or we would never go anywhere. We bid our farewells, with many hugs and vigorous handshakes coming from every direction. With Christmas around the corner, there would be no time to miss them. As usual, they would return home to celebrate with me.

After they had all departed, I waved until they disappeared around a corner. Knocking on James' study door, I waited for permission to enter.

The door creaked open a fraction, and he stood in the gap.

"Can I come in?" I asked.

"I'm very busy, Jane. Come back later." He huffed.

"I only want to ask if I can visit Mary. I will leave tomorrow and be back in time for the winter celebrations." Clutching my hands together, I squeezed them and tried to not look too eager in case he said no.

He turned his head to the side as if listening to someone and then replied, "Yes, yes, of course. Whatever you choose," waving his hand at me as if to shoo me away.

I allowed myself a moment of celebration. My hands shot up to my mouth, and I did a little jump.

I packed my bags that evening, trying to travel as lightly as possible. Three evening dresses, three daytime outfits, and my riding gear should suffice. I placed my silver and emerald drop necklace on my dressing table with my other jewels.

My mother had given me this necklace for my sixteenth birthday. It matched my favourite evening dress, and I loved the way the sun caught the green stone. Clearing away the surrounding mess, I went to take a bath before the evening meal.

Bess came in to help me dress in a yellow gown with gold trim. Once ready, I picked up the gold earrings from the pile of jewellery and headed down to supper.

"Can you just check I have packed everything? I'm sure I have forgotten something," I asked Bess before heading down to join the others.

The evening progressed as usual with James, the life and soul of his adoring followers. All the ladies played their instruments prettily while the men drank deeply. Now that our families had left, James and the blonde were becoming less discreet. They lounged on the couch as he toyed with her hair. Not aspiring to be pitied or mocked, I made my excuses and went to bed early. Seeing Mary would be just the ticket to get me through until Christmas.

The following day, I woke to the sound of carriage wheels crunching against gravel. The horses whinnied in excitement as they lined up on the drive. James prepared to leave, and I wanted to say goodbye before he went. I dressed and grabbing my bags I headed down the stairs to see him.

He and his party were standing in their travelling clothes, waiting to depart.

James waved both his arms at the group to usher everyone out of the front door. He merrily laughed at the chaos he created. I tapped him on the shoulder, trying to get his attention, and he turned on his heels with a shocked expression.

"Jane, why, whatever are you doing here? You don't even like the city."

"James, you agreed I could visit Mary. Don't you remember?"

"Why, old girl, I quite forgot; um, that's not going to be possible now, is it?" His face relaxed.

"Why? You're not here, and I will be back in time to order everything for Christmas."

"It's just that we are taking all the carriages and, well, you can't travel in your state, can you?" He looked me up and down.

"But you said — we agreed!" I pleaded, stepping away from him.

"It can't be helped. You are much happier in the country, anyway. I have to go now, Jane. Please don't cause a fuss!" His lips pursed as he left.

He strode through the door as if he hadn't shattered my world once more.

My first letter had only just left, telling Mary I would be arriving imminently. I would have to write again and explain. By the time my letter reached her, no doubt Mary would believe me lost. I walked to the door, watching the carriages pull away.

The group was hanging from the doors, yelling at each other and encouraging the drivers to race. I returned to my room to unpack. I pulled my jewel case from my bag and placed each piece back in its position. As I did so, I thought of the friend I sorely missed. Hanging the necklaces up, I reached into the case, expecting to find the emerald.

Perplexed, I ran my hand around again and then tipped it upside down, shaking the bag.

"Bess!" I shouted, and she came running through from

the dressing room.

"Have you seen my emerald necklace?" I asked.

"The last time I saw it was last night when I put the case in your bag." She stepped forward and gestured at the case in my hands.

"I can't find it," I said, puzzled.

"I'm sure it's dropped somewhere. It will turn up. Not to worry," Bess reassured me.

"I'm sure you're right. I can't seem to keep hold of anything."

Christmas came around, although the months between felt like they would never end. I couldn't wait to see Mary and my family. The snow had begun to fall the previous evening to the hoot of our collected guests and their children. Running out into the flurries, they threw snowballs and lay in the drifts, wildly flapping their arms and legs until they created snow angels. I happily joined them. My midnight blue skirts trailed in the frozen white, heavy with collected snow as the snow clung to the hem. My hair came loose from its fixings and fell about my face as snowflakes came to rest there.

My bump grew larger, and my face filled out. With James away and in my current condition, I had convinced the cook to allow me larger meals.

My sisters and I threw snowballs like children once more. We giggled and did not care for the disapproving looks of our husbands who gathered at the windows. My friend Mary had joined us with her fiance. Together with Harriette, we took on Sarah, Alice, Margaret, and Elizabeth.

Using hedges as shields, we hid. Sneaking around to attack from behind, we took the others by surprise. Against the snow, Mary's brown hair only made our seven heads of red stand out further. She threw a well-aimed snowball, which struck my shoulder, sending snow down the front of my gown. I gasped and hopped around as the cold, wet flakes melted against my skin.

The setting sun threw shades of brilliant orange, purple, and blood-red across the snow. It signalled the end of our games and time for the children's evening meal.

I watched as my family shook the snow from their clothes and laughed at the sight of glowing noses or tangled hair. Once again, the house was filled with warmth and laughter like the old days; how I missed them. Once inside, we took blankets, drying the wet flakes from the curls. My parents sat in the corner with beaming smiles. My sisters' husbands moved to warm their wives before the enormous fireplace.

As I moved towards the heat, a sudden pain struck me to the ground, like a lightning bolt down and out through my stomach. I clutched at the skirts, drawing my legs up to my chin, and groaned; the pain ripped through me again. Mary, who stood with her fiance, bent to kneel next to me. Her face turned ashen as she commanded the children to be sent from the room, and then she turned to my father.

"Mr Harris!" she called across the room. She stood. "John!" She shouted my father's name with urgency. "Jane needs you!"

My father rose, and seeing the worry in Mary's eyes, he ran across the room, pushing James to one side. He turned back to him. "Get the doctor!" he shouted. To my surprise, James did as he was told.

My mother ushered everyone out of the room, leaving me alone with Mary and my father. He brushed the hair from my brow, looking more concerned than I had seen him before.

"What's wrong with her? Can't you help?" Mary

questioned him.

"This is not my place. She needs her doctor, not her old father, for this."

"For what?" Mary continued.

The door opened, and Bess, accompanied by her mother, came in. They had been at the barn continuing our work and, hearing of the commotion, had come to the house. Someone instructed them to come in and help. Lifting me as gently as they could, each took an arm or leg, but every movement still caused further feelings of tearing. They moved me to the sofa, and I begged them to stop every inch of the way. As they placed me down, a patch of blood became apparent on my skirts. My father left the room, leaving only the women present.

"Help me!" I looked towards Lenora.

"I can't." Her eyes welled up.

The Doctor burst through the doors and came to my side. He shot a look of disdain at Bess and Lenora.

"Servants are not needed here. Be gone and do your chores!"

I heard the conversation as if on the edge of a dream and could only groan and rock. When the two women had left the room, Mary helped remove my corsets, unlacing them as gently as she could. Once my underskirts were removed, she stood, her hand over her mouth. The Doctor stood with her. I lay on my side with most of my clothing removed.

Not able to think about covering myself, my body lay visible to both. Now, evident healing bruises covered my arms, sides and thighs.

Months had passed between them, and some had faded. My damaged skin and the reduction in meals and strength meant my body healed slower. Even when they were faded, they were obvious to my friend and the Doctor.

Small scars dotted my body where my skin had broken, purple and angry.

The ordinarily stern old man turned to Mary. "My dear, she is losing the baby."

"No." I cried, suddenly lucid.

"You must inform her husband and family. Tell them she will need rest, and they must not disturb her for at least a week," The Doctor instructed.

"Of course," Mary said. She knelt beside me. "I'm sorry, Jane," she said before leaving the room.

A younger staff member, Isobel, appeared with fresh sheets and hot water. She and the Doctor set about cleaning me up now the pains had ceased. They sponged the sweat that had gathered across my pale skin. I let them move me as they wished, not caring about modesty anymore or thinking about covering myself. The rough flannel removed the blood that had pooled between my legs. Back and forth, washing it into the bowl of water as if it never existed. Discussion was had about the future of the couch on which I lay, removing any trace of my loss.

Isobel came and went, and the Doctor sat at my side, holding my hand. He assured me of the normality of such things and how my youth allowed plenty more time for children. I vaguely remember nodding along at his speech.

Once the rest of the house slept, Isobel returned, and with the help of the Doctor, they took me to my room. I lay awake until the sun rose the next morning. No thoughts that I can remember past the night. Only the shadows that marched across the walls until the sun cast them out.

At sunrise, I heard the sound of a coach on the gravel as it moved away from the house. Bess brought me water and washed my face without saying a word. She left a steaming cup of peppermint and red raspberry leaf tea.

I searched my memory for their uses. Lenora had once told me that peppermint would help with pain. The raspberry leaf would strengthen and clear the womb. I had turned away from the tea, not caring about either ailment. I shut my eyes.

When dark came again, James barged through the door, with Bess trailing after him. She looked defeated.

"Get her up!" he commanded.

"Sorry," she said as she moved my shoulders, trying to pull me into a sitting position.

"We are going to mass. Now, it is needed more than ever." He shouted at me, pointing a finger and waggling it as he spoke. "You lost the child, and now you must repent before we try again."

"James, I'm tired." I managed.

"The family motto is honor virtutis prœmium — honour is the reward of virtue. Jane, your virtue is in question, and so is my honour." His face turned a beetroot red as his anger grew.

"Sir, the doctor said she needed rest," Bess pleaded.

"Question me again, girl, and you will be out on your ear!" He stepped forward and made to hit Bess. "It's her soul that needs help now."

"James," I said, raising my hand in defence of Bess. "Don't. I will come with you."

He went to leave, then turned back. "I sent Mary home."

"Why?" I said.

"This is her fault for encouraging your behaviour last night. I won't have her influence in this house." He smiled as he said this.

"But I need her," I begged.

"Now, you will learn your lesson." And with that, he left.

"He did it to punish her," Bess said. "Mary told everyone

about the bruising, and the Doctor told them it was the reason you lost the child. We won't be seeing either of them again."

As I dressed, we heard raised voices from James' room. Not wanting any more drama this evening, I decided not to find out the cause. Instead, I tried to ignore the noise until, at last, a door slammed, and all went quiet once more.

I dressed in black, no doubt a bad decision on my part and one that would anger James, but I needed a period of mourning. I had lost a child and the future I had built in my head. As we walked to the chapel, I knew I would be correct in thinking he would see my outfit as a slight. He stormed ahead of the group, leading the way. Throughout the service, he sat with a determined expression. His attention focused entirely on the new clergyman.

This recent addition to the village had replaced the old man who married us. The poor man had died not a week after the wedding service, and he now lay buried in this very cemetery.

This new, younger man was full of godly anger and vengeance against sinners. He threw himself into his service, looking to impress the lord of the manor. He, too, had noticed James' attention and was lapping it up. It appeared he thought he was making the very best first impression.

His arms flailed as he lectured the worshippers, white cloth flying. The candles threatened to go out with every movement.

It would have been comical if it had been happier times. Once he had finished chastising the entire village, we moved as one to leave, our breath visible in the air.

I turned to see James clasp the man's hand with both of his, shaking it vigorously and inviting him to the house. On the walk back, my parents came to my side and took my arms. My father's eyes grew wide upon seeing my appearance.

"Why did you insist on coming out tonight, Jane? You look unwell. All colour is gone from you." His concern was written across his face.

I guessed that the story circulated amongst our guests differed from reality. Not knowing what else to do, I covered the tracks.

"You know how I love Christmas, and I wanted to see my family on this night." I squeezed his hand, bringing an end to the conversation, and conserving my energy for walking. I saw no need to add to James' anger.

I waited until dinner had been eaten. The clergyman had stopped sermonising over the candied fruit, and I made my excuse. Heading to bed, I reached the bottom of the stairs before James caught my hand.

"Wait, my dear," he said. The clergyman joined his side. "I have discussed our situation with my learned gentleman, and he has agreed to bless our union. He suspects the old man's bad luck cursed our marriage vows."

"Either that or you're a witch." The clergyman fell about, laughing at his own joke. "Sorry, forgive my jest. It was about an earlier conversation. There are rumours in the village of wise women doing dastardly deeds."

He waved his hands in the air as if casting spells, just missing the white berries that hung above his head. Poison inches from those fingers, a parasitic opportunist hiding in plain sight.

I clutched the long pearls that hung from my neck, my heart thumping hard in panic. "What rumours?" I asked.

"Oh, nothing; you need to worry your head about it," he replied.

He followed us up the stairs. "Your home is stunning, sir.

Might I congratulate you on such a respectable heritage?"

James huffed, and I smiled, knowing not one of those pictures was of his family.

We entered what I now consider my room. The clergyman bid us to kneel at the foot of the bed, facing the pillows. Raising his hands, he splashed strong scented oils. He blessed our union and crossed himself. Once finished, James saw him out of the room and to the top of the stairs. I stood in a daydream, waiting for Bess, but it was James who returned. I found a safe place deep inside myself to hide. Visions of the barn and my friends appeared behind my closed eyes. I removed myself from the present, choosing to hide in a dream.

As our first anniversary came and went, so did our second. My heart would break three more times during these years. Breaking for children that were not meant to be. More heartache followed in the passing of my father and then my mother. Leaving me utterly bereft and isolated from my family.

I would be dragged to visit Rector Farrow for a blessing each and every time. After a while, even he looked as though he were going through the motions. Where once feelings of sympathy for him might have stirred, only indifference remained. His obvious disdain grew with every loss, as though it offended his sensibilities. His eyes refused to meet mine, and he reserved his comforting speeches for James alone. Perhaps he had noticed that all who accompanied us to our blessings were James's guests. My family was conspicuously absent.

On our last walk back from the chapel, we were alone. James liked a crowd on hand to witness his majesty. I wrapped my cloak around me tighter, nervous about his change in routine.

"I wanted to talk to you," James said gruffly. "I have employed the services of a city doctor who will be arriving shortly."

"Of course, James." I replied with a sigh.

Surprised at this change of tactic, I agreed to see him. Nothing I had tried had worked, and I was resigned to the idea that my longed-for child was not meant for me.

Each village doctor had their views, and each one was promptly dismissed from their position after offending James in some way. He made it clear he was not interested in medical, only spiritual assistance.

I waited in my room, not wanting to face anyone before or after the new doctor's visit. Bess waited with me, ready to help in whatever ways would be needed. Neither of us knew what to expect or what tests could be performed, and my hands trembled. I sighed, tired of the intimate nature of the examinations, which took all my remaining strength to bear.

At last, the door handle turned and it creaked open. A short, balding man late in years stood in the gloom. His suit was freshly pressed, and a stern look spread across his face. Taking in the scene, his eyebrow raised before he strode in.

"Jane, I presume?" he said, looking at me, and his eyes barely flicked in Bess's direction. "You won't be needed, girl!"

Bess squeezed my shoulder before leaving us, and I clutched my hands together in my lap as if they could protect me.

Once alone, he placed a chair next to me with a thud and pulled a notepad from his pocket. Clearing his throat, he began asking questions about my childhood and what I had done with my time.

"My childhood was happy," I replied.

"Were you schooled like a lady in the art of marriage?"

"Of course." I kept the reading and other education to myself.

"Did you play like a boy? Did you climb trees?" His pencil paused in its scratched path.

"No," I lied, not trusting this man. "We would dress up and pretend to be getting married." I stole Alice's childhood memories.

"Do you want a child?" He leant forward.

"What a ridiculous question. Of course, I want children!"

He wrote furiously.

"Interesting," he said.

He continued prodding and poking at the corners of my life until, finally, starting on the miscarriages.

"How many now?" He waved his pen in the air as he spoke.

"This last one would make — four," I choked on the reply, remembering as if yesterday, every loss. My pain-wracked body was unable to stop the inevitable. I was left a husk.

"Why did you not want the children?" He repeated, looking into my eyes for the answer.

"Pardon? I already told you, of course, I wanted them." A tear threatened to spill down my cheek. My brow was furrowed and quizzical.

"Why did you have your friend lie about your husband?" Putting both hands on his notepad, he watched me intently.

"What lie?" I said, brushing the offending tear away.

"You colluded with your friend and the local quack to blame him for your loss," he said.

"I did not blame him or collude; they simply saw the

bruises he had inflicted," I spoke freely, my hands trembling.

"Isn't it true you're clumsy? Several people have told me how you fell on the stairs," he continued.

"I'm clumsy, but nothing that would damage a growing child." My hands went to my stomach.

"I'm the Doctor here, Madame. Answer the questions." He did not lift his eyes from his notes.

"I tripped. Ask anyone. I did not fall; I stumbled." I reiterated.

"Hmm," he pondered for a moment. "That will be all for now."

He got up to leave.

"Have you any answers or suggestions as to how to help me, doctor?" I raised my hand as if to stop him.

"Help with what?" he said.

I looked confused. "Well, seeing a pregnancy through to conclusion."

"How on earth would I know, Madame? I'm an alienist!" He looked baffled.

"No." My heartbeat thumped hard in my chest, and my breathing quickened. "James told me he was getting me a doctor. Why are you here?" My voice wobbled in panic.

"I'm here for your poor husband, Madame. The madness has taken you. You need care!" he said, raising his voice as if he considered me deaf.

"I assure you, Doctor, I am in my right mind. There is no madness, only fear and loneliness." I reached my hand towards him as if to stop him from leaving. As if keeping him here could change his mind.

"You see, right there, your eyes are quite wide, and your nostrils flare when you speak the lies of fear. How can you expect your poor husband to continue with a wife such as you? NO, NO. I will not let you damage him further."

The door slammed after him, and I found no words to use against him.

Bess returned as soon as the alienist left, and I poured my heart out to her.

"He's trying to send me away, Bess. I don't know what I can do?"

"We will think of something, I'm sure." She bit her lip.

As the weeks passed, I saw no more of the alienist, and hope grew that it would be a mere threat.

One afternoon, a letter arrived for James in a crisp white envelope with writing I could hardly read. He smiled as he read it and sat on the couch across the room from me.

He looked up.

"I've got news." He looked smug again, like on our wedding day. He straightened his back as if he had won some prize and I was his competitor.

"What is it, dear?" I asked, trying my best to sound carefree.

"My friend, the alienist doctor, is working on having you declared unfit. Not long now, dear, you will get the help you need in an asylum." He snorted.

"James, those are horrible places. You wouldn't be so cruel!" My hand grasped the arm of the chair, and I locked my ankles as if I could stop it from happening.

"Well, we will have to see, won't we? It would leave me free to marry again, and I would keep the house." He tapped his chin, pretending to think through the pros and cons and looking about the room. "We will see how much you try to please me. I will be away on business as usual, but when I am here, I expect the best treatment a wife can give. I will give you one year to produce an heir."

He stared at me, and his eyes hardened.

"Those are my terms, and they are non-negotiable."

I snuck through the dark corridors, taking only a candle. I carefully manoeuvred down the stairs, avoiding the loose boards that would give me away. One dog below stretched and looked up at me.

They were my birthday present to James, and I prayed they would be too lazy to move. The fire crackled, and the dogs shifted closer, rolling on their sides. I made my way through kitchens, past the smouldering fire and hanging meat. I turned the handle of the back door that led to the moonlit garden beyond.

It was good to feel the wet grass beneath my feet and the freedom of the night. I made my way to the walled kitchen garden, which, in its abundance, supported the lives of the house and estate. Fresh green shoots, bright with dew in the moonlight, made my heart burst with joy. Someone had brought the purple wisteria from strange lands. It covered the half-hidden wooden door to the garden beyond. I reached for the handle.

A droplet fell from the delicate purple blooms that hung in long garlands. They were low enough to brush the hair from my face and leave a trail of water across my cheek. It was cold and refreshing. A contrast to the backdrop of claustrophobic restraint that I had escaped.

I reached out and clasped the metal latch, trying hard not to make too much noise. I turned the handle, pushing the heavy wooden door and making my way inside.

The kitchen garden was brown, and the soil was freshly turned and planted for the new season. The skeletons of the beautiful fruit trees, trained in many shapes, stood along the walls. They reached across the hard brick behind. The herbs lining the paths released their scents as my shoes crushed the leaves. This would no doubt give me away to Bess in the morning, leaving a sweet-scented edge to the bottom of my gown.

I strolled towards the long glasshouse that stood against the wall. There were three: the alpine house, the pineapple house, and the largest of which I had claimed as my own. Each had their own atmosphere.

The Pineapple house was humid and smelled sweetly of rotting manure and seaweed. The resulting compost pile both heated and fed the tropical fruit. The Alpine house was home to ordered rows of succulents and low-growing mounds. My father had lovingly collected and collated these plants on his travels. I couldn't bring myself to visit since his passing and only felt sadness when I thought about his beautiful plants, now lying neglected.

My favourite was the Physic house, which housed the citrus fruits in my parents' time. Unlike the grand orangeries of the more extensive country estates, we kept a smaller array of these fruits. Dotted across the gravel in large terracotta pots, they edged the brick path. Amongst the fruit grew herbs, and overhead, a grapevine crept across wires.

At the far end stood a long bench curved around the base of the vine. The butterflies landed here during the day to rest for a while. I had cushions placed here to rest with them. As a child, I idled the day away here. I came here to mourn my father's passing, slouched on the bench, unable to face the world. My heart broke for a family I longed to be part of again.

I wanted to reverse time somehow and allow my girlhood self to tell him how much I loved him. And then the pain came in waves as my mother joined him. Passed only six short months ago. He had passed suddenly in his sleep, but she had lingered on wasting away, not sure of her purpose in this life. Two short months later, she, too, succumbed.

The night she died, I dreamt of a strange land with stone columns and white marble. They stood in groups, talking amongst themselves and wearing grey silk costumes. The image appeared like Roman statues in the British Museum, as pale as stone and equally as lacking in emotion.

My mother had approached me, the silk flowing in some imagined breeze.

"I am content now," was all she said, and then she was gone.

Both were now buried in the cold earth of our little village churchyard. They lay next to her parents and their parents before them.

I moved through the glasshouse, listening to the sound of the rain gently tapping on the panes above. I looked up, although it was dark, and I could not see the rain falling—only the traces of silver as it streaked the glass. I searched for the stars, but the clouds had drawn a curtain on the night. Closing my eyes, still facing the sky, let myself breathe, my chest releasing the tension it held.

I heard a sound behind me as if a breeze had blown across the room, dry leaves span following its path. I turned, expecting to find a gardener looking for an intruder. Instead, the room stood empty. Shaking my head at my foolishness for thinking I might have a moment to myself, I turned back towards the bench.

My breath was knocked from my body as I flew through the air. It was as if I had run full force into an invisible brick wall that had stood in my path. I found myself on the floor, my lungs unable to take in my laboured breaths. Using my elbows to push me up, the gravel digging into my skin; I struggled to move.

Looking up, I expected to see my husband. Instead, a large silhouette stood over me, but I did not recognise the shape. Tall with broad shoulders and a straight line running from there to the feet.

The candle had rolled to one side, and the flame flickered, threatening to go out. I could not distinguish who had struck me with such force. As the figure moved to strike again, the weight of him landed on my body, pinning it to the ground. The gravel dug into my shoulder as the force pushed me through it, and a sharp pain pushed into the skin on my chest.

My lungs burnt as I tried again to catch my breath. At that moment, realisation dawned that this might be the ultimate release I was looking for. If I died here and now, the days or nights with James would never come again.

I stopped fighting, and my body was more relaxed than it had been in years. I held visions of greeting my parents once more. Existing forever with them as the clergymen had promised. I took a deep, pained breath, closed my eyes, and waited for death.

The figure lurched forward, and his face stopped a hair's breadth from my neck. He paused and examined me, confused; he made to go for my neck again and stopped once more. The stranger released my wrists, nevertheless; I did not move. He took the weight of his knee from my sides, and although a breath escaped me, I lay still.

Disappointment took hold as I realised that he may yet let me live. Moments passed in which the searing pain in my shoulder grew worse as the gravel pushed deeper into my skin.

The figure changed to a crouched position next to me and then stood, tenderly lifting my body. Now, it was my turn to be confused. I opened my eyes, but I still could not see his face. A silver pin attached to the lapel of his coat hung in front of my face. A lady with wings stared back at me.

His hair must have been shoulder length; it brushed against my face as he held me. He carried me like this to the bench and laid me down.

Still, I did not try to flee.

"Why?" was all he said. His voice grew low, not angry or menacing, just questioning. "Why didn't you fight?" He repeated.

"I don't have any fight left," I explained, and I swung my legs down to sit, wincing at the fresh scrapes.

He sat next to me, and we stayed this way for some minutes.

He appeared to be pondering the situation. I jumped as he reached for the candle, holding it to my face. The flickering light reignited. In the flare, he caught sight of the purples and greens that now covered my cheekbone and eye. I shied away from the light, turning my face and closing my eyes against the memories of the blows that inflicted them.

"I understand," he said, sounding like a long-lost friend instead of my attacker.

"Are you going to kill me?" I said in a whisper, almost too quiet to be heard.

"I don't know. You've taken all the fun out of it."

His indulgent laugh caught me off guard and I caught the glint of deep green eyes below blond hair. He appeared five years older than me. His face was a little too sunken below the eyes, and his cheekbones a little too prominent. But his coat sat across broad shoulders. He obviously worked manually, with his muscles pronounced under his shirt. Otherwise, I would have said he was starved like the gutter waifs in the city streets. Something wasn't quite right about him, but I couldn't place my finger on it. Why did I even care? A moment ago, this man could have killed me.

We sat like this for what could have been hours in

silence. He made no movements, and it still appeared as if he was weighing up his options. In the end, I did as I had come here to do: sit peacefully and rest away from the horrors of the house.

At last, he spoke. "What are you doing out here in the night?"

"It's peaceful," I said. "My husband is cruel and I need the places I feel safe." feeling like I could be more honest now with the stranger than I had with anyone before.

"Have I taken a safe space from you?" he said.

"It depends; if you kill me, I will no longer need safe spaces. Death is the only true rest," I replied.

"That's a sad state of affairs." His voice grew low again.

"I wouldn't expect a man to understand. You have freedom." I countered.

He pondered this for a while.

"Anyway," I said, "you're a criminal; why would you even care? Are you here to steal?" I confronted him.

"I don't need your possessions. I'm hungry," was his reply.

It was my turn to think about his reply. "What do you do?" I asked.

"I'm a soldier, an explorer, and a mapmaker," he said, his back pulled straight and his shoulders back, as pride swelled in him.

"Goodness, all of those at once. How is it you have no money for food with this many strings to your bow?" I asked.

"It's complicated." Was all he would offer.

By now, the sun had started to light the edges of the night sky, prompting us to both stand. We made our way to the door of the glasshouse. It appeared he was in as much of a hurry as I was.

"I know this may seem a little strange, but can I visit

again? I promise I won't hurt you." He asked.

"I'm not sure my husband would approve. I'm quite sure he wouldn't." I took a step away from the stranger, taken aback at his request.

"No need for him to know." he winked at me. And with that, he disappeared into the night.

On the horizon, the sun sent a golden seam between the night sky and the new day. I headed back towards the house, remembering the gravel embedded in my shoulder. Cursing that I would now have to find some way of hiding the wound or an explanation, I quickened my pace.

Only the staff were up, making their way around the house. They were lighting fires and tidying away the signs of the guests the night before. I snuck upstairs undisturbed and came across Bess in my room already. I hurried inside and begged her help to clean and bind my shoulder, hiding it from James, his lover and his guests. He would be leaving for the city later that morning, and so I only had to keep up the illusion for a few hours.

I came to the door to wave my husband off, playing the dutiful wife. A flash of green caught my eye as the blonde stepped into the carriage. I squinted to get a better look and saw she was wearing my emerald necklace.

"James." I grabbed his arm. "That's my necklace; where did she find it?"

"Don't be silly. Why would she want your necklace?" He shook my hand free.

"I don't even know where she got it," I said.

"You're losing your faculties, Jane. You know she has enough money to buy her jewels. Why would she need your trifling ornaments? You're running out of time. Don't you think you ought to concentrate on fulfilling your duty?" He left my side and went to the carriage.

Never yours

As they moved away, I saw my jewellery adorning the neck of my husband's lover.

CHAPTER FOUR
Monkshood

The next day, the heavens opened, and I found myself wandering the house. Rain pelted the grey, flint-covered walls outside. The silence smothered me, a constant reminder of how empty the house was. It drove me mad. I paced its corridors, rediscovering its rooms, hoping this would lift the feeling of dread and hopelessness that had settled over me.

Our ancestral home was laid over two floors, with attic rooms and two tower rooms that stood alone up winding staircases. The family and guest rooms were on the second floor. The ground floor entrance held the hall, with its cold stone floor and grand wooden staircase.

I hopped down the steps and slid across the smooth floor into the sitting room. My hose slipped easily, gathering dust as they went.

A glint of my childlike playfulness made a brief appearance. The room had large windows that overlooked the garden. The drizzle sent rivulets of water running down its surface. A stone fireplace now crackled with a freshly laid fire. I paced around the edge, looking out as drops bounced in large puddles on the path outside. Despite the fire, a gloom enveloped the room.

My feet led me to the dining room, which had a long, elegant table big enough to hold the entire extended family. Most days, I sat alone, staring into the distance, my head full of dreams. The empty chairs only reminded me of the family I longed to see.

Dust motes hung in the air as I crossed the hall to a door that led to James' study once my father's. I remember running there as a child, often muddy, looking for a hiding place from my sisters. My father would let me crawl under the desk. When anyone came looking, he would gruffly tell them he was too busy for all this interruption, sending them packing before I crawled out giggling. Now, I could only stand at the locked door and wonder at what was kept within.

I continued upstairs to the first of the tower rooms. I climbed a small wooden staircase which wound around until it reached a dark room. It had a larger window that overlooked the topiary garden. The white-washed walls were peeling, revealing the mottled beige lime plaster below. They were damp to the touch, and the room smelt musty and unloved. Dust covered every surface; as my skirt dragged across the floor, it sent plumes into the air, clogging my nostrils. Sneezing, I flung open the window. I sat on the wide ledge, thinking I might clear my lungs with the fresh, damp air.

Despite the rain, the view was breathtaking, and on a clear day, I could have seen forever. Past the woods at the edge of the estate, even the village looked tiny from here. I hadn't been further than the coach house barn in so long. Even this allowed me an escape from the prison my home had become.

Farm workers were busy in the fields. Little pillows of smoke rose high into the air from the cottages. I squinted to make out the steam train moving across the horizon toward the city. That would be the train James would be on, taking him far from here. I longed to be on that train. Not with my husband, just to be going somewhere and to be someone else. Perhaps some young woman off to see her lover or a man on his way to do business in the city.

From here, I could see a world that I did not belong to, something I wasn't allowed to be part of. I was so tired of being sad, tired of being ground down and hanging on for any little pieces of mercy, of peace. I was tired of being an extra in the story of James's life.

Reflecting on all those I had lost, they no longer had these earthly cares. How blissful nothingness must be. I remembered the stranger who attacked me and the feeling of peace after accepting my fate.

James could marry again, and my sisters had families. I had nothing to lose, no love, no child and no parents. What was there to live for anymore? Bess, her husband Jack and her mother Lenora would be fine. The new mistress would need staff for the time they spent here. A shell of my former self, I hadn't felt like a person for a long time. I existed to be James's and do as he wished, and only then when he wished it, or else I was to be a ghost. Well, no more.

Emotions no longer played a part in my decisions, only logic. James did not want me, and I couldn't have children. There was no point in my existence. The only problem was that I wasn't sure I could be brave enough to do what was needed.

Getting onto my knees, I balanced on the window ledge. The gravel below appeared to rise and fall in waves. My head spun, and I gripped the window frame. The walls of the room closed in on me, and I slipped back to sitting. My fingers left little blackened imprints on the dusty white wood.

I decided a daytime display of that would not be fair to the staff. It would make too much of a mess that would need someone to clean up. I couldn't put anyone through that. I shuddered; no, that was not for me. I made my way back downstairs.

The light faded outside, and I made my way to the library. Isobel finished making the fire; she curtsied and left. Its walls were no longer visible behind deep wooden bookshelves and many books. I don't think I could finish them in my lifetime. The smell of old paper, earthy with a hint of vanilla, filled the air. I decided that while the weather kept me from the garden, I could spend more time in this room. I lost myself in paper worlds and slouched in one of the two large, soft leather armchairs.

The back of the chairs faced the full-height window, and opposite them stood a fireplace. A mantelpiece sat above the fire with a large vase of flowers. This room had a second floor with a short staircase to reach it. Rich, dark wood panelling filled with more bookshelves surrounded me. I moved around the bookshelves, running my fingers along the leather-bound spines. Feeling the rough, well-read ones and the shiny new, hardly touched ones. I read each title as I went from the Greek myths to encyclopaedias and, of course, the Bible. I climbed the tiny staircase to the upper levels and found the section on plants and gardens. One caught my eye: a large red leather-bound book; the pages were edged in gold and looked untouched. I took it down from the shelves and read the cover.

Poisonous Plants of Great Britain
by

Professor Arthur Merryweather

I took the volume and went to sit in one of the leather armchairs as Bess came in.

"Would you like something to eat, Jane?"

We had gone beyond formal titles, at least when James wasn't around. By now, we both knew each other too well.

"Yes, a little something in here, if that's not too much trouble?" With that, she left, and I relaxed into the soft chair with the warmth of the fire on my face.

She returned a short while later. She set a tray down on the small table between the chairs and left once more. Leafing through the book, I admired all the glorious paintings of plants. There were some which I recognised and others I had never seen. I picked at the cold meats and cheese, wiping my hands on a cloth between mouthfuls to avoid making the pages dirty.

I read a page on foxgloves, the sort that flowered pink and white, in the woods on the estate. Digitalis was used in some preparations, but too much proved toxic to be of any use. Letting the pages fall open where they chose, it landed on Monkshood. A blue flowered plant I had seen in our gardens. The description made the reader aware that the taste would be off-putting.

Next came the nightshade; again, the symptoms sounded less than tempting.

It did have a recommendation for making an eye drop, like the Greek ladies, to widen the pupils. I didn't feel like any of these were going to do the job.

As I cursed my cowardice, there came a tapping at the window. I turned, thinking the rain had gathered pace once more since it had persisted at the edge of my hearing. It started again, louder now, and made me jump, the window pane rattling along with each tap. Although the curtains were wide, I could not see who was making the noise. It was pitch black outside, and the light from the room I occupied hid them from sight. Only the room's reflections and my visage were shown in the window, as if I were looking into a parallel world. The knocking shook me from my musing, and it was even louder this time. I got up from my chair and moved to see if I could make out the intruder. It wasn't until I was upon the window that I finally saw who lurked beyond; this did nothing to settle my nerves.

Again, the knocking continued, this time so loudly that I feared one of the staff or dogs would hear. The hairs on my arms stood on end, and goosebumps sprung up. My breath caught in my throat, and my eyes widened. The idea that James would discover that a man had been at the window sent a shiver through me. If the staff heard, there was no telling what his reaction would be or what more leverage this would give him over my fate.

I reached for the latch, opened the window a tiny amount, and whispered, "What do you want?"

"Hello to you as well, my lady." The attacker from the glasshouse made a low, slow, exaggerated bow and then lifted his face to smile at me. "It's only me, your neighbourhood villain, looking in on his latest victim."

As he turned, a scar appeared; it ran from the bottom of his right eye to what was now the upturned corner of his lips.

"That's not funny. What are you doing back here?" I demanded.

"We agreed. Don't you remember? I could return to talk," he said.

"I'm not sure, agreed, is what happened? Why? What would we have to speak about?" I replied.

"Oh, I don't know, I have been to many places." he held his coat lapels.

"But I have not. I fear I will only bore you." I went to shut the window.

"You're not boring me thus far," he shrugged. Come on, let me in; it's wet out here." He exaggerated his shiver and ran his arms around himself. I will tell you a story."

"Ugh," I groaned. "Please be quiet. Someone will hear you." I swung the window open wider and stepped back. He stood still. "Well, what are you waiting for? Come in, come in."

Placing one hand on the frame, he leapt into the window, landing on the ledge. For a moment, he crouched, looking like a crow, taking in the surroundings. His eyes betrayed an intelligence I did not expect to find. The birds are known as thieves and pranksters, and this image suited the visitor well. Although, as a group, they were known as a murder. I would need to be on my guard in case more of his ilk was secreted nearby.

"Why thank you, my lady." He shook water droplets from his coat.

"Stop calling me that," I said as I stepped back out of reach of the wet.

"What should I call you?" he said as he stepped off the ledge and stood in front of me.

He stood at least a foot above my head and taller than James. He was wearing a long, rough, black cotton box coat, which had only added to his wing-like appearance. Its gold buttons glinted in the light as he undid them, contrasting with the silver pin. He threw his coat over the back of the chair next to my own, his ruffled black shirt creased from travel.

"No wonder I couldn't see you out there. You're dressed like the night," I said.

"Ah, but I could see you, and that's what's important."

I was reminded of the wolf from the Little Red Riding Hood story. I moved to my chair as if it could offer protection. He slipped into the chair next to me, slinging his leg over the arm and resting his back against the other arm, facing me.

"What are you reading, little bird?" He enquired.

"Why little bird now?" I let out a frustrated sigh.

"Well, you're caught in a gilt cage, aren't you?" He gestured at the surrounding room.

"That's none of your business," I hissed.

He held his hands up. "OK, I promise that the next time I give you a name, it will be one you aspire to be called. How's that?"

"I don't know. It's a bit strange, don't you think?" I said, my brow creased in confusion.

"No. I know other people call you the name your parents gave you, but I will find a name only I will use. Then you will know it's me." A smile curved at the corner of his mouth.

"I don't think we will know each other long enough for that." I tried to let him down gently.

"Ah, is that why you're reading about poisons?" he nudged at the book on the table between us.

I grabbed the book and slammed it shut, a little louder than I meant to, causing the plate and tray to wobble and clatter against each other.

I placed the book on my lap and sat up a little straighter.

"Again, that's none of your business." My voice grew more agitated now.

"Well, I don't know. Maybe I can help," he offered.

"How?" I asked.

"Give me six months." He leant forward, dropping his leg from the arm of the chair.

"I'm not sure I have six months, and what if I don't want

six months?" My eyebrows rose.

"Look, at the end of six months, if you still no longer want to live, I will help you with that. But give me six months to show you what there is to live for," he said.

"How will you help me?" It was my turn to lean in towards him. I already knew he was dangerous; perhaps this was the coward's way out I was looking for.

"I won't tell you now, but two weeks before the end of the bet, I will tell you how I will help you." He sat back.

"It's a bet now, is it?" I chuckled.

"Well, we may as well make this interesting."

"What is it you want in return?" I eyed him suspiciously.

"I will tell you that two weeks from the end." He sat back in his chair once more.

I studied his face, trying to discover what those things could be that could not be known until the end. His face appeared different from the last time. His eyes weren't desperate or sunken, and his cheeks had filled out. I considered his offer, turning to the fire as the flames licked across the logs. After a few moments, I turned back to him. He hadn't taken his eyes off me, and I squirmed in my seat.

"It's a bet." I sat up a little straighter, trying to gain a sense of command over the situation.

He held his hand out as if to shake it. His green eyes sparkled now as he looked into mine. After we had shaken, I pulled my hand back, uncomfortable at the familiarity of the touch.

"Good." He smiled again. "But tonight we'll just talk. In two days, I will be back, and we can start."

Eager to change the subject, I interjected, "You said you would tell me a story?"

"Ah yes, so I did." He leaned back in his chair and watched the flames dance as he started.

"I met an old man once; he must have been around fifty-seven. We met in London on the banks of the river Thames. He had a mop of black hair and a big bushy beard that hung longer than his arms." He gestured theatrically as he spoke, showing the beard stretching out before him.

"His navy jacket and trousers were stained with ground in dirt and coal. Only his eyes were visible above the beard and below the hair; the rest was covered in mud.

"This man sat every day on the road, with his cap before him, hoping the passersby would donate to his meal. Most did not see him. Those that did kicked yet more dirt in his face. They repeated the same old tired admonishments for not having work or family.

"No one knew his story, no one cared, and he considered himself unlovable and uninteresting. He didn't understand why I sat with him to talk. But as I said, everyone has their story. I discovered that the mud had come from the river foreshore. Where every day he would trawl through the wet earth looking for treasures.

"Occasionally, he would find a lost trinket or coin that would save his life for another day or two. But his most valued treasures had become the things he could not sell.

"In his inner jacket pocket, close to his heart, he kept rocks. These rocks had strange shapes in them—curious curving or tangled creatures from long ago. His fingers had polished them. Night after night, he smoothed them, his fingers travelling every inch, as he sat below the street lamps, admiring his collection.

"This man, whom no one thought about, himself thought a great deal. He was an explorer of his corner of the world. His story was interesting."

"What happened to him?" My voice cracked. Although our lives were very different, I sympathised with his loneliness.

"The same thing that happens to all old men," he said.

We talked long into the night about his military service and my oils. I told him my deep secrets about the miscarriages and finding my husband's affairs. As time passed, it was wonderful to talk with someone new. I felt I had dominated the conversation and sensed that he had more information about me than I had about him.

"I must be leaving," he said, standing to go.

I looked at the wooden grandfather clock as it struck four in the morning. "Oh my, I've kept you too long."

"No, you've kept me the right amount of time."

"Can I ask your name before you go?" I said, realising I hadn't asked.

"Of course," he said, taking my hand. He bowed low and kissed it before looking at me again. "My name is Sabrett."

"That's unusual. Where does it come from?" I asked.

"A question best answered next time, I think," he replied, dropping my hand once more.

And with that, he took his coat and climbed back through the window.

Bess didn't try to wake me until after lunch, which I was grateful for. When she came to my room later that day, we sat sharing a tray of fruit, bread and cheese. We chatted about the glasshouse, now brimming with seedlings, close to growing everything we needed, even building a surplus. We had started supplying oils to neighbours and travelling salesmen, earning a few coins to give Bess and Lenora a better life. Of course, I was the silent partner, as I would draw too much attention.

"We are agreed, then. I will spend the remainder of today and tomorrow in the glasshouse tending the new plants," I said.

This was a plan I heartily looked forward to.

"I'm afraid I cannot help this time, and I may be too busy with my work to be found," Bess replied.

Bess would be busy with chores for the next two days, and I would not see her much. I knew James had set her many tasks and I did not argue with her.

As I pottered in the physic garden glasshouse, the earthy smell of damp soil drifted through the humid air. I went over the details of my conversation with Sabrett, turning green with envy of his ability to travel. I pondered how nice it must be to walk alone and talk to strangers with no care or fear. How free he must feel. I had no measure by which to compare and imagining a life that different proved difficult. It must be akin to when I watch James' carriage disappearing up the drive. A sense of relief and a relaxing of shoulders so knotted from being bunched up, that they groan at the change. Most of the time, I didn't even know they were hunched up. Breathing easier, knowing that if I chose to kick off my shoes and walk barefoot in the grass, I could. But that was as close as I could get.

I picked up a trug and headed into the garden to harvest lavender. The heady scent filled my nostrils and permeated my skin and my clothes. I sneezed; the strength of it had that effect sometimes. Brushing my hair from my face, I continued working until the trug became heavy with stems. The fading light spurred me on to the barn to hang up the harvest. Drying these would ensure next winter would not be such a barren affair. There were strings stretched between the shelves, criss-crossing each other in many layers. I tied them in bunches with coarse string and hung them from the rust-brown nails that stuck out from the wall at jaunty angles. The walls were now so layered with the scent of oils that the lavender's potent perfume barely added to the fragrance.

As I turned, my eye caught a movement in the tree line. I stopped, peering through the barn door. The last rays of the sun had disappeared below the horizon, and moonlight instead lent its gentle light. My eyes struggled to adjust as I searched for the source of the movement. There it was again, in the corner of my eye, small but still there.

"Sabrett," I called, but there was no answer. "Sabrett," I called again, but this time, an owl sent its screeching reply.

I put the movement down to animals and took a candle to light my way back to the house.

I crept across the courtyard in front of the coach-houses, passing the horses as quietly as I could. I reached the end and turned the handle to the staff entrance. One horse pounded at the floor with his hooves. Grunting and letting out a loud whinny, he kicked at the door, all the while staring up into the night sky. A tile slipped from the stables' roof, falling silently through the air and smashing on the cobblestones. The other horses joined in, the noise becoming deafening. The stable hands and grooms ran out of the surrounding barns. They pulled on their trousers and shirts and stumbled sleepily across the cobbles. Running to calm the horses and see what had spooked them. I ran inside and up to my room.

CHAPTER FIVE
Vanilla

Dear Harriette,

I have wanted to write for so long. I know I won't send this letter, but one day, it will be in your hands from someone other than me. I wanted you to understand my actions.

Most days, I move through life completing meaningless chores as though there is no end, as if time is not ticking away in the background, as if I have forever.

I hope this is something you will never experience and that your life is blessed.

It's hard to imagine that someone hates you. My first reaction was disbelief. I never considered myself a bad person. I tried to make the right choices. Of course, I failed, as everyone does. No person in the world has made all the right choices. But nothing was ever malicious, and I remained convinced my choices had only ever hurt me. The aim was that they only ever hurt me. I never wanted my family to know my shame.

Then deep, deep sorrow hit. I tried to love him, but he hated me. It hurts so much more if they are meant to love you. The pain will rip and tear at your insides, becoming physical. Your heart hurts; it aches so profoundly you're not sure it will ever stop. You live every day hoping to change something in you that will make them love you.

You question yourself and examine every detail and flaw. You examine yourself deeply, tearing yourself open, trying to get at and cut out the rot inside you. I hope you never know this loss.

The withdrawal of love without explanation is awful. Sometimes, the explanation itself can be torture. They will tell you that you are the monster. They can't look at your deformities any longer; now, for their safety, they must withhold their love.

The darkness fogs your memories.

It makes it impossible to remember if you ever felt their caring touch. Have they ever shown you the love you feel the loss of? They will claim that it is your bitterness, how could they have shown you when you were so cold and hard?

How could you have been cruel and singled them out in such a way as to hurt them? Twisting and turning your words and feelings. You question every memory of every decision. You look back on fondly held memories with the most pain, knowing that what you see as happy, they see as a mirror image. What to you is white, to them is black.

Their smiles and soft eyes turn to stone with new understanding.

Their words repeating over and over in your head haunt your nightmares and daydreams. A black void opens, threatening to swallow you. Sometimes, oblivion seems like an easy answer because living is pain. You must indeed be a horrible person for the one you love to want to cut you down so badly.

I cannot continue in this life. I hope you can forgive me.

All my love

Jane

I slipped the folded letter between the pages of my book

before I left the more mundane letter to Harriette, filled with inane catch-up chatter, on the hall table. While waiting for Sabrett to return, I pondered what he would be showing me over the next six months that could change my mind. After all, the critical component wasn't going to change. My marriage to a hateful man continued, and I couldn't see a way out. I remained set on my decision. What a strange situation this was. A new acquaintance, not a friend that's too informal, who could kill me at any moment. Unlike James, this man's intentions had been laid out before me from our very first meeting and yet I no longer cared about my life. It was not some precious jewel to protect. I no longer feared death. I welcomed it.

I sat in the library for the evening, hoping that since this was the location of our last meeting, he would appear at the window again. Now and then, I got up and paced the room as the hours passed, thinking myself a fool for believing a man and his word. Then I would sit and chastise myself. He must be busy; why else would he keep me waiting? Before pacing and cursing again.

As nine o'clock approached, I stormed out of the library, cursing the day I trusted a man. Isobel hurried across the hall.

"Where's Bess?" I yelled.

This took her by surprise. I wasn't the yelling kind.

"She's in the kitchen garden, Mistress." She held a curtsy as I hurried past. I wasn't even sure what I planned on doing when I found her.

I hurried through the formal gardens, past the sweetly scented roses, and through the heavy wooden door. I stopped after stepping inside, looking around and spotting Bess near the apple trees at the far end. My eyes were drawn there by flapping white material. I was momentarily confused as the washing lines all stood in a courtyard close to the stables. I headed down the gravel paths that flanked the beds, now bursting into life.

The month of May had rushed in abundant and fresh. Green pea shoots poked up through the soil next to last year's winter cabbages. The apple blossom had now faded and fell like snow to the ground. Large sheets were strung from the branches, the flapping corners were tied tight as I approached.

I could see a light behind them as the sheets were pulled taut. It illuminated the figures of Bess and Lenora, her crooked stance unmistakable. A broad-shouldered man, whom I took to be Bess' husband, Jack, stood with another two figures I could not place.

As I turned the corner, the other two men came into view. Sabrett was one, and he appeared in animated conversation with the other shorter gentleman.

On Seeing me, Sabrett turned.

"Ah, here she is. A little earlier than expected, but so be it."

Bess shifted awkwardly.

"I was going to come and get you when we were ready." She had a wry grin on her face.

Blankets were strewn on the ground in front of the sheets and a little table teetering on the gravel somewhat precariously. The little man rushed to push it down into the stones, securing it before the little mechanism containing the light fell.

"May I introduce professor Arthur Merryweather?" Sabrett held out his hand in the direction of the smaller grey-haired gentleman.

At which point, the stranger tipped his glasses down his nose to look at me

"Hello, m—y dear." He spoke quietly, and there was a

trace of a stammer hidden beneath the words he chose. I recognised that name from somewhere, but couldn't quite grasp it.

His left hand was missing the last two fingers from the knuckle. He pushed his glasses up again using the stubs, which were long healed over, leaving no trace of the wounds that had caused their loss. He wore a waistcoat and striped shirt with cufflinks at the wrists.

"My friend here was in York, giving a talk, and I was sure he would be the perfect person for this job," Sabrett added.

"And what job is that?" I asked, feeling the anger from earlier dissipate, opening instead into curiosity.

"I'm going to show you the world with the help of friends, of course." Sabrett gestured to the guest.

"Oh, Jane," Bess said, looking so excited she might burst. "There's a little box with a light in it, and it has pictures."

I chuckled, caught up in her infectious excitement. "What are you talking about?"

"Come sit down, ladies and gentlemen," Sabrett said.

We settled on the blankets, as comfortably as possible, facing the taught sheets. Sabrett sat next to me.

"I hope you don't mind me borrowing your friends, but I needed a little help," he whispered in my ear.

The professor stood before us.

"Today, I'm going to presen—t to you a few illustrations from m—y travels. I hope you enjoy them." His voice betrayed the nervous edge of someone who was used to having to prove himself, and with that, he returned to the table.

Movement flickered on the sheets, and a colour picture appeared illuminated there. Bess gasped, grasping Jack's arm, and Lenora crossed herself as if in protection. Before us was what looked like a painting of a strange landscape. Large mountains were in the background. Soft brushstrokes of colour across glass captured a magical world.

A group of people, whose skin shone in tones of umber and ebony, carrying packs or loading horses. I gazed in awe at the image brought to life in front of me. Like no painting before, it stirred feelings I had not experienced.

The image was vivid, like looking into another world, not static and unchanging like the art gallery pieces. There was beauty and danger in equal measure within these adventures. My eyes moved across the image, taking in all the tiny details. Then another appeared, making Bess jump. A detailed view of a beautiful and strange plant. Petals of deep red spotted at the edges with white no plants in our gardens could compare.

I turned to Sabrett.

"The book in the library?" I gasped.

"The one and the same," he said of the author and now our guest.

I turned back, disappointed to miss the last minutes of the image, only to be greeted by another. A river in full torrent dashing through a cut in the jagged rocks. It made me feel quite unsteady to think of the danger of that water. Then, a small village appeared with huts covered in plant material. Little fires surrounded by women cooking. Bess gasped louder now, and Lenora tutted audibly. Jack chuckled under his breath. The woman pictured wore nothing on their breasts and only a small covering across the rest of their body. Sabrett laughed loudly at the reaction of our companions whilst I tried to hide my shock.

"Ah," said the professor, his cheeks flushed. "I'm sorry, ladies. This show is meant for learned gentlemen."

Another slide clicked into view. This time, I recognised a

younger professor Merryweather. He stood triumphantly on top of a mountain. It was a nighttime scene, and two porters were setting up the camp. At the back of the illustration, a man crouched over the campfire, tending it. I looked closer to make out the man further, his face illuminated by the flames. I could swear the man was Sabrett, but where the professor looked younger, he looked the same. This man's crow-like stance was the same as I had seen when Sabrett entered the library.

Sabrett must have seen my puzzled expression as he leant closer and whispered.

"My father, some say we look remarkably similar."

"Is he alive?" I asked.

"Oh no, he passed many moons ago." With that, he turned back to the pictures, eager to change the subject.

The slide changed again, and I saw no more pictures of Sabrett's father in the collection. Once the show had finished, we all applauded the professor, who blushed and bowed his head.

"That was amazing," I said, clasping my hands together in front of my face as if in prayer. "Please, come up to the house for some supper, and you can tell me all about your travels. Bess can make sure you have a room for the night. Both of you." I gestured at Sabrett.

I turned to Lenora, Bess, and Jack, "Please, come eat."

"Not me; I'm afraid I need to get back to the village. It is late already, and Jack will need to help me." Lenora declined.

"I will stay until morning to make sure everything is taken care of," said Bess.

Our little party separated, Lenora and Jack disappearing into the dark. The professor joined us, blowing out the light, and packed his magic lantern into its box to carry it back to the house. We took down the sheets and Sabrett picked up the little table, slinging it over his shoulder easily.

When we got back to the house, we sat in the dining room and Isobel brought the soup from the kitchen. The professor ripped some bread apart. He used it to soak up the thick liquid before stuffing it past his moustache. The fluffy growth held some of the vegetable soup back each time, building up a thick layer. His little glasses perched on his nose. Bess sat with us as she did when James wasn't home. We chatted about the illustration. I learned that the exotic flower was called an orchid, all the rage now in the fashionable houses.

"I can't say this house has been called fashionable for many years now." I laughed.

It proved refreshing to have new company, and the professors' stories were fascinating. As was his habit, Sabrett slung his leg over the arm of the chair opposite me while he lay back and took in the scene.

"You haven't touched your food?" I said.

"Don't worry about me. I ate earlier." He held his hand up, palm out, as if stopping any further offers of food before they were given.

Bess jumped in, "It's alright. I made sure he was fed before we started. We were keen to surprise you."

"Well, you certainly did that. I must apologise to Isobel; she must wonder what on earth was going on."

The professor, arms stretched high over his head as his mouth widened in a yawn, "Sorry, it's been a long day."

"Of course, we must find you both rooms for the night." I stood, making ready to find space for them in the house.

"Not for me, I'm afraid. But I have arranged for the professor to be taken back to York tomorrow. If it is not too much trouble for him to stay, that would be kind," Sabrett said as we walked into the hall.

"No, of course not, but it's past one in the morning. Are you sure you want to leave now?" I walked with him into the hall, our feet echoing across the stone floor.

"I have an early train to catch. I have left instructions. In two weeks, Jack will take you to the train station and you will meet me in the city." Sabrett announced another surprise.

"What? No, I can't leave. What if James finds out?" My hands trembled at the idea.

"I've made sure with Alice and he will still be in the city," Bess explained.

Alice worked in the London apartment as a maid and had grown up with Bess. They often wrote to update each other on the households, ensuring that the master's wishes were obeyed.

I turned to Sabrett, looking for reassurance.

"Don't worry, it's a big place and he won't see you. I will meet you at the train station at 9 o'clock. We will go by the cover of night, and you will return early the next morning to avoid too much speculation."

"But what will we do?" I asked.

"That is for me to know. I didn't agree to tell you what I would show you, did I?" He opened the door and stepped into the night. Only his blond hair betrayed him in the dark. "Until next time."

The weeks dragged by, and I grew restless as fear bubbled up inside me, accompanied by excitement. I was torn between wanting to experience more and the fear of being found out. If I had known how to contact Sabrett, I would have cancelled numerous times, but I could do nothing but wait.

I distracted myself by making oils, and the barn shelves groaned with the many tiny vials. The professor had promised to send his newest book,

The Plants of South America, and a week after he left, it arrived.

This time, the book was bound in deep blue leather and brown paper packaging with a string tied around it. The botanical illustrations were even more fascinating than the last volume. I gladly added it to the library and sat reading it most evenings, wondering at the amazing lands the professor had visited. They were covered in lush tropical foliage or deep blankets of snow. I lived vicariously through his adventures.

At last, the day came, and Jack brought the little cart, big enough to fit two comfortably and four with a squeeze. It was painted in yellow and black with large wooden wheels that seemed to catch every lump in the road. It was attached to one of the stocky working horses; the hunting horses were not to be used for pulling carts. The large, muscular, tan colour horse looked at us. It judged us as if weighing up the journey it was to embark on before snorting its disapproval.

It took us most of the morning to travel the unkempt, rough roads through the village and out the other side. Finally, the train station came into view, usually only visible from the tower room. The platform, raised above the tracks, stood almost empty. The guard didn't venture out of the lone timber building that housed the waiting room.

I waited on the platform, wearing my city clothes. A practical white high-collar blouse with the sleeves slightly puffed at the shoulder. I had pinned my favourite brooch at the front, a red ruby set in silver to go with my hair. A simple black travelling skirt and a black hat with a small veil. I pulled it further across my face, hiding in case someone recognised me. Of course, I so rarely ventured out that it was doubtful, but I still could not stop my hands from trembling.

The large steam engine in royal blue heaved into the

station with a loud screech of steam. I grabbed my purse to my chest and jumped backwards and my ears were left ringing.

The doors were flung open, and I climbed into the carriage, pulling my ticket from my purse as I went. To avoid unwanted attention, I found my seat next to a young couple with their child. I sat next to the window to watch the world go by. The gently rolling hills flattened out into fields interrupted with thick hedges.

The train rocked back and forth as we travelled; people came and went, families on a day out and older couples travelling home. Young men full of life, looking for adventure in the big city, poking fun at those around them. I kept to myself as much as I could, my veil still pulled across my face. At last, the edges of the city started to blend away from the countryside.

The sun setting on the horizon sent oranges and yellows softened by the smoke that started to rise from the chimneys. More and more houses appeared until the rush of the train made them combine as if they were one. Windows lit from within, a glimpse into other people's lives. The view moved steadily. Blending from the poor, un-curtained and crowded rooms through to the wealthy inner-city drawing rooms. The smut from the train stained each house the same muddy brown colour, no matter the class of the residents.

The station loomed into view. Its tall roof lets the standing trains' billowing steam escape. It rose high above the heads of the crowds of people.

I stepped out of the carriage, feeling like I needed to regain my balance after the long journey. It was like my feet had forgotten the solid earth. As I stumbled to the side, a firm hand gripped my arm. I looked up to see Sabrett's green eyes shining in the gloom. He replaced his dark glasses, concealing his eyes once more. The top hat added height to his already tall frame. He led me to a waiting taxi outside, and we took the carriage through the streets. As people pushed past us and the crowds made their way through the station, I realised I hadn't remembered it as being this busy. The rose-tinted glasses of youth colouring my memory.

He lifted my veil. "You won't be needing that here. Nobody will recognise you in these crowds."

"What is going on?" I asked.

"You do live under a rock, don't you?" he said a little more cruelly than I hoped he meant. "It's Prince Albert's Great Exhibition. They built a crystal palace to house the wonders of the world, and now everyone is here to see it."

"Of course, I have heard that. I didn't expect quite so many people," I said, with a little sarcasm in my voice. "It's so loud."

We stepped out of the carriage, and the vast glass building loomed over us. It stood taller than even the tower rooms in my home. Breathtakingly beautiful glittering in the evening light, lit from within, it reminded me of a diamond on the neck of a beautiful lady. I was not the only one admiring the building. Huge throngs of people stood open-mouthed, gaping into the night. Dust clouds were thrown into the air by the carriages as they brought more people, who stopped and stood with us. The enormous number of candles flooded the building with a flickering warm orange glow, like a lantern. People in strange clothes moved through the crowds, and we made our way to the doors.

Sabrett's arm was wrapped around me, holding me close, trying to protect me from the worst of the shoves and elbows of the overexcited populace. As we entered, the roof stretched far above, housing entire trees inside the glass walls.

Voices surrounded us, chattering in excitement about

giant creatures and mechanical wonders. The heat of the crowds was stifling. We pushed through the bodies, looking for the exhibits.

At the building's heart stood a crystal fountain. The water bubbled up and then cascaded down, much to the delight of two small children. Dressed in their Sunday best, they trailed their hands in the waters as they ran in circles, giggling.

We climbed the stairs to look down from the first floor at all the exhibits. Moving among the crowd were beautiful dark-skinned ladies, turning the heads of the gentlemen who passed by. Jewellery adorned their necks, and the earrings they wore were bell-shaped. Even their noses had large jewelled hoops through them. They bowed gracefully with their hands together in what looked like prayer. Their bangles clinked and slid down their arms as they did, revealing bruising I recognised only too well.

"Who are those women?" I asked.

"The British call them coolies, not a nice word, I know. They are likely Indo-Caribbean, probably working in the the colonies before coming here."

As their bright clothes disappeared into the crowds, I wondered at the cruelty of mankind.

We stepped around a tree trunk that grew up through the floor. Its deep-lobed and bright green leaves spread above our heads as we walked through the canopy. Below us, a man swung an umbrella about, wielding it like a strange weapon, to the giggles of some ladies who whispered to each other. We climbed down some stairs and admired striped skins pinned to a wall. There were giant twisted horns and antlers larger than the cart that had taken me to the station.

A huge grey beast loomed above my head as we turned the corner. Its trunk curved high in the air. It was draped in delicate red cloth and carried a gold-tented chair high up on its back. I stepped out of its path in case the elephant was about to tread on me, but it did not move, frozen in time.

"Poor thing. How could someone kill something so majestic and bring it across the sea?" I wiped a tear from my cheek.

"Come, there's much more to see." Sabrett took my hand.

He led me further into what appeared to be a giant trophy case. Walking until we came to a display barely visible through the collected people. They vied to view it: the huge Koh-i-Noor Diamond. It was displayed between what was rumoured to be the finest ruby and the finest emerald known to the world. Two young men pushed us from the exhibition. They were desperate to win their female companions' favour by showing them the jewels.

We found a table set with exquisite orchid flowers and seed pods. Next to it lay dark, luxurious pieces of chocolate.

"Would your dame like a taste?" the man with a French accent asked.

"That's something you would have to ask her. Well, Mon amour, would you?" Sabrett asked.

I blushed. "Thank you, I would love to."

A silver tray produced in a flourish held small squares of dark chocolate. The aroma of sweet cocoa beans filled the air. I placed a morsel on my tongue and let it melt before chewing, releasing the perfumed, fruity flavour of the vanilla. I played with the greenish-yellow flowers. The extracts from the pods filled my senses with exotic flavours. I thanked the man, and we went to see the machines with the taste still lingering on my tongue.

Giant clanking metal monsters sent steam into the air, turning enormous cogs. In another corner, soft silks were draped. I heard words I could not recognise on the lips of people from far-off lands. I couldn't imagine how all this might be possible. The entire time, Sabrett walked with me, letting me lead the way and watching as I took in the sights. Suddenly, I turned, burying my face in Sabrett's chest. As he looked up above my shoulder, a dark-haired man and a lady strode by.

I felt James' eyes boring into my back, and Sabrett said, "Women, easily shocked by all of this." The man smiled and carried on. "Your husband, I take it?".

"I'm afraid so," I said. "Do you think he saw me?"

"No. I don't think so; his attention was on the lady with him."

I looked at the crowd and made him out. He had his arm around a dark-haired lady I did not recognise, who was examining some silks.

"It's time we left," Sabrett said.

We moved, following the crowd, until we could make our escape into the night air once more. We walked for a while in the park before leaving to catch a carriage back to the station. Once there, Sabrett walked with me in silence to the side of the train.

"Thank you. It has been a lovely night."

He tipped his top hat in my direction and removed the dark glasses. "It's been my pleasure."

"When will I see you again?" I found myself asking.

"Well, that is all for this month. I have work to do, but I will spend one week with you at your home. Bess is making the arrangements."

"I get the feeling you know Bess more than I imagined."

"Ah yes, her family and mine go back quite far."

"I never asked you about your name," I remembered.

"It's biblical. I was born in the Americas to a devout farming family."

At that exact moment, we reached for the silver handle on the door of the red-painted carriage. Our hands landed, his on top of mine. He pulled his back, his skin stroking across the surface of my own.

"My apologies," he stuttered.

"My fault entirely," I said, feeling my cheeks flush.

The whistling of the trains began once more, joined by the guards' whistles, signalling the imminent departure. They drowned out my small voice.

"Pardon?" he asked.

"Oh, it does not matter. I will see you when you arrive then?"

"You will, safe journey," he replied.

I climbed back onto the train, looking forward to sleeping the entire trip. My dreams were instead haunted by James. I started awake at every turn of the door handle, convinced he would appear at any moment.

CHAPTER SIX
Chrysanthemum

James returned a few days after my trip to the city, announcing that he would be staying for longer this time. He intended that we try one last time for a child before he travelled out of the country. His business took him to the Americas, where he planned on acquiring new suppliers. I had never cared about what his family business entailed. This time, I reasoned, taking an interest might give us something to talk about. He would be here for a couple of weeks, after all.

Since being married, this had been the longest I had seen him in the house without his entourage. Time would tell how it would affect his mood and if this would be my last chance to stir some feelings in his heart.

Dinner proved to be the perfect time to attempt to make conversation. My isolation often made this difficult; I had never had the social skills of my sisters. Lacking practice in recent years. I preferred my own company most of the time. People other than my family, Bess and Lenora, were a mystery to me. Even Jack found the conversation stilted, as I couldn't help but wonder what I could say that was of interest to him. This was only made worse by James. He had a habit of pointing out all the flaws in everything I said. Mimicking my voice, joking about my opinions, and labelling them the ramblings of an uneducated child. I cleared my throat, ready to start my attempts at a civil marriage.

"How long do you think your business will take you away?" I tried to sound as casual as I could.

"It could be some time. I suspect at least two months."

"I wasn't aware." This had indeed surprised me.

"Yes. I have several visits planned to research potential partner mines. You know how long these ship journeys can be. I suppose you don't, do you?"

I ignored this jibe.

"Write to me, won't you? It would be lovely to hear about all the exciting things you do and see. Could I could come with you next time?"

"Let us see how the month goes, shall we?" he reminded me of his plan

"I could invite my sisters to visit while you are away."

"No," he paused to finish chewing. "You don't need to over-exert yourself with children running around. You will have to stay here, resting to produce our child."

"Surely Harriette could attend to me."

"I said no. Let's not press the subject further." He slammed his fork down on the table.

We finished our meal in silence whilst I tried to rally, thinking of more things to say. All the while, his chewing drove me to distraction.

After the meal, we retired to the little sitting room. Pulling the stool out in front of the piano to try a little tune I had been practising, I sat down and lifted the lid.

"Jane, not tonight. I don't fancy a headache. You will have plenty of time for practice while I'm away."

Instead, I picked up my copy of *Plants of the Americas* and sat next to him on the couch.

"Did you know the scarlet runner bean was domesticated in the Americas?" Reading aloud, I hoped to start a discussion about my interests.

"Hmm," he mumbled, still facing the fireplace.

I sat up a little straighter. Encouraged, I continued, "And the Aztec staple crop was a plant called Amaranth. And chocolate comes from—"

"Sorry, were you speaking?" He interrupted.

"Um, yes, I'm telling you about—"

"Never mind that now. I believe it is time to complete our last attempt at a family." He stood to leave.

I sat on the bed, my stomach churning. It was Bess's night off. I undressed and waited for him. When he had finished, I got up to clean myself before bed, wrapping a sheet around myself. I made my way across the floor, a green glint caught my eye. There, on the carpet next to my dressing table, lay my emerald necklace.

"James," I said, "did you put this here?" Reaching down, my fingers grasped the gold chain of the necklace.

"No. Why would I? See, I told you my friend wouldn't want your jewels. You're clumsy, you must have dropped it." He dismissed my concern.

"I've searched for months and would have seen it." I insisted.

"You should question that servant girl. She looks like the type to steal," he said as he buttoned his nightshirt.

There was little point in continuing the conversation; if I pushed him too far, it would risk Bess's arrest. My mind was now a jumbled mess, trying to work out if I had seen his lover wearing it or if it had been my imagination. I lay down, still going over everything, and drifted off.

A scream jolted me awake. I sat bolt upright, listening. James had not stirred. Again, a scream rang out clear as day—a woman's screams from inside the house.

I darted out of bed and ran to the top of the stairs, half expecting to see someone murdered below. Nothing moved, not even the tan and white pointer dogs, who lay on the rug as if nothing happened. I ran back to the bedroom and shook James awake.

"What is it?" he murmured, half asleep.

"James, I need you. Someone is in trouble." Fear gripped me.

"What are you talking about?" He rolled over to face me.

"A lady is screaming!" I whispered.

"Where?" he asked.

Staying still, trying not to create any noise, I listened again. "There, this time, it's coming from the garden!"

"I didn't hear anything," he sighed.

"Can't you hear that? James, it's scaring me." The noise rang out again, clear as a bell.

"There's nothing there," he insisted.

"James, tell me you can hear that." The scream echoed around the house, and my fingers wrapped around his arm a little too tightly, causing him to yank it away.

"Go to sleep. There's nothing there." He rolled over again with his back to me.

Covering my ears and curled in a ball, the screaming continued, on and off, throughout the night. It caused every muscle in me to tense. I had heard foxes bark and was conscious it wasn't them; it had to be a person, but James had me doubting myself.

Never yours

By the time I woke, every part of me screamed in pain. Sleep came fitfully, with each muscle pulled tight against my bones. Hoping to keep the screaming out of my head by sheer force of will. Halfway through the night, I started to doubt my mind, and eventually, I drifted into a deep sleep filled with haunted dreams. When I went down to breakfast, James had already dressed.

"Ah, Jane, at last, I was going to suggest we go for a ride today," James said brightly.

"You want to go riding with me?" My eyes grew wide.

"But, you are looking peaky. Do you think you are up to it?" He lifted his hand to my face.

I took one step back. "I would love to. I don't remember the last time we rode together."

"Go dress, and I will meet you at the stables." he reached down for his riding crop, dropping his gaze, and I hesitated, one foot towards the door and the other stock still as if I expected his mind to change. "Well, go on then. We haven't got all day."

My heartbeat sped up in panicked thumps as I remembered the haunting screams from the depths of the night. Pushing these thoughts from my mind, I pulled on my riding gear and headed out into the June sunshine. The summer sun was not yet too hot, it soothed my ragged nerves.

As I walked towards James, the horses in the stables made gentle snuffling noises into their hay wracks. Lifting my face, allowing the gentle breeze to caress my cheek, I wondered what on the rooftops could have spooked them before. The smooth, tiled roof gave no clues.

We made our way out through the woodland, following the paths between the brambles. The pine, beech, and oak trees stretch above, shadowing the mountain ash and elder below. Once out the other side, we rode across gently rolling hills of grass cut short by the cattle and sheep. Wildflowers punctuated the green. We headed towards the little town that lay past our village.

My black mare pulled hard, excited to be able to run. The presence of James' white stallion only made her pull that much harder. I envied the carefree animals but revelled in the ride. I made sure to let James take the lead, although I longed to let my mare go. He slowed at the edge of the estate and suggested we stop for lunch at a little tavern to rest the horses before we headed home.

I slid into an alcove with a table while James ordered our lunch. He stopped to talk to a couple of men at the bar. They were hunched in conversation, their hats pulled down over their heads, concealing their faces. They left the establishment shortly after. I enquired about their business to James, who ignored my questions and drank deeply of his ale.

We devoured our meal, hungrier than I had been in weeks. The trip to the city and now this was more than I had done in years. I was happy to allow the silence to be filled with the meal instead of trying conversation.

A small child watched us. Leant on a low wooden stool, she stroked her rag doll before her mother took her hand and led her away. To the outside world, I imagined we would appear as if we were on a tryst. When we had finished, we headed out and mounted our horses, once more moving through the town and out into the country.

Heading across the fields, James picked up pace and pushed his horse hard. Foam began to form at the corners of its lips, and its eyes grew wide and wild. I struggled to match him without pushing my mare to the same excess. Falling behind, I thought nothing of it as I had travelled the woodland paths many times.

Never yours

I slowed my horse so as not to wear her out, picking our way through the mottled sunshine. Leaves moved gently in the breeze, and I closed my eyes briefly. Feeling the strong muscles of the horse below me and the soft wind blow across my cheek. I let my arms drop to the saddle, allowing the reins to droop as the mare's gentle rocking motion led us along the well-worn path.

Startled, the mare reared and jumped to the side. I clung on with my knees, close to being flung from the saddle, regained my balance and looked around. I searched for what had made her jittery but saw nothing. We moved on, and then, in the corner of my eye, a flash of white; by the time I turned in its direction, it had gone. Nervous, I urged her on a little faster, trotting now, another flash of white in the trees to my left. I caught a fleeting glimpse of long hair and the curving figure of a woman. I stopped the mare, peering into the gloom of pine trees.

"Is anyone there?" I shouted. "Hello." No reply came.

And then that scream rang out again, piercing the summer day. My fingers turned white as I gripped the reins. The noise rocked me to the core. I urged the mare on into a gallop. When I was convinced I had escaped, the scream rang out again from behind a large tree a few feet ahead. I pulled the reins hard, swerving around the trunks, and thundered along another path. I kept my eyes on the path ahead, scared of what I might see as the horse's hooves tore up the ground.

We careened back to the stables, swerving unpredictably, the mare's fear matching my own. I half fell off, launching myself straight into James' arms. My mare reared in a skittering, fearful way, her eyes wide and foaming at the mouth. Two stable hands pinned her in a corner. She reared again and pounded her hooves on the ground before allowing them to grab at her reins. One stroked her forelock and spoke soothing words close to her twitching ears while the other checked for injuries.

"It happened again, the screaming lady." My eyes were as wide as my mares', and I dug my fingers into his arm.

"That's enough, Jane; no one here heard it." He shouted, "I know you don't want me to go away, but this insanity is getting too much."

I was sobbing now, realising that the stable hands and grooms were all standing watching this unfold.

"I — " Words failed me as I stumbled towards James, trying to make him listen.

"Get a hold of yourself, woman," he shouted and stepped away from me, pulling his hands out of my grasp.

Looking around me for someone to help, I saw only blank stares. I ran into the house, embarrassed at the scene I had caused.

James marched up to the bedroom an hour later, flinging the door open.

"I called the doctor." The frustration was evident in his tone.

"Not the alienist. I promise I will not mention it again." I begged.

"Not this time. I believe the village doctor will suffice." He patted my arm, and I pulled it back.

As he said this, a portly gentleman in his early twenties, I guessed, entered the room. This wasn't our old village doctor who helped me with my first miscarriage. Nor was it any of the doctors that had followed.

The medical man gave me a pitying look as I described the night and day's events. This time, he prescribed laudanum, a bitter concoction that dissolved my cares and allowed sleep to come. I stirred only occasionally. Once, when James appeared to be above me, grinning and pushing himself against me. His face hung over my face, and it rippled and moved as if he were holding me underwater. His words were dulled by the sound of crashing waves in my head, and then I faded again. I woke up the next morning, and James was there to give me another dose of the medicine.

Hours became days, and days became weeks, speeding past in a blur, punctuated only by a vague sense of the nights and James taking his pleasure. During the days, I could not make myself care enough about the nights to remember the details. Either way, I didn't hear the screams again, and I don't remember seeing Bess, only Isobel. Every time I remembered to ask after her, the question floated off like a wisp of smoke.

I awoke again to find James dressed in his travelling clothes.

"Is It that time already?" I managed.

"Rest. I'm travelling today. I will write to let you know when I will be back." He leaned in to kiss my forehead. "If you are not pregnant now, you have only yourself to blame. Isobel will tend to you," he whispered before barely touching my skin with his lips.

"James — " I managed, but that was all, and I fell asleep once more.

Bess's face swirled in a mist, dipping in and out of my vision. Her face creased with worry. Darkness fell again, but voices interrupted my dreams. They were close but tantalisingly out of reach of understanding—two of them. Bess's voice filtered through like a song while a man's tone accompanied it. His voice was low and gravelly—one I recognised. I fought the smog that had filled my head, looking for a name. Sabrett.

My eyes fluttered open again; this time, my head split in

pain, and I held clumps of hair in each hand. Grasping at it, crying out. Bess mopped my brow with cool welcome water, but I couldn't stay awake.

I tossed and turned for what must have been days, my bed sheets soaked through with sweat.

Bess helped me by day, changing my clothes and keeping me clean. By night Sabrett came reading to me from *The Plants of South America* by the professor. Twice more, I heard screams, the first time the lady's again. I informed Bess, whose brow furrowed. The second time, a deep guttural cry of a man rang out, and then it was gone.

On the fourth night, Sabrett brought me a bunch of flowers from the garden. The laudanum had worn off enough to allow me to sit up and smell them. Their floral perfume was such a welcome scent. The stale bedroom was claustrophobic, and I desperately wanted to get up and walk in the gardens.

"Soon," Sabrett said, keeping his voice low.

"Where's Isobel?" I asked.

"She isn't in your service anymore." His answer was matter-of-fact.

"Where did Bess go? Why was Isobel here instead?"

Sabrett leant forward, his hands clasped in front of his face and his head bent towards the floor.

"The flowers are beautiful," I said. "Do you know what they mean?" I teased.

"Why don't you tell me?" He sat back in his chair.

"They are all chrysanthemums, although different colours and forms. Some are pom-poms, their petals thick from the centre and showy. Others are simpler, like the golden one with red stains along them." I traced my fingernail along their path. "The violet ones are dainty with smaller heads but are meant to wish someone well. Most appropriate. The red, well, they are a proposition I think best skipped over for now. But the whites are most important; they are for truth and honesty." I sat back, observing his reaction.

"My turn. Did you know that in Japan, the emperors sat on thrones of Chrysanthemums? They are viewed as perfection in physical form? A symbol of the sun and the opening of the petals revered." His fingers played with the petals as he spoke. He plucked one free and dropped it in my glass of water. "One single petal is meant to give health and a long life."

As it floated gently to the bottom, it rested against the crystal-clear glass. The red of the petal was magnified, filling the water with unspoken meaning. A moment of silence hung heavy in the air before he continued.

"Bess sent word for me to return from my trip earlier than planned. Both she and Lenora had grown concerned when James had sent Bess away. She had been told to take a paid holiday, unheard of for your husband. Then Jack had seen your breakdown in the stable yard."

"But why?" I asked.

"Together, we discovered that James paid Isobel to help. They had planned to drive you mad, and they wanted witnesses. It would make his alienist friend's case." He now looked for my reaction. "They had schemed with Isobel's two brothers and sister to make you think you were hearing and seeing things. They had even gone to the lengths of drugging the dogs; it was fiendishly clever and cruel, even for him."

My shoulders slumped, and my eyes glistened in the candlelight. "What about the doctor?"

"No. He wasn't involved; he was only another witness to add to the list," he reassured me.

Convinced I knew his depths; he would always find a

way to plumb a new one. My attempts to be a good wife and any hope were dashed again. I saw no way of avoiding the fate he had intended. Despite me laying down and turning my back to him, Sabrett sat silently and kept me company.

I woke again to find Bess plumping pillows and fussing over me.

"Has he left?" I asked.

"No. He works during the day and will be here at night. We set him up a place to work and sleep in the tower room."

"No, of course. I owe you both more than you can know." Reaching for her hand.

"His work is important, though, and he only agreed to stay if no one disturbed him there. The staff have all been told." She pressed the point home. "I'm afraid that means it's off-limits, even to you."

CHAPTER SEVEN
Harebell

July came hot and humid, keeping me housebound in the cool of the stone walls by day. By night, Sabrett would walk with me through the grounds, talking or in silence, enjoying the breeze and stars above.

I summoned the doctor to discuss my treatment. He agreed that I appeared much improved and that it would no longer be necessary. I had recovered from my malaise now that Isobel was not around to administer the laudanum. I decided not to argue that it wasn't necessary in the first place, not wanting to raise suspicions in case we needed his testimony in the future. Unsure if my mind had cracked under the constant attacks, an eerie feeling settled. On some nights, our walks felt as if they were observed from the woods. I confided this to Sabrett.

"I hope you don't think I'm mad, but the woods feel as if they have eyes," I said as I hung on to his arm.

"What do you mean?" he urged.

"I'm not sure. There's a feeling. It's like when you turn

and catch someone looking at you across a room," I tried to explain.

"Hmm, you had better stay clear of them at night. In case the brothers are still hoping to get their pay on James's return. You need to take companions with you on your trips to the barn. I'm sure Lenora and Bess would be more than happy to do so." his eyebrows furrowed.

Observing his complexion in the moonlight, I recognised a pattern emerging. He was almost statue-like, marble cold and hard. Then night upon night, his skin would grey and fade until he looked as at our first meeting, drawn and sallow. The process took four to five days, and then the next night, he would appear refreshed again. I made up my mind to confront him about it, as he looked renewed once more.

"Are you sick?"

"Why do you ask?" He laughed.

"Stop answering with a question; it's infuriating! Your skin reveals more about you than you think."

"Oh no, I'm aware of how my skin appears." he avoided the question.

"Well, are you sick?"

"I have a condition, yes." He fiddled with a button on his coat.

"What sort of condition?" I started to sound like a curious child poking at the adult in their company.

"It's a blood condition. Resting a lot and getting treatment every few days helps." he sighed, looking me in the eye.

"Is that why you look unwell some days and then almost perfect others?" I let this slip out, and my cheeks grew warm and pink. "Well, not perfect, but you know, better."

A grin had spread across his face and he did a little bow.

"You flatter me."

Butterflies flitted around my stomach. "How are you finding the tower room?"

"It suits me well." He shrugged his shoulders.

"Don't you find it damp?" Reflecting on my visit to the room.

"It hasn't bothered me, and now the summer is here, it's drying out."

"How can you work when the window is so small? You know you could have a guest room?" I offered.

"No, I'm far more comfortable away from the hustle and bustle of the house. You forget I'm used to travelling in rougher settings than this." He straightened his back.

"But you could at least work in the library during the day if it's quiet."

"No, I'm out most days seeing colleagues. If not, absolute silence is needed, and this is best achieved away from the main house. People would start to talk if my presence became more obvious." He was determined. "You don't want it getting back to your husband, do you?"

"No, of course, you are right." I agreed.

"It's getting late and you need your rest. I'm going away for a few days, but on my return, there's something I'm going to show you." He changed the subject.

"Are we travelling again?" I asked.

"Not this time. This time, it's right here waiting for you," he answered cryptically.

"Oh please, tell me. You can't leave me like this." growing frustrated.

He laughed out loud, "Yes, I can, I will."

He was toying with me now, and it reminded me too much of the words James had used. Flicking a curl of hair that had escaped its pin, I pretended as if it didn't affect me. We finished our walk and didn't mention it again.

Lenora met me at our barn, ready to use our harvest. The thyme and lemon verbena were now abundant, and a heavenly citrus scent drifted into the air. It clung to the wooden shelves and lingered in our clothes. While James was away, I no longer cared about changing my dresses. Although highly impractical, wearing some of my best clothes meant breathing in the oils whilst sitting at dinner in the evenings. This little act of rebellion felt like I was reclaiming a part of my life.

Lenora and I were abundantly aware of the suspicion of eyes on us, following our every move. Neither of us strayed far from the mouth of the barn alone. Another reason not to hang clothes on the branches of the trees as we would when James was home. Whoever lurked beyond the edge of the gravel track made that impossible. Sabrett's instructions had been clear: stay away from the woods.

Distracting myself from the threat, I took out my notebook, which was thick with pages of writing and pressed flowers. There were stems poking out from the sides and a ribbon was needed to keep it shut. My head felt as stuffed with information as my little book. I gladly used it daily to create potions for anyone who needed them. I flicked through the pages, although my eyes were focused somewhere in the distance.

"What is it, honey?"

Lenora rested her hand on mine.

"Is it that obvious?"

"I can see you have more on your mind than Isobel and her despicable family."

"I wrote to Harriette telling her a little about what happened with James. The mail is so slow, I had hoped to hear something by now. I believed she would help me." My voice wobbled.

When I stripped the tiny leaves from the stems, the scent of thyme filled the air, mingling with citrus, and my fingers turned green.

"Try not to worry too much. I'm sure she will write soon." Lenora replied.

"I know you must be right; I'm anxious to hear a friendly word." Rubbing my forehead, I tried to shut down the doubts.

A voice came from behind us, making me jump out of my skin. "What's that? What words do you need? I can say them." Jack had crept up on us; all smiles, as if completely unaware of the edge my nerves teetered on.

"You oaf," Lenora snapped, "Don't sneak up on an old woman like that!"

Jack routinely met Lenora after he finished his work and walked her home. They would escort me across the stable yard; we figured anyone lurking in the woods would be a fool to attack him. Occasionally, the horses would rear up as we made our way past them and then settle again. This would cause me to grab Jack's arm and hide behind his solid frame. Once inside the house, a feeling of safety would return.

Sabrett stood before me with a small red leather case held in his palm. He pushed the box towards me. The smooth surface looked new, and the hinges moved easily. The lamp light flickered across a pair of gold Etruscan-style earrings. Wire and bead-work created a highly decorative and detailed surface. Hanging at the bottom were two perfect sparkling gems. They were filled with different flecks of colourful light.

"Fire Opals," he said, watching my face for clues.

"They are lovely. But you didn't need to get me

anything." Feeling myself blushing, my cheeks grew warm.

"It was nothing. A jeweller owed me money, and seeing these, I picked them out for you, taking them in Lew of the debt." He brushed off the gesture.

"They're gorgeous, thank you," I said, running my fingers over them.

"Promise me you will wear them."

"Are you going to tell me where we are going?" I pushed for an answer again.

"No." He maintained.

"But what do I wear?"

"Bess has laid out your clothes. Why don't you go change?" He gestured up the stairs.

Laid out across my bed was a simple white blouse and black skirt with a slight ruffle at the bottom. The style of clothing you might find a farmer's wife wearing. They did not indicate a trip to the theatre or other public places unless we were to go in disguise.

But what threw me was the cloak. It brushed the floor and was the colour of the night, in velvet, with a large hood that almost covered my face. Wrapping it around me, I was glad the nights were cooler; sure, I would faint if I wore this in the heat of the day. The combination of simple white cotton and the deep blue-black velvet was strange. Hooking the earrings through the lobes, the opals glinted out from the darkness of the hood. I glided back down the stairs to meet Sabrett at the bottom. He pushed the hood to one side.

"Beautiful," he said, brushing his fingers against the earrings.

Catching his eyes on mine, my heart thumped harder.

"Shall we?" he said, taking my arm in his, and we made our way out into the dark.

The evening was still, and the stars shone brightly. We

headed through the stable yard and past our little barn towards the woods. The horses watched our passage, barely registering our existence.

He must have seen me hesitate. "Don't worry, nothing is in there tonight."

His confidence made me brave, and I pulled the cloak closer to my body, ensuring I did not catch it on the brambles. The darkness filled this place, with all traces of light blocked by the trees, but Sabrett pushed on. I followed close behind as the well-worn ground was now too narrow to walk side by side. His blond hair, tied up with a leather thong, swished along with his long, confident strides. His high-necked white shirt sat on broad shoulders, and his strong arms held heavy branches out of our way. At last, we emerged from the trees into the bright moonlight of the meadow beyond.

The meadow looked ethereal in the silver light, and we continued to walk towards a small hill. As we approached, thousands of little harebell flowers became apparent. Their nodding bells cast a blue aura, shining in the light of the moon. On the crest of the hill, a small orange fire illuminated five cloaked figures. Sabrett climbed higher, and I reached for his hand again, my footing slipping on the dew-damp grass. Once we reached the top of the slope, the illuminated faces became clearer.

Lenora, Bess, and two other women from the village were joined by another unfamiliar woman. Bess stood with Lenora, their hair braided the same as the others. I recognised the baker's wife. The other village lady took me a while to place, and then it dawned on me that it was the Blacksmith's wife. She was a strong-looking woman with arms to rival Sabrett's. The fifth lady was a stranger; her white hair matched Lenora's, and her face was wrinkled and sun-worn. She held herself with an air of command, shoulders back and with an unblinking gaze.

Sabrett left my side and went to the edge of the hilltop, laying back in the grass and flowers, his head against a rock. I was left alone to face the women, who all stood around the fire in a circle. They undid the fastening on their cloaks and removed them, placing them at a slight distance from the fire. I flung my hood back, smiling nervously at Bess, and copied them. I was unsure what was expected of me, but I felt this was what I should do.

"Welcome, Jane. My name is Flora, and I am the coven leader," the white-haired stranger began. "We meet to practise our craft." Flora's long, almost silver hair tangled and blew in the wind.

She was willowy, and her long fingers were gnarled and bent with arthritis. Her fingers pointed towards her thumbs in a painful, twisted form. Her kind expression did not betray the pain she must have been in.

"Witchcraft," I gasped.

"Yes, Jane, and you are hereby invited to join us." Flora stood with arms spread wide.

Bess smiled a huge smile.

Lenora nodded. "We have taught you some of our ways with your oils and potions. But you have power deep inside that we are going to teach you to tap into."

"I don't have any power, and the oils are things, not witchcraft," I replied.

"What do you think witchcraft is, Jane? Flying on broomsticks, casting the evil eye or keeping black cats in a cottage in the woods?"

"Well, maybe not exactly that, but it's a little of what I assumed." I shrugged my shoulders.

"How cliched. It may even shock you to know we don't eat children." Flora moved as if to raise her claws and bare her teeth in a mocking gesture. "Keeping cats in a cottage in the woods is an unattainable dream for most of us." She smiled at me.

"Now, I didn't think children were being eaten." I scoffed.

"Good, then we can continue. You need to forget all the stories you have heard; we do not live in nursery rhymes. We are real, and we always have been."

"I'm sorry; perhaps if I had some warning of what to expect, I could have prepared myself." I looked at Sabrett's lounging form.

I knew Bess and Lenora, and I didn't think they were evil for a moment. I had to trust that what they wanted to show me was good. It may have been naïve of me to think that Lenora's teachings were simply midwifery or healer knowledge, but she had never given me a hint of magic.

"You need to start by remembering. You might have to dig deep. It may be a long way back; you have lost your powers in recent years. Think back to any times you can't explain." Flora urged.

Reflecting as far back as I could across the years of my life, I dug deep. My memories had become mixed up, confused, and, in some places, too foggy to see.

"Let me help. Bess has told me about your wedding day." Flora interrupted.

"What of it?" My hands clenched together, the knuckles turning white.

"Do you remember feeling faint?" she probed.

"Of course I remember, but what has that got to do with power?"

"What of the old clergyman?" she continued.

"He fainted as well." My eyes flicked to each face in turn, gauging their response.

"Did he?" She sounded like she had already discerned the answer.

"Well, it was his heart," I replied.

"At the exact moment you grabbed the altar, feeling faint? He had a heart attack? Think back to how you felt." She began to make me doubt myself.

"Well, angry and then faint and — tingling." I cast my mind back.

"That's it, Jane, think about that feeling." she leant forward.

"Well, it sort of rose in my chest and then moved down my arms into my fingers." I traced the feeling of its movement through my body.

"And then?" She leant in further.

"It grew unbearable, like sparks and heat." Realisation was starting to dawn.

"And you grabbed the altar for support?" She encouraged me.

"Yes," I paused. "He looked at me. I remember now the look that crossed his face before I fell. I saw his eyes." My brow now creased with concern.

"It's buried deep, but it's there." She spoke slowly, as if comforting me.

"But I didn't mean to hurt him," I spoke to the group as if they were accusing me.

"We know you didn't, and we are going to teach you how to harness this power so that you don't hurt anyone again—unless you choose to." She left this sentence hanging. Tonight, we will try a simple ritual to raise power. Nothing too taxing. You can copy the chant we do, and if the feeling takes you, some of us will dance.

"Um, I'm not sure about any of this." My emotions were everywhere. Guilt from the old clergyman mixed with sadness and now confusion. My face contorted through all of these, one after the other.

"If you must simply stand and observe, do not move out of the circle."

I followed her instructions and watched. The other ladies shook off their earthly cares before a low hum started. Each lady tuned her voice and her frequency to the air around her. My muscles relaxed and loosened their grip on my limbs as their attention was focused elsewhere. I breathed in and out in time with their tune, which had become a rhythm pounding at my soul.

A low primal drumbeat that took root deep inside me. It pulled at my chest, and the rate of my breathing increased. My heart sped up, thumping hard, and I panicked at what was happening. I looked at Bess. She was glowing from within, fully immersed in the ritual, and she started to sway. Lenora's head bent forward, a deep voice emerging from within. She and Flora began to the chant, and the others followed, well practised.

"Ancient mother, we feel you,
"Ancient mother, we feel you,
"Walk with wisdom in this place,
"Walk with us as we celebrate,
"Your divine strength to grant,
"In the fire, our hearts rejoice,
"Ancient mother, we feel you,
"Ancient mother, we feel you,"

The swaying became graceful movements, and the chanting continued, repeating the same words. Perceiving the rise and fall of the beat deeper inside me, familiar, warm and protective. And then the tingling started. It moved in my chest like a snake, uncoiling and stretching out through my arms. I had the irresistible urge to hold them out. As though the snake could break free from my hands and move off through the grass. At the same time, the other ladies also held out their hands. All of us palms to the night sky, our heads bent, facing the moon.

A pulse of energy moved in waves from the swaying bodies of the surrounding women. An invisible force linking us. My fingers tingled as the feeling concentrated at the very tips. The feeling built to a lightning charge in the pit of my stomach; our bodies jolted as one, and the feeling turned to sparks that leapt from my fingers. A golden ring appeared briefly in the grass. Joining us, and then rose into the air above us. It hung for a moment and then exploded across the fields, a shower of sparks dissipating as it went. I gasped for air and tumbled to the ground.

My eyes opened to five female faces hanging above me. Bess, with her hands clasped together in front of her mouth, grinning.

Flora helped me to my feet. "How are you feeling?"

"A little shaky." I let the older woman lift me, unsteady on my own feet.

"Sit next to the fire. We can eat now, and this will help you feel better." She gestured towards the bright flames as sparks rose into the air.

I sat near the warmth of the glowing embers where a pot had been hung. In it bubbled hot stew, the smell of which made my stomach gurgle loudly. Holding my belly as if I could stop everyone from hearing, my mouth started to water. The Blacksmith's wife shoved a wooden bowl of piping hot food into my hands.

Everyone sat, and as we ate, they introduced the remaining two ladies. Lettie, the Blacksmith's wife, and Tansy, the baker's wife. Tansy was rounded at the waist, as one would expect from someone who loved to taste the food she made. She wore her brown hair in a long braid, tied with a leather thong and the occasional glimpse of a silver ring in it. She wore a moss green dress with fine silver needlework to match her hair accessories. On the sleeves were embroidered runes and knotted patterns with strange creatures. More silver rings were wound into the sleeves and hem of her clothing.

Lettie stood tallest, and her arms strained against the short sleeves of her dress. A leather apron was worn over rough brown cotton. Her Jet black hair accentuated her grey eyes, which matched the smut on her cheek. She was beautiful and strong. Her voice was confident and heard above the others in the conversations that flowed around me.

Flora reassured me that it was normal for me to feel the effects of the ritual for many days.

"It has awakened something inside you, long forgotten," she said. "Give it time."

"I promise I will. I'm afraid of what more I will find." And yet doubt still lingered that the power even existed.

"It's not new to you or your family." She looked into my eyes as if examining my soul.

"I don't understand."

"This power is ancient. I suspect there are more of your ancestors who had it. But we all know what happens to powerful women."

"Do you all have it?" seeking answers in their faces. My eyes cast about.

"No, magic is different for everyone. Most people learn to harness it in physical ways. Tansy bakes spells into her food or weaves them into clothes. Lettie is a smith and forges items with spells woven into them. As you know, Bess and Lenora are wise women, as were their ancestors." She gestured towards the group.

"What is your power?" I asked.

"I'm a conduit, a diviner, a teller of fortunes. I look only when asked. Too much trouble comes from giving an unrequested reading." She looked at the floor.

Sabrett moved, making me jump. I had forgotten that he had watched the entire thing. We made our excuses and parted with the group. Making our way back across the fields in silence as I contemplated tonight's experience. We reached the edge of the woods, and Sabrett stopped; he turned me towards him, his face glowing in the moonlight. He pushed a stem of the blue harebell behind my ear, and the bell-flower tickled against my skin.

"I have a name for you," he announced, grabbing both of my hands.

"What is it?" Butterflies flitted around my stomach.

"Sekham," he pronounced.

"What does it mean?" my eyebrows furrowed.

"Powerful or mighty, it is an ancient Egyptian word," he explained.

"I don't feel either of those things." My shoulders sagged.

He pulled me closer, taking my hands in his, and green eyes shone in the moonlight. "You are more powerful than you realise."

CHAPTER EIGHT
Passiflora

The little blue harebell lay between two sheets of White tissue paper, the paper wrinkled as I touched it. They were pressed between the pages of *Poisonous Plants of the United Kingdom*. The leaves were edible, and it was said witches used the flowers to turn themselves into hares. They were more likely to use them to treat a malady or earache, but why should facts get in the way of a good story?

In my other hand, a letter had arrived from James. It described his journey in more detail than I expected. Perhaps he was still playing the dutiful husband for anyone who would be watching. No doubt the alienist had advised him to do this, adding more proof to his expanding case against me.

In the weeks that followed, James Letters became more frequent. Unlike his first letter, he managed to say very little in as many words as he could muster. Something of his politician grandfather had rubbed off on him. His journey had been fruitful; one mine, in particular, had been added to the company's portfolio. He hoped to find my position as fruitful on his return, which looked to be around the end of November. My stomach flipped as I now had a date for the dreaded reunion. I spent as much time as possible living in the moment instead of counting down the days. But now its was made solid and concrete in my mind. I placed the letter and book on the table.

Bess had become round with her child and my envy grew with her, despite being my closest friend. Occasionally, I let jealousy slip into the open with a comment or a look that, if she noticed, she did not speak of. At the same time, I was glad for her and Jack; they reminded me of my beloved parents. They were obviously in love, and having a child would complete their family. She had involved me in planning her lying in. Privileged at being included in such deeply personal time, I had invited her to have the baby at Wendsum Hall.

Lenora would be a midwife, helping her daughter, as she had helped many before. Jack practically skipped around each day. Looking forward to carrying his child high on his shoulders. We had a room prepared despite it being many months before the baby was due. My family had collected a few small items of clothing for my child when the time came. Tears stung my eyes, knowing the sickness should have started by now, but there was nothing. No cravings or turning stomach. Giving up all hope of a child, I presented the little white hand-stitched tunic and cap as a gift to Bess. I wrapped it in the same tissue paper in which I had pressed the little harebell.

"Are you sure, Jane?"

Her look of pity hurt far more than when James' friends had looked at me in the same way.

"Honestly, Bess, you have been everything to me. I want you to have it. It's not my destiny."

"It's beautiful. Did you make it?" she asked.

She examined the intricate embroidery. The beautiful greens of the leaves and tiny white star-like flowers sat next to vivid purple berries. Stitched into the white cotton, the elderflowers and fruits were a powerful ward against evil.

"Oh heavens no. My mother gave it to me, and it has been passed down through her family." I laughed.

"Well, I'm worried it will get ruined; our cottage isn't like your home. I'm afraid the damp would damage it. How about I borrow it? Then it can come back here where it belongs." She looked at the floor.

"If that's what you want," I said, in part glad that the heirloom would find its way back.

She tucked it neatly in her bag before we made our way to the gardens to meet Lenora and Tansy. Today's job was to collect herbs and produce for the harvest celebration.

Lenora waved impatiently at us as we walked through the gardens.

"Come on, girls, we have lots to do!" she shouted.

We hurried to the garden, and when we reached them, we set about pulling courgettes from the plants. The hairs on the leaves left our fingers feeling sore, like small glass shards piercing our skin. After the last of the vegetables were gathered, we took our knives to the herb garden. Great bunches of mint sent a beautiful aroma into the air, joined by wafts of the onion smell of chives.

Lenora grabbed Bess by the arm and carefully removed her herbs from her hands.

"Go wash your hands immediately!" she commanded, her voice laced with urgency.

"But why?" Bess asked

"You were cutting parsley and Clary sage. Pregnant women should never touch or eat these herbs. It will be fine;

you would need more to do damage, but let's not take any risks. The oils of these herbs will bring about your contractions early, and the baby isn't ready yet," she soothed Bess, her voice filled with care, stroking her hair as she explained.

Bess hurried off to wash her hands, and Tansy took the herbs.

"Don't worry, I will dispose of them," she said, before leaving us alone in the gardens.

We broke bread on the last Sunday in July. Tansy baked it in the shape of the god Lugh, wielding his spear. The bread smelt heavenly as its warm steam escaped into the night air. Flora took little jars out of a bag at her side. She had brought preserves made from her garden and honey from her hives. We celebrated the Harvest festival on the hill in the meadow.

Lenora brought butter supplied by her husband. Bess brought fruit and nuts gathered from the hedgerows. My contributions included wine, ale, and crystal glasses. Lettie had cooked a side of ham in the forge, and steam rose into the air. We feasted and made oaths to each other, clinking together our glasses in cheer. As the wine and ale flowed, our cheeks became rosy. We all made an oath to Bess to protect and care for the child as if it were our own. But as much as I would have loved to stand by my promise, fear gripped me that I wouldn't be around long enough to see the child born.

The meat and bread went well with the chutneys, sweet and savoury, mixing in perfect unison; we groaned and loosened our skirts. Before too long, the wine and ale produced a warm glow in our stomachs. Once more, lifting our glasses to the sky, we toast Lugh.

As tradition prescribed, competition and sport were to be part of the ritual. Lettie had brought heavy metal hammers with her, and we set about taking turns to throw them as far as we could. Bess, of course, was not going to win this one, taking care not to throw too far in case it hurt the child. Lenora and Flora were well-matched.

Tansy and I took our turns and a cry ran up from us all as Tansy's hammer whirled past my own. Lettie won the tournament, as we were no match for her strong arms. Swinging the most enormous hammer with ease, her muscular arms sent it arcing through the air. It landed with a thud handle up, and the head buried in the soft earth. Again, a cry went up, and we all patted her on the back in congratulations, toasting her and her craft.

We collected the hammers and settled around the fire. Sat on large rocks that became more comfortable with every tip of the glass. We were stargazing as the sparks from the fire drifted up into the heavens and flora started to speak.

She told the story of Lugh, who fought to free the grains and seeds for mankind. She used large arm movements with the confidence of someone who had told many tales. At times, the story alluded to the two gods fighting over a woman, not the seeds that would feed generations. When she had finished, Flora made an offering of corn into the fire. She held it high above her head and chanted in reverence to the god of the harvest.

For my part, I would be happy to stay here forever if I had a choice. As the sun rose, we all parted company and headed our separate ways. My blurred vision caused the golden rays of the sun to make everything glow. The effects of the wine and ale were taking their toll.

My footsteps were unsure. The path wound its way back to the house, drifting through the deep dark of the woodland. Stumbling, my hand grasped a tree, feeling its rough bark beneath my warm fingers. A feeling of contentment settled over me. Stopping at the door to our barn, taking in the heady scents, my head grew light and spun. I balanced myself once more. Making out what looked like daisies within circles around the wooden door frame. Tracing them with my fingers over the rough edges as the wood splintered and sizzled under my touch. They were carved with such care; how could I not remember seeing them before?

Butterflies were thick in the air, surrounding the tall bush with deep purple flowers. Browns, oranges, yellows, purples, blues, and white painted across their wings. Fluttering from flower to wall, settling to sunbathe. Lined up, all with wings pointing in the same direction, soaking up the heat on the brick. Examining the detail in awe of such beauty in something so simple.

The professor had sent me a collection of prints of butterflies from his travels. They were simply magnificent. Their wings were gossamer and the colours were so vivid they appeared as if they would fly from the page. Our butterflies were as much an inspiring sight. I flitted through the garden, following the fluttering wings. Darting from plant to plant until I found what looked like a butterfly buffet. Sat on the grass watching their delicate wings and whiling away the afternoon. I had wandered the gardens, enjoying the sun and letting it soothe my aching head. Rising late and taking a little brunch when the professor's parcel arrived. I spent half the day reviewing the pictures in awe and then decided a walk would do me good.

I scribbled on a sheet of pale blue paper describing the scene to Harriette. Her last letter had arrived over a month ago but contained only brief news of her pregnancy. It did not address my last letter of admission to my marriage's failings. The tone was wrong. Instead of her flowing writing with lengthy descriptions, the words were stilted.

My heart yearned to see her, and my letter invited her to stay until James came home. Now I knew for certain he wouldn't return until November. There would be plenty of time for her to arrive. Even if he found out, I'm not sure what other threats he could possibly level at me. It occurred to me that it might be possible to even tell her of his plans to have me committed.

Sabrett had promised more than magic. Surely, that was the pinnacle of possibilities. Then I was convinced the same about the magic lantern show and meeting the professor. At every turn, Sabrett surprised me and showed me more than my upbringing had allowed me to believe possible.

The professor had become a friend, and we continued our communication. His letters were more frequent than my own family's. They allowed me to live through his eyes, experiencing the things he had been doing. His letter gave me hope in curling black ink.

Dear Jane,

I hope this finds you well. I'm excited to tell you I'm actively looking for benefactors. However, this grows increasingly difficult as age catches up with me. Despite this, the Alps have been calling to me, and the search for new and mysterious plants is months away. I'm sure that they could hold the answers to questions not yet asked. I have been lecturing at Oxford University and built up a small following of students. They have read all my books and seem keen to follow my plant-hunting exploits. Young blood, all with wealthy families, I'm considering taking a party to fund my next trip.

As always, I will send you the first copy of any new book from the expedition. I miss our conversations and hope you will write

soon. You remind me so much of my own dear Eleanor.
Yours Fondly
Arthur

Having no funds of my own and assuming it was pointless to ask James, I was unable to help my new friend. I didn't want James to know I had people to talk to, or he might find some way of getting rid of them, as he had done to Mary. There had been no word from her since that fateful night.

In my writing to Harriette, I included a note asking her to pass on a letter to Mary. All the while, fearing myself now abandoned as neither had returned my correspondence. I sat half curled up in the armchair in the library, reading and rereading Arthur's letter.

So many things had occurred I never considered would ever be part of my life.

Sabrett had sat in this very room, betting that he could show me what there was to live for. I was left with amazing memories of the glorious sights at the Crystal Palace and all the beautiful people. Sabrett had gifted me more at this time than James had in our entire marriage. Although I was glad I had experienced these things, if anything, they only solidified my wish to die.

At some point, this reprieve would come to an end and James would ship me off to an asylum. The alienist had all but sealed my fate. A few months certainly wouldn't be enough for me to harness the powers needed to change that. It could only make things worse. The possibility of being accused of witchcraft and locked up set my nerves on edge. The doctors would come with their needles and experiments, poking and prodding.

I was now accustomed to Sabrett joining me late in the evening, as his work never finished before sunset. I held my hand out in front of me, tracing the lines in my palm. A warm glow tingled in the centre, and a faint light illuminated my keen expression as I practised, raising my power. In youth, it had come naturally, only to be stifled by my mother's harsh punishments.

"Sekham," Sabrett whispered in my ear.

July had faded into August, and the sun had barely gone down. Usually, he would take his time, but today, he materialised as if he were waiting for the last rays to disappear. I quickly folded my fingers into my palm, quashing the light.

"Sabrett, what are you doing lurking around?" I gasped.

"Come, let's walk," he said.

He clasped my hand in his, his skin cool as usual. He never broke a sweat whatever he did for work. This time, he led me to the window he had entered during our second meeting. He flicked the catch and pulled the heavy frame; it slid open easily on the rope runners.

"You don't expect me to climb out, do you?" I gestured to my clothing.

"Trust me. This way, we can sneak away without prying eyes knowing your every move," he said playfully.

He climbed through first, reminding me again of a crow hopping down out of a tree. Landing as if he had pinned a rabbit to the ground. He stood and held out his hand. I collected my skirts together and clambered up onto the sill. I swung my legs out, sitting now, and hopped down. Sabrett caught me by my waist and lowered me to the ground as if I weighed nothing.

He held me a moment longer than needed. His hands were firm, but his face displayed the grey tone it took as his health declined. His green eyes glinted playfully as he lingered in the moment.

"Where is your pin?" The silver ornament from his lapel was made conspicuous by its absence.

"It must have come loose. No matter. Come on then," he said, releasing me and running off towards the formal garden.

Doing my best to keep up my skirts, catching on plants and gravel as I lost sight of him in the hedges. I slowed, trying to creep through the tall yews on crunching gravel, my skirt caught twigs that dragged, giving me away.

Sabrett jumped out from behind a twisted yew, pouncing fingers in claw-like shapes. I yelled and jumped backwards, nearly falling into a flower bed, before regaining my composure. Then, taking my hand again, he led me towards the wooden door in the wall of the kitchen garden.

He reached up, picking an exotic-looking passionflower. It had creamy white petals with streaks of purple. The centre stood tall with purple and green stamen, heavy with pollen. Abundant orange fruit hung from the vines between. He handed it to me, and the heady scent of spices and sweet tropical fruits flooded my senses. I placed it as a buttonhole on his shirt, my fingers brushing against his chest.

We headed towards the glasshouse as the air crackled with the sound of a summer storm. The clouds rolled over, and spots of rain began to fall. The glasshouse was the very place where we first met. I could feel the power of the lightning anew, as if I had never experienced a storm before. Goosebumps rose on my arms, the hairs standing to attention, and the storm ionised like static on my skin.

I reached for the handle, and my other palm pressed against the cool glass panel of the door. Sabrett's hand clasped over mine, pausing the handles turn. He reached up and took my other hand, his fingers pushing between mine against the glass. His body pressed against my back, pinning me. The flower was crushed between us, releasing the scent of spices and fruit once more. He bent his head, his tongue licked at my earlobe, and he nuzzled into my neck. My breathing grew short. Releasing my hands, his fingers grasped my waist in a firm grip, and then he allowed them to travel to my hips. I slipped from his touch, my head spinning.

The glass-panelled door opened lightly, and he shut it behind us. He paused his hand against the door with his back to me. The flashing storm sent light through the glasshouse, casting long shadows of the plants across the room. The shrubs in pots stood tall around us, the foliage brushing across our torsos as if we were walking through a humid jungle. Pulling my hair free of its braid, I let the wet, red strands fall across my shoulders. The power of the storm was glorious.

"Ancient Mother," I whispered.

Sabrett caught my shoulder and turned me to look into his eyes. The lightning appeared in them as if it was born there, and the electric current ran through me. There was a powerful pull in the pit of my stomach as it fluttered nervously. I had never known an attraction like it, and it scared me.

Turning away from him, I walked to the bench where we had sat so many nights ago. The memory of the desperate look in his eyes as he struck me to the ground nudged at my mind. I tried to keep the vision of this dangerous side of him. Trying to prevent the mistake now being considered. He joined me on the bench and took my hand. The scar on his face shone brightly in the flashes of lightning.

He looked into my eyes. "Sekham, I will ask your permission before I do anything." He kissed the back of my hand.

My skin tingled; the touch of his cool skin was

distracting.

"I want you to feel tenderness." He continued.

"I would like that," I admitted, taking myself by surprise and looking at the ground.

He stood, taking my hand and pulling me up from the bench into his embrace. With one hand on the small of my back, he pulled me close. Brushing my hair from my neck, he bent in to kiss it. His lips were light as air, placing small feathery kisses down my neck to the top of my blouse.

I let my head fall to the side, allowing him more access. My eyes closed now, feeling the tingle move through me. He looked at me again, and my eyes opened to see his smile. The butterflies in my stomach skittered around. The tingle drowned out any sensible notions, overtaken with longing.

"Do you want me to stop?" he whispered.

"No," I said, lifting my hands to hold his back and feeling him through his shirt. He leaned in and kissed me deeply. It was as if I were in free fall. His teeth lightly grazed my lips. I was lost in this world, wanting to stay in his arms.

He moved, walking me backwards to the warm wall of the glasshouse. His weight leant into me, the warmth of the wall and the cool of his skin through his shirt. Every sensation was heightened, and my skin prickled with need and want—two things I had never experienced before. Expecting to be struck at any moment, my mind could not fully let go of the memories that raced through it. I wanted to enjoy this moment but rising panic was engulfing me.

He stopped again, looking at me, trying to read my mind.

"I won't hurt you. You will not leave here with bruises."

He brushed my cheek and kissed my forehead. The breath left my body as his kisses landed once more, this time with more passion. Small nibbles at my neck, and my eyes close once more. My heart thumped in my chest.

His hand slid down my back and over my buttocks. He bent to scoop me up. I wrapped my arms around his neck as he carried me to the bench and lay me down.

I did not resist, but tensed when his hand moved again to my skirt. He gradually pulled it up enough for his fingers to slip beneath. Squeezing my eyes tight, embarrassed and afraid of what might come next, I still did not resist. He knelt at the side of the bench and kissed me again. His light fingertips traced swirling patterns on the soft flesh of my inner thigh. His hand moved so slowly it tickled, the feeling verging on pain and exhilarating all at once. My head spun. I wanted him to move faster and wanted him to stop. My mind was on fire. His fingers moved over the lace of my drawers, and he found the opening and the warm flesh beneath. It was gentle, as if it were the most natural thing. At that moment, the glasshouse and the whole world melted away.

The only things that existed now were his lips and the movement of his fingers. They travelled my body in ways I didn't know where possible, finally finding a spot that sparked at his touch. I didn't know what I would have begged for, but his slow teasing brought me to the point of desperate need.

It started as an ache, a warm glow like the embers of a fire. The lightning crashed overhead, and my body arched, and I let out a moan. His finger moved faster now. The glow started to spread and sparked again. Intense feelings like being on the edge of something, about to fall, and all my muscles tensing again.

A warm glow burst out through my body. Sparks electrifying every inch. My muscles jolted, my body riding the wave of fire, releasing all the tension in one glorious moment. My body spasmed as he released the pressure. Still, he kissed my neck while I floated back to earth.

My eyes opened in time to see a ring of fire released across the sky, half hidden by another burst of lightning. He kissed my lips again, holding me until I was brought back to this world and existing again at this moment. He stood up, leaning over me and lifting me into a sitting position. His every touch set my skin alight again.

"This is how it is meant to be, Sekham," he whispered.

My eyes glistened in the lightning, which startled him a little. Then he held me close, allowing me to release all the sorrow in that moment.

"I'm sorry. You didn't hurt me, it's — I've never felt like that before."

He held my face in his hands, turning it to his. "You will only ever feel this way from now on." I thought he told a beautiful lie.

This year, the Lord of the Harvest was declared to be Tansy's husband. He took his role very seriously, negotiating the wages of the labourers for the next year and organising all the men into action. The feast and party were a triumph under his command. As they announced his arrival, the men dragged their scythes along the ground in a procession. The metal rang out in a solemn song that told of the ending of the farming year. As the men marched, their heads hung low, and the scythes sparked against the stone. The crowd grew quiet in reverence.

George had taken his sharpest knife and diligently cut the last sheaf. He now carried it in outstretched arms to present to the waiting crowd of villagers. His attention to his duties was not surprising, as his living would be determined by a good harvest. This year there were more strange faces at the party. A travelling group of labourers camped nearby, looking to find work.

We were lucky and had prospered in the last few years, but other villages had not been so fortunate. Whispers of curses and bad luck caused by witches were circulating. The Rector attended to bless the ceremony. He added an air of fire and brimstone, dulling the party atmosphere. Standing on apple crates to gain height on the collected worshippers. In the dirt yard of the big barn, he sermonised to the party, casting all witches and demons and their familiars to the depths of hell. Bess, Lenora, Tansy, and Lettie joined me as we watched. He wound up his sermon and beseeched the onlookers to dance and eat freely.

We turned to each other and whispered, "Ancient mother, we feel you," under our breath and rolled our eyes.

What no one had considered was that the witches in these parts had helped our luck not hindered.

Lenora's husband took her hand, and although now bent with age, he swung her in circles and stared into her eyes. Bess sat out the dancing, her sickness making her skin pale, and she waved off any offers of food. Jack sat steadfastly by her side. Tansy's husband relinquished the last sheaf to the Rector. He then joined her side. The Rector would take it to decorate the little chapel.

"This is George," she told me, gesturing at her husband.

A tall man with grey streaked hair, as if the flour from his bakery was permanently ingrained. It flopped over one eye in a rakish fashion. She ruffled his hair fondly, and he took her hands, leading her to the dance floor. Stopping briefly to put down his glass, he's flirtatious, winking at the women he passes. They giggle and wink back as he returns to his wife. His customers like to buy his bread, enjoying his jokes as he serves them. Lettie stood with her husband to the side of the dancing and nodded a greeting in my direction.

I Observed all the couples and how they behaved

together. This time, a little of the spark they had for each other warmed my own heart.

CHAPTER NINE
Daisies

Month five of the bet arrived in September, under cloudy skies. The warmth of the summer still lingered on. The heat hazes were gone, but warm breezes travelled through the fields and garden, moving the grasses with them. The animals enjoyed the last of the grazing before the weather started to turn. I reflected on how the months had passed in a whirlwind of experiences.

Anticipation grew as I waited to discover the secrets Sabrett had to impart in our final month. I dined alone once more, seated at the large table. The room housed a long wooden dining table with many cushioned chairs. It had once welcomed my family in happier times. My parents, now long since passed, had sat at each end of the table, inviting guests from across the county. Regular visitors had eaten fabulous meals created by some of the invited chefs. Our cook catered to our family on more intimate affairs.

Ghosts of the memories of my sisters and myself appeared to tease and torment each other across the wooden battlefield. My father pretended not to notice as his paper grew higher over his vision. Sarah flicked peas across the table at Marguerite, who giggled and created volcanoes of mashed potato. Alice stuck her tongue out and aimed a pea at Harriette, but inevitably, it strayed, hitting mother, who would then put an end to the shenanigans.

The visions fell away like mist as Bess interrupted my musing. She carried a bundle of letters tied with ribbon.

"A man brought these to the house," she said, handing them to me.

"That's Marguerite's writing."

"There, see, they have written," Bess said.

My hands shook as I hurriedly opened the letter at the top of the pile, eagerly pulling apart the folds of paper.

Dear Jane,

Harriette has asked me to write to you in the hope you will answer.

I am saddened that you have become distant and disappointed that you have chosen to stay away in Harriette's hour of need. We are all unsure of what we have done to offend you. I would not have otherwise imagined you so heartless.

Your sister

Marguerite

I searched the pile of letters for evidence of what she spoke of. My hands shook as the fear grew, and I fumbled over the pile, spilling them onto the table. Picking them up, the postmarks stood out, stamped and re-stamped one over the other. It was revealed that my mail had been redirected to James in America before they reached my hands. The postmarks were clear. This meant the bundle had travelled the globe more than once before reaching me. Someone had collected the letters over the months and sent them all to my husband. I pulled the following letter from the pile and tore at it, dragging it from the reluctant envelope. All love and comforting words had gone from my sister's writing.

Jane,

I am begging you to attend to Harriette; she is gravely ill. We are all here with her, but you are conspicuous by your absence. What is it we have done to offend you so much that you will not talk to us anymore? We are your family; even after our parent's deaths, we are still here; we have not gone anywhere. What are we being punished for? I cannot imagine what slight we have extended upon you that you would treat us so badly. But to ignore Harriette is low, I would not expect it of the criminals held in the prison hulks on the shore. She has treated you with nothing but love and care and wanted only the best for you.

If you do not reply, I will treat you as if you were a stranger and will no longer look on your face.

Marguerite

Fearing what would come next and tearing open the envelope, lying inside a simple few sentences told me it was too late. Reading all the letters together with no way to undo the damage done.

The final letter is a white envelope tied with a black ribbon. Stamped with Harriette's husband's family crest. My hands trembled again as I hesitated before opening it. Inside lay an invitation to Harriette's funeral. The date written in black ink revealed a whole month had passed since her body had been interred. Marguerite had not written since; her anger at me must have been too great to discover my excuse. The scrunched-up letters hit the wall and bounced onto the floor. A guttural howl released from my chest in anger and grief mixed into one.

My long-imagined Christmas meals with my sisters would never happen again. It had not crossed my mind that one so young would not be here to enjoy dancing and snowball fights. A small note inside the invitation, written by Alice, told me that Harriette had been lost, giving birth to a beautiful daughter. After months of bed rest and sickness, the blood loss was too much for her slight body to bear. The redhead child had quickly been christened Eve before Harriette had given out. She signed it, but there were no sisterly words or personal messages. The letters read as information being passed between two people, who might as well be strangers.

I wanted to write to explain, but unsure who could be trusted, I was unable to communicate my situation. Aware that my post was being watched, I feared my letters would be discovered. Six of us were left, and it didn't feel right not to have the seven sisters abroad.

My head rested in my hands, and what was left of the soup was pushed to one side. I was no longer interested in eating. The chair screeched across the floor as I pushed it backwards, and the noise of it echoed around the room. The gold trimming of the curtains was dull and lifeless, and the day held no interest for me.

I sensed someone moving my hair and sat up, startled. Sabrett sat next to me on my bed, brushing my forehead.

"I don't feel like going for a walk tonight," I said, rolling over so my back faced him.

"It might do you some good to get some air," he replied.

"What good will it do? Will it bring my sister back from the grave?" I said, throwing my hands in the air, my voice taking a harsh tone.

"Of course not," he sighed.

"Will it make the nightmare of my life better?" my temper flared.

"Perhaps." He shrugged.

"That's a bold promise. What are you going to do?" I mocked him now, the sarcasm dripping from my words.

"It's easy to take this out on the people closest to you."

"Close to me. We barely know each other. This is all a game, remember? Well, I'm tired of the game." My hands, now fists, pressed hard into the covers.

"It's not long now," he soothed.

"Well, maybe you should leave and not come back until the bet is done. I'm tired!" I shouted, "I'm done with playing everyone's games!"

He got up to leave.

"What do you want from me?" I screamed as the glass from my bedside table crashed against the door as it shut behind him, sending shards across the room.

Dressing in black every day, the weeks passed in sullen moods. My skin shrank from my bones, and meal after meal was refused. Most days, water would be the only thing to pass my lips and only at the insistence of Bess, whose face betrayed her growing fear for me with every passing day. I refused to walk in the garden; instead, I took to my bed early and rose late. Sitting on the window ledge of my room with all but one curtain drawn, hiding from the world, I gazed out to the woods beyond.

On more than one occasion, movement in the dark of the trees would catch my attention in the dying light. I was growing convinced someone was watching me from the rooftops of the stables. An eerie feeling grew inside me, as if hidden eyes followed my every move. I threw the curtain aside and glared out into the night, daring them to do their worst.

I missed coven meetings, and the group sent gifts of herbs and food to make me feel well again. But these were pushed to the back of my cupboard, gathering dust and mould with the little oil bottles. When Bess returned from the barn, I could smell the oils on her, but that didn't tempt me to leave the house.

My sadness grew deeper than it had ever been, sinking deeper with no way out. I spiralled out of control, wanting only an end to the pain.

Bess knocked at the door on the thirteenth night, and when no answer came, she knocked louder.

"What?" I lifted my head from the pillow.

"I'm coming in," she shouted.

"Please don't!"

The door opened inwards, and she appeared in the gloom.

"Don't be mad, but there is someone with me."

"Who?" I asked.

Sabrett entered, framed by the candlelight behind. His eyes were sunken, and his cheekbones protruded.

"She's worried about you." He sounded angry. He was distant and cold and reminded me of our first meeting.

"I told you to go away!" I crossed my arms.

"You did, like the spoilt brat you are." He stood his ground.

"Deuce take you!" I slammed my fists down.

"Language, dear." He smiled.

"Patronising ass."

"I have been called many things. Do you think you can do better?" He crossed his arms and tilted his hips to the side. "Stop being pigeon-livered, and say what you mean."

"You Ratbag, hornswoggler, addlepate,"

"Blowsabella," he fired back.

"Bull calf, blunderbuss."

At this, he started to chuckle, which slowly became a full-on guffaw, holding his stomach as if it would split.

"It's not funny," I screamed, still indignant.

"What a do," He snorted.

My arms still firmly crossed, I sat on the bedside, waiting for him to stop.

"Bull calf blunderbuss," he repeated my insult and burst into hysterics once more.

His laughter became infectious, but anger still bubbled within me, not wanting to concede the battle.

"Ass."

"Are you done?" He moved to leave. "I want to show you something."

"Wait, I'm not dressed." I scrambled to find something to wear.

"Throw something on. It's not cold." He stormed from the room.

I grabbed my cloak, which lay on my dressing table, discarded from the last time I had used it, wrinkled and not cared for. Pinning it about my shoulders with only my long white linen nightgown on beneath. I hastily slipped on bright yellow-gold silk slippers with a bow on. I looked a frightful sight. Hurrying after him, we made our way across the stable yard. I could not help but think about the shape on the roof and the urge to look over my shoulder followed me. His journey finished at the mouth of our barn.

"Look," he said, pointing at the wooden door frame.

"What?" I said, "It's dark."

He huffed and grabbed a candle from inside the barn, lighting it before joining me again.

"See," he said, pointing again.

"Do you mean the carvings?"

"Yes," he huffed.

"What about them?"

"Do you know what they are?" His voice was still raised in anger.

"Daisies."

"No. These are ancient protection symbols. Hexafoil. Carved in the wood of all your precious spaces by your friends." He pointed to the shapes I had seen before, half asleep from wine on our last coven meeting. There were six petal shapes within a circle; it certainly looked like a daisy.

"For me?" My hand clutched at my cloak.

"Yes, you damned fool. Your friends have been trying to protect you."

"But James isn't going to take much notice of those." I scraped my foot in the dust, staring at the floor.

"It's not for him." he turned away from me.

"For who, then?" I threw my hands in the air, becoming increasingly frustrated with this conversation.

"It's not a who either." He turned to face me.

"What do you mean?"

"I've been trying to work that out. I'm not sure what's lurking around, but I catch a sense of it now and then. It's ancient." He looked out towards the trees.

"What are you talking about?"

"I left instructions not to go into the woods. Well, when you were recovering, and we had removed Isobel from the house, she went missing. Her brothers went looking for her. Not one of them returned."

"That's horrible!" My hand shot up to my mouth.

"We were hoping they had skipped town, but my sources say there's no trace of them."

"Your sources?"

"I have connections." He waved this off, and then he

stumbled to the side, catching hold of the barn door.

"Are you alright?" I reached out as if I could catch him.

"It's my disorder. I'm not feeling myself."

His face showed signs of degrading further, with the skin hanging loose and pale, as thin and papery as birch bark peelings.

"Do you have your treatment nearby?"

"Not quite."

I guided him into the barn and helped him sit on the bales of straw. "What can I do?"

"Nothing, there's nothing you can do." He patted my hand.

"But there must be. How do you normally treat it?"

"That's not something I'm ready to tell you. We have another month to go." He pushed my hand from his.

"Don't be ridiculous. What happens if you don't last till that month?" My concern was growing.

He shook his head. "That's not a problem."

"Sabrett, I'm worried you look very sick. Can't I help?" My forehead creased.

He looked torn and paused before breathing heavily.

"I don't know that you're ready, Sekham."

"If you truly think that is my name, then I must be ready. I've seen and done so much now, I'm not sure anything can surprise me."

"Sit so you can't run." My heart thumped louder in my chest. Finally, the secret that had been niggling at me since our bet would be revealed.

"Please, listen until the end before you react. Promise me." I nodded encouragingly, but he hesitated once more.

"My blood disorder wasn't inherited; it was thrust upon me. Before you were even a glint in your father's eye." He checked my face, which creased in confusion.

"My parents were farmers, and we settled in the new world, the Americas. We were devout and prayed many times a day. We were hard-working, tilling the soil and looking after our cattle. Life proved tough and remote, a hand-to-mouth existence. A stranger came to the farm one night and asked for a guide to the town. He paid my father more money than we had seen in a long time, enough to feed us through the winter, and so I left with him.

"We travelled through the mountains, reached the snow, and set up camp. He said he needed to rest, too tired to travel through the day. We made camp and I slept beside the fire while he had a makeshift tent. When I woke the following evening, he stood over me. That's when he attacked.

"I was trapped with nowhere to run. He ripped my neck apart, and my blood gushed into the snow, staining it red. He left me for a moment.

"My fingers dug into the snow, pulling me forward. I tried to crawl away before he noticed, but he was too strong and fast. Then he gave me a choice: die on that mountainside and be consumed by the wolves, or he would save me. Only this stay from death would last many lifetimes.

"I have travelled the world and seen many amazing things, but I will never see the sun again. Without consuming blood, this existence would cease. It can be volunteered, but the hunt is exhilarating."

I stood up and hovered in front of the barn door, then sat and then stood again, unsure how to process the story he told.

"You mean?" I couldn't bring myself to say it. "But the scary bedtime stories of demons with teeth ready to rip your neck were simply tales. Weren't they meant to keep naughty children in bed? Surely you jest." a mirthless laugh sprang from my mouth.

"Believe me when I say that I won't hurt you." He reached for my hand again.

"You're lying. Why would you lie to me? When we met, were you going to kill me?" I pulled my hand back.

"Yes, I needed to feed. I told you that." He nodded.

"You were going to kill me then. Why not now?" My arms crossed over my chest as if they could offer protection.

"Yes, but it's different now." He leaned forward.

"Is that how I will die?"

"If that's what you choose. But that time has not come," he replied.

"And what about you? What were you going to win in this bet?" I kicked at the dirt.

"You." His green eyes shone in the dark.

"Me, how?"

"If you want to die, I get your blood, But Sekham, if you want to live, I get your life." He was matter-of-fact.

"My life?" I asked in a low voice, shrinking from him.

"Yes, I want you to join me. You are powerful and have depths you haven't even discovered yet. And if you join me, you can easily be rid of your husband." he reached up to brush the hair from my face. "You are like air to me; I breathe you in, and if I want to see the sunrise, I need only to look into your eyes. I have been alone for so long that I did not know I needed someone until I met you. I cannot exist without you." He leaned forward and kissed me.

When I could gather my thoughts once more, I asked, "How could I be rid of my husband?"

"You will hold all the power, and his fate will be in your hands."

I pondered these words, turning them over in my head like a toy.

"I would hold all the power. And you want me to join

you?" I repeated.

"Since the moment we talked in the library."

He leant heavily to one side.

"But what can we do to help you now?"

"You can't; I need blood, which means leaving to find some." He shook his head.

"Where? Is there some blood storage you pop along to when you are peckish?" I sneered.

"Sekham, you are not that naïve. Blood has to come from people," he tutted.

"What people? How do you find — victims?" This word disgusted me, but I could think of no replacement.

"I will go out into the world and hunt," he replied.

"No," I paused. "Stay, I will give you mine. You don't look as if you will get anywhere like you are. Volunteering is better than knowing someone else suffered."

I pulled my cloak from my shoulders and said, "You don't have to take it all, right?"

"No, just enough to see me through." He got on one knee, half crouched on the straw in the pose of a proposal.

"Will the bleeding stop when you're done? And my neck, will anyone know?"

He leant towards me, his cheeks hollow, how gaunt he looked.

"With your permission, I will take it from somewhere no one will see."

Putting his hands on my shoulders, he guided me down to lie on the straw.

He moved his hand down my leg, sliding it up under my nightgown and lifting it as he went. My whole body froze, and a shiver ran through me, scared of what might happen. The breath escaped me as he moved down and started to kiss my ankle and then the round of my calf. He moved his lips over my skin's surface and stopped every inch to kiss again. The kisses were soft, but his teeth, now brushing my skin, were sharp. Soft lips, then a sharp scratch. The danger behind each kiss set every nerve on edge. When he reached my thigh, he gently parted my legs to better access the soft inner flesh.

His hands made small circles on my skin, sending ripples through me. His teeth are so sharp they puncture the artery with only a moment of pressure. Then his tongue moved gently, licking at the red viscous fluid that flowed forth. His mouth warmed now. Drawing heat from my body. Eagerly sucking at my thigh, drawing forth a rush of blood that made me giddy. My senses whirled once more, and a moan escaped my mouth as he ate hungrily. His mouth left my thigh and found the secret folds of my sex, his tongue lingering there for a moment, moving back and forth.

He climbed above me. His face was an image in shadow, hollow-cheeked, with a mouth full of sharp teeth. The look turned my insides cold, and then, in a flash, it was gone as if it never existed, replaced with a look of fire in his eyes.

Lost in those eyes, caught up in the need and desperation that overtook the fear. The Sabrett I knew, appearing again before me, pulled down the loose top and bit into my breast. Once finished, he caught me up, pulling me close. His salty, metallic kiss sent shivers through me. His eyes glistened in the night as he stared into mine, and I wanted him at this moment more than ever before.

I begged him to be with me here and now, whispering my lust into his ear as my heartbeat pounded in my chest. He pulled me up to sit on his lap, and I was aware of him through his trousers. The blood had risen in him, and he was animated now, pulling me close.

His strong arms held me tight as he kissed the curves of my breast. His tongue flicked gently as his teeth grazed my nipple. We rose and fell as one, beads of sweat running down my back until my body could take it no more.

Sabrett apologised for taking more than I offered, hushing him, saying that it was what I wanted to. I turned to face him. Laying on my front in the straw, my ankles crossed as they swung gently back and forth in the air. My fingers stroked his skin, teasing more information from him about his condition. He lay on his back, his arm raised above his head, and his skin looked flawless once more.

I stared into his face, my chin on my hand, looking into his sparkling green eyes as he explained. My fingers danced along the lines of the tattoo inked into his shoulder. A simple tree, a teenage rebellion on a long sea journey. The ink faded at the edges but had at one time been black with red material wrapped around it. The one above his heart, though, was a different story. He told his tale as he had told the tale of the old man on the night of our bet.

"I have many tales to tell, and maybe one day we will travel the world as I tell you the stories memorised over decades. But for now, my own tale will have to suffice.

"As my body lay dying, the snow falling around, my eyes pointing to the starry sky, and my attacker did his work. Incantations and strange words had flown from the stranger's lips. He scratched a new tattoo onto my skin. Knowing that he could only turn me once the work was complete. A crude woman shaped with wings, her arm outstretched, holding a screech owl. And next to it, as was the older man's tradition, a binding rune. Alien Letter after letter piled on top of each other, etched into my skin.

"Hours passed in paralysed agony. My skin burnt and my blood all but gone into the frozen earth. When he finished, he stood looking down and admiring his handiwork. Then, the attacker had bitten his own skin. His wrist, torn open and bloody, shoved into my mouth. At first, holding back on the brink of death and unable to move.

"Then, as the blood trickled down my throat, it found my wound and mingled with my own blood. Like a parasite, it invaded its host, taking hold and taking over. Every part of me changed, becoming stronger. My heart had slowed to the point of death, no longer needed, as the blood crawled along my veins. My organs turned as if to stone with each agonising invasion. My body died a little more, replaced by a vessel for the new blood. This blood needed no food other than more blood. Which would be consumed replenishing the contents of this vessel of my flesh."

He described how his mind became invaded, as did his body. Although pieces of him survived, like the knowledge of his previous life. He was now a different man from the one who had left his family farm the day before. He was like a child again, learning anew the ways he would need to make his way through the world. Part of something alien to him.

He explained that vampires live for an eternity, but not forever. They were bound by blood and needed it to survive. Without food, they would wither away to dust, still existing in maddening swirls. Sunlight, as every schoolchild knows, would burn through him. Boiling the blood in the veins that ran close to the surface, he ventured out only at night. He needed no sleep but still rested to allow the blood to recover wounds and prepare him to hunt again.

The blood inside him wanted to reproduce; it urged him to make new vampires. Each one would take a piece of him, so he had resisted until now.

He had seen his maker increase the brood at the behest of the first of the clan. Once his reluctant companion, now a madman, his maker's mind was lost in fragments for each new vampire sired. He would sit in corners, rocking and pulling clumps of hair from his head. The clumps would promptly grow back again. Eventually, his mind cracked, and Sabrett could only leave him with the clan.

There is a hierarchy in the clan, and you do not question your place in it. The firsts were the ancient ones; they were the ones who walked alone. He was initiated into a clan of vampires whose purpose was to find Lilith, the mother. The first of the clan became increasingly obsessed and maintained that the mother hibernated somewhere in the world. Other clans exist, but there are only three in total.

The Sekhmet clan uses its resources to find the daughter of Ra's resting place, believing her to be the only true mother. The others are Strigoi, an ancient race whose first became cursed for his crimes in life. They believe in no mother and hide in the earth, only rising to kill. They are a lonely race of creatures all others shun. Their bodies are twisted by their sins.

"Is that why you wear the silver pin? It feels familiar," I asked.

Both horrified and fascinated. I pushed him further for his connection to Bess and Lenora.

"During the witch trials, the vampires had seen the destruction of hundreds of women. At one time, the number of bodies grew so great that they could have filled the city of London. The piles of rotting corpses would have shocked the most murderous Strigoi. The firsts of all three clans had come together, something unheard of, and stood on the graves of these women. They agreed that if the madness continued, their food source would dry up, and no adult woman would be left. And without women, there would be no children, and the human race would cease to exist.

"After they finished with witches, attention would be

drawn to new victims. The strange and unusual would stand out as a target. Putting us all in danger. The story went that they had come to an agreement with Hekate, the goddess of magic, the night, and necromancy. The vampires would kill or glamour all who threatened a witch. Be it an informer or Witchfinder General until none existed. They could be called upon to help if a witch needs protection.

"Hekate herself could not be involved; if she used magic to help, it would only confirm the fears and stoke the fires of those that would do them harm. The wording of this agreement had been left open. This means that, across the years, it has been used by many to help with all kinds of situations. As long as the need was genuine." he twirled my hair around his finger.

"What did the vampires get out of this deal?" I asked.

"Two things were given in return. If the vampires ever joined together again to request it, an army of the dead would be given. That army could be used to destroy their common enemy.

"Hekate would be held to her promise: to raise from the ground any witch who had passed, and they would be bound to serve the vampires. For the second gift, each clan would be given an amulet. The amulet would help them find the deity and mothers they searched for.

"Of course, the Strigoi needed no amulet, as they did not have a mother belief system or any belief system. Instead, they requested to be allowed to make witches into new Strigoi without consequence. They had been doing it for centuries. They were drawn to witches and criminals and turned them whenever they could. But they were hunted by witches for their crimes.

"Hekate had wept at this, but she saw her sisters burning and hanging limp from trees. Their spirits had accompanied her. They wanted revenge on those who had persecuted them. They wailed and cursed like banshees until she complied.

"However, her trick had been twofold and only discovered once the agreement was made. The vampires had upheld their end of the bargain. It's all in the wording, you know. Always double-check your contract wording, especially with a goddess." Sabrett added,

"What possible tricks could have been played? It seems like the vampires are holding all the cards," I asked.

"The amulets merely pointed at clues and not to the actual resting places of Lilith and Sekhmet. This angered the Children of Lilith the most, stuck in their library. They were furious that the first had fallen for Hekate's tricks. The Strigoi found that they, too, had been tricked. Their love for chaos had outweighed their annoyance at the agreement's small print. I am unclear as to how they were duped, as I don't have any contact with them. The witch trials were long since finished, but the agreement must still be honoured. Even now."

"How did you come here?" I sat up to see his face.

"Bess and Lenora had called me in when some of their friends had disappeared. Of course, Lenora's mother was my contact before Lenora was born. I responded to the witch's calls when needed," he explained.

"Did you find the friends?"

"Not until it was too late."

CHAPTER TEN
Gypsophila

"Let's have a dinner party," I suggested. "We can combine Mabon with a celebration for you and Jack."

"Here, of course. We can all cook and eat together." I gestured around the room.

"Are you sure, Jane? Won't people talk?" she replied.

"Let them," My posture defiant with one hand on my hip.

"Sounds fun. This place needs livening up." Sabrett chimed in as he slumped in his chair with an arrogant air about him.

"You told me you liked it here?"

"Sekham, you know I do, but everyone needs to let their hair down."

As the end of September approached, James' ultimatum was still fresh in my mind. The end of our six months was in sight, and along with it, a new choice—a new trajectory—but the cost weighed on me. Death might no longer be the end, but instead a new beginning.

To have justice and a future, though, I would need to give up myself—the very essence of me—and give myself to a clan, strangers to me. I would be bound to them and their beliefs, obedient to their laws and, first, a leader I didn't know.

"Why did you call me a name connected to a different clan?"

"Well, it suits you. I also recognised that if the other entity lurking around is the Sekhmet clan, it would protect you. A name is a powerful thing, and invoking Sekhmet in your name means they cannot touch you. This brings protection; they won't dare attack someone with that name. To make Sekhmet angry meant plague and disease on those who did, even vampires."

"Ah, cunning, but is protection needed?" I nudged him with my elbow as he came to stand next to me.

"A precaution," he assured.

"Are there more of you close by?".

"Some of the Lilith clan are close, and at least one Sekhmet clan, but I don't know any Strigoi," he replied.

"Can we meet them?"

"I don't see why not, now that you know everything." he shrugged his shoulders.

"Why don't you invite them to the party?"

"I'm not sure." he turned away from me.

"Oh please, we need some new faces." I squeezed his arm.

"I can't answer for the Sekhmet clan, but I'm sure the Lilith clan will attend. I will send word." he stroked my hand.

The coming days were spent distracting myself with preparations. The celebrations were for both the autumn equinox and the life growing in Bess. At six months pregnant, her bump could not be hidden; there could be no denying it now. It would be a February baby, in time for Imbolc, a festival of rebirth and fertility; Brigid had truly blessed her.

Candles were strewn about amongst sunflower heads now full of seed. A few stems of gypsophila, their delicate white flowers, hung between them. They brought memories of my wedding day and the sisters that were lost to me. Lenora had told me that the villagers called it baby's breath as it smelled of sour-sweet milk. Resembling the scent a mother would find on her baby's breath. Perfect for celebrating Bess' condition. We collected as much as could be found, but it was late in the year.

Invites were sent out for the coven to stay at the house for four days of celebrations. They were to bring their husbands and family with them. The house would be filled with life again to fight off the sense of death that lingered there.

Accommodating everyone would be no trouble, but the puzzle of how to house Sabrett's friends needed to be solved. We found the rooms on the darkest side of the house and set about boarding up the windows of three of them. Two were for the Lilith clan and one for the Sekhmet clan, who surprised Sabrett by sending word that he would attend. An invitation was also sent to the professor, who had returned from his European trip. This might be my farewell party, after all.

The house glowed warmly, reminding me of the beautiful memories of my family living here. It had a soul again. The thought occurred to me to ask them all to stay forever, but James had written. He was due back in the first days of November, in time to ruin Christmas and my new yule traditions. I crushed the fleeting thought, balling my fists up at my side.

He had never left me an address to reply to. He had no idea whether I was destined for confinement or the madhouse, either would be fine with him. By now, he expected me to be six months pregnant. On his return, seven months would have passed, and he would know by setting eyes on me which way this would play out. My choices were bleak.

Brought back from my train of thought by the arrival of Lenora, she flung her arms around me.

"Blessings," she whispered in my ear.

Her husband stood at her side, his large hands clapping me on the back.

"She is very much looking forward to trying the beds," he laughed. "Old aching bones," he added, rubbing his back. My stomach knotted in a twinge of guilt.

Bess was close behind, with Jack, unloading wooden crates from the little cart they had ridden in. Despite a meagre existence, they had brought contributions for the feast. I rushed to help her before leading Lenora up the stairs. At that moment, I decided to place Lenora and her husband in my bedroom. Once in my parents' room, it seemed the right thing to do, as Lenora had been a mother to me for the past few years.

Bess gasped as she entered what had been Elizabeth's room. A grand four-poster bed sat in the centre with pretty floral curtains hanging around it. Bess giggled and clasped her hands in jacks, swinging them, leaving them to relax. I chastised myself for not inviting my friends into these rooms before now, pulling my fingers through my hair. Moving my things into Marguerite's room, I contemplated the hierarchy in which we had been brought up. For the most part, I had still treated Bess as a servant despite becoming close. Weighed down with disappointment and shame, I finished unpacking.

More effort could have been made to change things

before now, as my friends had done with me. They had let me join them and treated me no differently. I had been slow to truly let them in, but fear had kept me from seeing the wall built. The fear of James and what would happen if the status quo changed had me in a stranglehold. Only now was the veil of trauma thinning enough for me to start seeing through it.

The younger me wouldn't have thought twice about playing with Bess or begging for her to stay over. But that is the innocence of childhood. Something that you are expected to grow out of. To take your place in society. The natural order had been something James said once. Or was it about husbands and wives?

A few hours later, Tansy arrived, followed closely by Lettie, both bringing with them more wooden crates. By the time Flora arrived, a stack of boxes lined the kitchen table. I had sent the few remaining maids and cooks away. That way, we could say and do whatever we wished without being observed.

Flora was alone; her partner had died some years before. She had never married, choosing to live with her lifelong partner, Daria. This had caused rumours of unnatural behaviour. But they had put on a front of women, keeping each other company in spinsterhood.

People got on with their lives, forgetting about them. The rumours would start again whenever they refused a man's attention. Time made people blind to them. As age took its toll, they were forgotten, and people decided they were old women living out their lives together as companions. But the journey to this had been challenging.

In recent years, the death of her other half had made her bold, taking charge of the funeral service with all the involvement of a spouse. Now, though, she looked like she had fully embraced her existence, flaunting it, daring people to question her life choices. Her tiny village had been unsure how to react; secrecy had been easy for them.

Leading her up to Alice's room, we passed Harriette'. It would be only fitting to leave Harriette's room locked; no one should stay there, my grieving incomplete.

The rest of our party would arrive after sundown. Sarah's room would house the two Lilith clan members, and Sabrett would have to bunk with the Sekhmet clan member. The professor was put up in the second tower room that overlooked the drive. Once settled, we went to prepare the meal. I would mostly be taking orders, with very little experience in this area.

Tansy and her husband made use of their skills preparing bread rolls. After cleaning the cobwebs from its surface, Lettie and her husband cooked meat on a spit. Henry's scar shone across one eye. Damaged by a white-hot shard of metal when striking his anvil three years previously. Blind now, milky white, it stood out against his hair, jet black. His arms, I'm sure, could crush anyone who imagined they could challenge him for Lettie's affection. He expertly lit the fire below and ordered me about.

Bess sat at the table, sharp knife in hand. She sliced easily through the carrots as Jack hauled the crates, packing everything away. Lenora and Flora were gossiping in a corner, whispering between them as they sorted the plates.

My skirts were in a whirl, dashing back and forth, bringing everyone what they needed, looking like a scullery maid by the end. The doorbell rang, and before checking myself, I ran upstairs, taking two steps at a time, to answer it. Opening both large doors in an extravagant gesture of welcome to the party of five that stood on the doorstep. They turned from the conversation and looked me up and down.

Sabrett and the professor stepped over the threshold whilst the others waited.

"It is polite to invite your guests inside, Sekham." he nudged.

"Sorry, of course. Come in, come in." I stuttered.

"You mustn't forget, a vampire can only enter once invited," he reminded me.

"Sorry, I'm not used to all this yet." wringing my hands together.

Holding hands, two tall, slim vampires stepped into the hall with long white hair falling down their backs. Each lady wore a deep purple gown. They accentuated every flawless inch of their bodies. They were perfectly identical. Their skin was like porcelain, and their eyes piercing grey.

I had never met twins before, and I gushed, "I know this is strange, but I'm sure I've heard of you before. It escapes me where, but you are most welcome here." I reached for their hands in greeting.

In unison, the twins spoke, "Madame, we must admit, this is not how we imagined you from Sabrett's description." The effect was of one voice with two notes to it, harmonised and lyrical. Neither lifted their hand to return my greeting.

My hair tumbled loose from its ties, and I wore an apron soiled with dirt and cooking fat.

"I'm mortified; if I had known you were arriving so soon, I would have changed."

Embarrassed now, I was unable to stop comparing myself to the beautiful people before me.

The third, a man at Sabrett's side, was the Sekhmet clan member. His dark umber skin and curly black hair reached his shoulders. He smiled at me and bowed, taking my hand and kissing it.

"Ignore them. You are every inch as beautiful as I

imagined."

Blushing, I made my excuses to change. Adding insult to injury, I tripped up the stairs as I went, cursing myself under my breath. I reached the bedroom and hastily chose a satin claret dress with black details. Pairing it with the earrings that Sabrett had given me. The opals flashed in the light. The touches of green in its swirling-coloured centre complemented the emerald pendant.

Sabrett caught up with me as I closed the door of the bedroom. Reaching around my waist from behind, he held me while kissing the back of my neck. Then, turning me effortlessly, he kissed me deeply. His teeth poked through, sharp and white, in the dark of the corridor.

"I wish we were alone," I whispered.

Kissing him back, I led him to my door. Reaching out and opening it behind my back, half falling through as he moved down my neck.

Returning to my guests, I found everyone dressed in their finest. They sat around the dining table deep in conversation, food piled high in the centre, waiting for me so they could begin. Sabrett went to sit at the head of the table, his leg slung over the arm in his now familiar way. My chair at the other end was waiting empty for me.

The Sekhmet clan representative sat beside Sabrett, and everyone else scattered between. The twins sat on either side of me, which I found quite unnerving. They examined my every move, and I squirmed under their gaze, chewing slowly and deliberately so as not to drop a crumb. I was overtly aware that we ate in front of people who had long ago forgotten the taste of solid food. Instead, I tried to take the focus from myself by asking the questions.

"Sabrett neglected to tell me your names."

The twins looked at each other, and the one to my left answered.

"I am Xanthe, and my sister is Trillian."

"I apologise if I find it hard to tell you apart," I said.

"It's simple. Each of us wears a glass vial containing a trophy. Each trophy is different," Xanthe replied.

I looked closely at her vial. It contained a liquid, and an eyeball, perfectly preserved and still blue, was suspended in it. The strings of nerves and veins trailed behind it as it gently spun.

My nose wrinkled, and the corners of my mouth turned down as realisation dawned. I turned to find what the second vial would hold. Gently swirling liquid revealed her vial contained a finger with a gold ring. The nail still appeared perfectly trimmed as it bounced against the sides.

"In life, we had been made to marry two brothers. Princes from a far-off land. We were promised as children to the neighbouring kingdom to seal the two houses as one. But our betrothed had decided on a different fate for us.

"The headdresses we wore matched. With bright blue sapphires, fine silver wire work and silk veils. But they had been laced with slow-acting poison that sat on our skin throughout the ceremony. Seeping into every pore. By the time we were to retire, we were sick. Our husbands consummated the marriages. Making sure they inherited all our kingdom had to give. They left us for dead.

"Our fate changed with a vampire. On seeing us lying dying, he offered us the chance to kill our husbands in exchange for eternity with the Lilith clan.

"We did not hesitate and moved quickly. First, taking the lives of the brothers and their mistresses, whom we found lying together. Then, their father, mother, and the entire wedding party were all in the same house, still drunk from the feast.

"We occupied the castle and used the village for generations. Until the people moved on and the village was left desolate.

"At first, we worked as map makers, keeping the castle as our home. We found our way to the first of our clan and pledged allegiance. He welcomed us, and we were appointed as part of the council and, more importantly, enforcers."

"A job we take very seriously, and enjoy," Xanthe added.

"And the trophies?" I gestured.

Trillion spoke this time. "Xanthe scooped out the eye of her husband for looking at another woman. I took the finger of mine for procuring the poison and for dusting it on the veils. Do you remember the crunch of bone as I cut, sister?" Trillion cawed.

"I do, sister. Do you remember the screams as I plucked the eye, sister?" Xanthe smiled.

"I do, sister," Trillion replied.

Both laughed as if recalling a fond memory. By the time I heard the story, I looked to escape their company. I signalled to Sabrett, who moved to my side. He made the excuse that Adio had not made my acquaintance yet and took me to his seat.

The stranger's dark brown skin reminded me of the ladies at the Crystal Palace exhibition. His black hair was shiny and full; it bounced with curls that lay on his shoulders. His dark eyes smouldered and glinted with mischief. His white teeth showed two longer pointed tips that could belong only to a vampire. He wore a yellow gold long tunic that hung to his knees and covered matching trousers below.

They had been having a good-natured but heated debate about Lilith's existence over Sekhmet. Each wanted to tell me the tale and get my opinion.

Sabrett started, "Adio here would rally against this, but Lilith is said to be the first mother. Wife to Adam and made from the same clay. They had many children together. But as Lilith became weary of Adams's insistence on being on top. In bed and everywhere else. Lilith asserted her equality. This made Adam angry and dissatisfied, and he demanded that she be cast out. She was sent away, turned into a demon, and roamed the desert.

But that was not the end of her torture; the Christian god had cursed her to lose one hundred children, for every day that she did not submit. The story goes that she created her own demon children to serve her and that she proved a devoted mother to them."

"Ha," Adio mocked. "To believe that, you would have to believe in the new god. Sekhmet is much older, the daughter of Ra, and vengeful. Her bloodthirst could only be quenched by tricking her into drinking the Nile—colouring it with pigment and flavouring it with beer until she grew too drunk to continue." He slammed his glass down with fervour. "She is the true mother!" His voice now raised as if in cheer.

I considered both, not wanting to hurt either vampire's feelings. "The stories sound very similar to the uneducated ear. Are they not both women who have been punished in some way?"

"Hmm, a Very tactful answer," Adio replied. "I like it. Of course, I don't agree, but I like the answer." He slapped me on the back and went to talk to the twins.

I breathed a sigh of relief, seeming to pass some tests, I hoped.

"How did you two meet? I presumed you wouldn't be allowed to mix?" I gestured towards Adio.

"Strictly speaking, no. Going back to my days with the

professor." He raised a glass toward the old man, who sat with Lenora in discussion. "We met halfway up a mountain. He was on his way up, and I was on my way down. We immediately recognised we were from opposing sides, but he did not attack me. I stopped to greet him. He asked if there was anything to be had from continuing; if it turned out to be a dead end, he would rather not waste his time further. I didn't have to be honest, but I saw no harm in it. Letting him know that there were no clues to be had where I had come from."

"That's very sporting of you," I replied.

"Well, it worked in my favour, as the next time we met, he helped me out, and we have been doing the same thing ever since."

"What is it you both do?" I asked.

"We are map makers. There are many jobs in the clan. We all have our part to play in serving the first and Lilith's chosen children," he replied.

"Who are they? Aren't you all chosen children?" my forehead creased.

"No, we are all children, but the chosen children are the sect part of the clan. They are zealots and need others to help them with their search. While they stay in the library researching the myths and legends. There's the council and the cleaners, who sort out any problems that might alert the humans. The enforcers who tend also to be on the council. They make sure our laws are upheld. The map makers like me are the ones who get to explore the world. Checking for clues we find and making maps of the areas we journey through. The Sekhmet are much the same," he tried to explain.

The professor interrupted, "We have had many brushes with the others, have we not, Sabrett?"

He poured himself another drink. A dribble of wine escaped the bottle and over the edge of the glass before he could right it.

"Yes, professor, but you are retiring from that life now, and well deserved to." he raised his voice.

"Have you always travelled together?" I asked them both.

"Oh no, Sabrett here came to me from sol — from soldiering," he hiccuped.

"Yes, it's easy to hide on the bloody battlefield, and there's always a war somewhere." Sabrett nodded.

"Weren't you afraid they would notice?" I asked.

"No, if someone gets suspicious, you simply lay down and play dead amongst the corpses. It's not wise to survive off the already dead for too long. But it will suffice until your company has moved on. Then you stand up and join the other side, relieving some soldier or other from his uniform."

I made a face, wrinkling my nose at the idea of cold, rotting blood.

He continued, mistaking my face for encouragement. "Well, after all, what do I care which side wins as long as it advances our cause and I get to the places I need to go"?

I was a little taken aback by his cold, callous answer when many died for other's beliefs in far-off lands. I sought answers in his face, but none presented themselves.

"I must show you the slides from our trip to French Guiana," the professor offered.

"I would like that," I said. "What year was it?"

"Oh, now I think it must have been 1803 or 04," the professor replied.

"It was 1802, professor, the year you graduated, and you wanted to get your career off to a flying start. I believe your uncle put up the money, didn't he?"

"Yes, I was telling Lenora here about the Amaranth flower. Cultivated as an edible grain there, and here they are, a cut flower. She says they call it love lies bleeding, if you will." He chuckled.

The food had now gone, but the drinks were flowing, and we decided to move to the lounge. Sabrett joined me while we ushered the party through the door.

Lenora and Flora stopped in front of me, looking intense. They each placed a hand on either side of my stomach. With their other hands on the small of my back, they closed their eyes for a moment, as if listening. The rest of the party stopped to take in this spectacle, and they both stepped back.

As one, they pronounced, "You are carrying a child."

My face grew pale. "That's not possible."

"Ah, but it is. There is life," Flora said.

"But my husband has been gone too long, and I'm not showing."

They both looked at Sabrett accusingly.

"It's rare but not unheard of," Lenora answered.

Sabrett sat heavily in a chair beside the fire and stared into the flames. I blushed and sat on the couch, rubbing my hand across the material as I remembered my first miscarriage.

"There's more to consider here." Xanthe stepped forward.

"This is an abomination," Trillian added.

"Now, wait one minute." I started.

"You have no idea what you're dealing with here, witch." Xanthe aimed at me.

"What do you mean, dealing with? It's a child."

"Dear gods, think about it." Trillian condescended.

"Sabrett, what are they talking about?" I admit I had been naïve up until this point, only thinking of having a child.

"Let me," said Adio, taking my hand as he sat beside me. "This is forbidden for many reasons, dear one, but mainly because Sabrett here is not living. He cannot bring up a child. It shouldn't have been possible; only a few vampires have managed to sire a Dhampir. Those children are cursed."

I looked into his eyes. He had no reason, I could see, to lie to me

"But why are they cursed? It must be like me; otherwise, it wouldn't exist."

"It's not as easy as that. These children are torn between two worlds; they will either go mad and hunt us down. Taking out their father issues on us, or they will turn and become one of us."

Sabrett looked up, his eyes sad. "I wanted you to join me in eternity. How is this possible now?"

I hadn't considered that. Only the joy of knowing I could have a child. Only the idea of my longed-for child and with someone, I assumed, would stick by my side. I hadn't considered that the love may have been selfish and conditional on me living as long as he did. My sadness only deepened. This distressed me because I knew that my situation with James would only be made worse. I paced around the room, hoping an answer would present itself with every footstep. My only way out had been snatched from me. I couldn't let my body die now; it was the only thing that could bring this new life into the world.

"Surely, I can have the child and then join you after?" I asked Sabrett.

"Who would bring it up? You might kill it in your hunger. New vampires don't have control over their thirst." His expression was blank.

I considered what he said, running my hand through my hair. I wanted to bring it up, love it, and have it love me.

Trillian and Xanthe, as one chimed, "It's not your decision."

"What do you mean? Surely, it's only my decision; it's my body and my child." I grew aggravated.

"No, the council will decide; we are enforcers. Since we were here to witness the abomination, we will take Sabrett back to face the council."

Sabrett stood and walked towards the twins.

"Wait, you can't go," I said, moving to take Sabrett by the hand.

Adio grabbed my arm. "He has to; he has to be judged. If he doesn't go, they will kill you now and be judge, jury, and executioner. They have the council's support in anything they do. This is your best bet. Let Sabrett argue your case and pray he wins."

As Sabrett moved past me, he lurched forward. Missing the twin's grasps by millimetres and pulling me up, he held me close. "We will find a way. I won't let you both die. Trust me," Sabrett whispered.

With that, the twins grabbed his arms and dragged him from the house.

Adio stood, "I must leave too. My council must also be told this is a threat to all of us. At the very least, instability will show cracks in our clans, which could force a war no one wants."

"It's just a baby." I cried as the coven gathered around me.

CHAPTER ELEVEN
Love Lies Bleeding

As Samhain approached, we prepared a giant pyre on the hilltop. Branches and logs from the woods were dragged through the brambles and across the grass. We had all become keenly aware of being watched. Everyone sensed the presence, and we sensed its eyes on us as we worked. The feeling grew strongest near the woods. When we crossed the boundary from the house, the hairs on the backs of our necks stood on end.

We assumed the clan would send people to ensure I didn't run, and we went on with our lives as best we could. Of course, it had crossed my mind to take flight and find somewhere new to live, away from everyone who would do us harm. James' purse strings were held tight; this meant I would have had to sell things, which took time I did not have. I couldn't be sure his spy wouldn't notify him, and I couldn't get far or give my child a decent life without money.

Flora had recruited an apprentice to teach everything she had learnt. Not wanting her knowledge to leave her village when she passed on. The young girl was an orphan; her Romany parents had died from typhoid, and she had been left with no family. The rest of the village saw her as unclean and left her to fend for herself.

At fifteen, she was as fresh as a daisy and just as delicate. Flora found her begging for scraps and became the only one willing to take her in. The girl quickly took to helping, and Flora slowly taught her all the plants. She appeared unfazed at her guardian being a witch, bringing our little coven up to eight. A new stone would be added to our circle. We would take ash from the Samhain bonfire and place it underneath in a well-practised ritual.

The cattle and sheep were being slowly moved to low pastures, close to the houses for winter. The apples in the gardens were all but picked and beans were withering on the vine, ready for use as next year's seed. Kitchen windows propped open to release the sweet scent of jams and chutneys. We packed a little food into one of the wooden crates that still stood in the kitchen. Everyone returned to their own homes shortly after the twins left with Sabrett, leaving me alone again.

I had grown to hate my own home, empty of love and waiting for the moment it became my prison again, or worse, my grave. James' arrival drew near, and no one had heard from Sabrett. I would be at my husband's mercy once more, only now I was pregnant with another being's child. There would be no way I could pass the child off as his; too much time had passed. I was only a month into carrying the child. The sickness had started, but I was stronger this time, and my body had become healthy. There were no dips between my ribs, and I had meat on my hips. Despite the danger it represented to me and my child, I had a hunch it was meant to be this time.

Never yours

I would do whatever I could to make sure it came into the world and that I would be the one to hold it. I had cast every charm and said every protective word I knew over the house and garden, doing everything I could to ward off any harmful influences. Inviting only joy and friends through the doors.

Positive light glowed from me most days. When melancholy came upon me, a dark grey mist swirled around the house. My powers pulsed as though they were growing along with the child. Bess, too, glowed with her pregnancy, and together, we amplified the rituals.

Samhain was going to be a powerful time for divination, and I was excited to join the coven. Flora and Lenora were busy getting together everything we needed to greet the thinning of the veils. Lettie had set herself the challenge of constructing a heavy metal cauldron to be hung over the settling embers of the bonfire.

Tansy was channelling her Irish heritage and baking Barmbrack; the bread was heavy with raisins and sultanas. I had been practising in the kitchen and supplied the candied citrus peel. The chef had been remarkably patient with me. Treating me like a curious child and starting with small cakes and biscuits, graduating to preserve foods. Not all had gone well, as I had burnt the scones so much that the windows had to be thrown open, allowing the smoke to escape. The less said about the soup, the better. I still had a long way to go before I would be able to throw a dinner party.

I walked into the gardens, helping to harvest the apples from the trees. The windfalls would be used for cider, and I was thoroughly looking forward to trying it the following autumn. But for now, I was to settle for water and juices.

My favourite foods now made me ill. Even the smell of frying foods would send me running for the water closet.

Lenora would be a midwife to both me and her own daughter. Because of my complicated situation, she tried to find out as much as possible. But there was little to no information on such a rare pregnancy in a small village.

I had written to the professor, and he had promised to go through the university library to see what he could find. I had heard nothing since. Turning my library upside down, I had set about reading as much as I could. My hopes of finding a birthing manual for a half-human, half-vampire child were low. But with little else to do, I continued anyway.

What I did find was an old family bible. A dusty tome hidden in a dark corner on the top level. After generations of fingers had rubbed the surface, its faded lettering became hard to make out. I ran my fingers across it, feeling a connection to the ancestors within. A blue spark shot from my fingers, jittering across the book and dying at the edge. I opened it and found pages of handwriting. The sheets of delicate paper recorded lists of births and the years. Each page had a different family name.

I thumbed through each page, skimming and reading before I ended at the last page. I suddenly recognised my own name at the bottom. I read the page from bottom to top. Following from my name were my sisters in order and then my mother and father. I flicked back a page to find my mother's parents' names. At the bottom was my mother's name and then, in birth order, her sisters. I counted seven children in total.

I flicked back to another page. The writing getting harder to read now, but I recognised my grandmother's name at the bottom. Reading through each of her sister's names and her parents at the top. Seven again. My heart skipped a beat. I flicked back again to find her mother's name at the bottom and six sisters listed before her parents. Three more pages all revealed the same pattern. The last had only five children, two females and three males. It was a record of my family for eight generations, with only the first containing any male heirs. I had heard the rumours of female children and red hair, but considered it a recent occurrence. Nothing that wouldn't be broken in time.

I sat contemplating the number seven. That would make me the seventh daughter of the seventh daughter. An unbroken chain for generations.

Samhain was upon us, and I was thrilled to be a part of something so powerful. My stomach was in knots as I looked forward to the night's activities. The sickness had grown with my child every day. I met Bess and Lenora at our barn, and we walked along the path through the woods, listening to the owls and other creatures in the undergrowth. The various snuffles and growls made us jump, but we walked on.

The pyre was waiting along with the rest of our party as we made our way up the hill. Lenora and I linked arms with Bess to help her. Lenora predicted there may be twins, and it was taking a lot out of her to grow these children. Jack's pride, already at bursting point, had positively exploded on this news. He had been strutting around like a cockerel ever since.

We arrived at the top of the hill and took our places around the stack of logs. Flora said a small incantation under her breath and lit the fire. Welcome, sister, to the place where the world of the dead meets our own. From now on, we must be careful in what we say and do, as the veil is fragile in this place. She nodded to her protégé, who stood off to the side, and we all made room for her in the circle. The flames licked higher up the stack of logs, making it harder to see everyone's faces. The orange glow rose above us and cast long shadows down the hill.

The heat warmed our faces while the cool of the night was on our backs. This made the feeling of being surrounded by waiting spirits more real. Grace brought with her a stone so large she struggled to carry it. It was flat on two sides, and she looked it over and chose the side she placed on the ground. Freckles covered her cheeks and nose. Her short, auburn hair almost matched mine; she could have been mistaken for part of my family. Still gangly and finding herself, she wasn't comfortable in her body yet, which showed as clumsiness. Flora raked some embers from the fire and placed them below her stone. Then, we renewed the ash below each of ours, tilting the well-worn stones. The heat from the embers warmed them before being extinguished.

We sat and talked and cooked in the new cauldron. It worked extremely well, and we all clapped Lettie on the back, saying we all wish we had one at home. The bar back was sweet. Its fruit went well with the crumbly cheese, although the others scoffed at my choice. As it happened, Grace could play the penny whistle, and the music rose with the smoke. We all took to dancing, our black cloaks flying about as we sped up, circling the fire. Looking out across the field, soft glows dotted the dark.

The spinning may have affected my eyes. I swore faces started to reveal themselves in the glowing lights. Some were too far away to make out, but the closest ones became clearer as our dancing continued. And the one appeared to step forward, closer than any of the others. Mists swirled about her, but the female form began to crystallise. I recognised the face of Harriette and my heart skipped a beat.

I gasped, not wanting to stop in case the spell was broken. I danced and swirled around to see her smiling at me and clapping; she laughed as I spun past. I circled, and she moved into view; her wild hair now flew about her pretty face. The tears stung my eyes. The emotions were too much to bear, but I couldn't let this stop. The dancing continued for so long that I was convinced my feet would break. I watched my sister the whole time, looking truly happy, and she danced along with me. She spoke with me as she circled the hill; the others joining her until the whole field danced with us. The spirits rose and fell as if their dance floor was fluid and moved in waves. She was glorious in death.

And then she stopped. Raising her hand, her face cracked into a scream. She pointed behind me and looked at me; her face contorted and white. I stepped back in shock, but her scream made no sound. The horror was no less, and I stopped dancing and spun around to find what she had pointed at. The spell was broken, and the spirits had left us, disappearing in a retreating mist. Only the woods lay behind me, and I couldn't see anything in the pitch black. My head spun, and I took my seat to let it settle. The others gathered around, and I explained what I had seen.

Flora spoke, "It was an omen, and your sister was trying to warn you about something to come. The danger did not stand behind you, but was approaching in time."

"The warning must be about the clan decision and my child." I was shaken to my core.

We collected the embers of what was left of the fire. Placing them in the cauldron prevents it from spreading through the dry grass. Planning to collect it the next day to use the ashes for future divination.

When we returned, we would check on the rocks on which we sat. If one had moved or was mislaid, it was a bad omen, meaning the death of the occupier.

We parted ways. Flora and Grace walked across the fields and home, and Lettie and Tansy returned to the village.

Lenora and Bess would walk with me as far as the courtyard and then take the little track back to the village. The moon was still full in the sky, its light helping us on the paths. We hugged and said our goodbyes at the mouth of the stable yard. I watched as the two shapes disappeared into the dark.

Breathing in the cold night air relieved some of the sickness. I looked at the few clouds that floated above my head. I turned, thinking a shape had moved in the corner of my eye. Examining the rooftops, I remembered the one I had seen before, thinking it was a trick of my mind. The night had caused my anxiety to peak, and I didn't think it could be trusted. I started my journey across the cobbled yard.

The horses, nodding in their stables, looked up when I passed. Softly chewing or rubbing against the brick. As I reached the centre of the yard, each horse turned to me. At once, the mood changed, pounding at the stable doors again. This has happened before. I couldn't think what I was doing to cause the fuss. I went to soothe them by stroking the forelock of a sizeable black mare called Tess. Her eyes were wide, so wide you could see the whites at the edges.

As I soothed her, a dark shape dropped between me and the door to the house. The horses brayed and bolted around their stables, kicking as they went. The shape was hunched, as if a sack had been dropped from the rooftop. Then it unfolded to stand.

"Sabrett", I called into the dark. "Is that you?"

My chest heaved, and my breathing became panicked as no answer came. I judged the distance and could not reach the door; the only other exit led to the woods or the barn. I remembered the hexafoil on the barn door frame and decided, at that moment, to run there.

My cloak billowed out behind me as I dashed, slipping on the damp cobbles and twisting my ankle, sending a sharp pain through it. I stumbled on, fearing for my life. As I turned the corner, I saw the barn, and the door stood open.

I heard a loud thud as the gate behind me hit a wall and splintered as wood shards flew around me. I didn't look fearful of the knowledge of what was following me. If I could reach the safety of the barn, then I would confront the creature.

The barn was almost within grasp, and as I reached out my hand to grab the door, an ice-cold wind rushed past my cheek. Appearing in front of me, the figure grabbed my outstretched arm, and I came to an abrupt stop. The sudden loss of momentum jarred my limbs, and the breath knocked from my body. I flew backwards as my arm was twisted and used to send me flying to the ground.

Getting to my knees, my face covered in dirt and gravel. I tried to crawl back towards the stable, coughing with the effort. The figure reached down, looming over me. He grabbed both arms, ripping them from under me, and held me, lifting me. He turned my body to face him and then lifted me higher. My feet dangled until my toes dragged against the rough ground.

My attacker's face was hidden from view by the folds of a hood. The dark space within seemed to go on forever, and then he loomed close to me and I could smell him. The scent of moist earth, freshly dug, mixed with the putrid smell of rotting meat, made me gag.

It was only now that I saw him. His face was long, his head shone in the moonlight, and his black eyes reflected the pale disk. His nose was missing. Two holes were flat against his face as if the protrusion had rotted off. His hollow cheeks only accentuated the missing parts of his face. He turned to look around us, revealing pointed ears. He wore a simple, long black coat. It was torn and covered in loose earth, which fell to the ground every time he moved.

He sniffed at me and leant in further, taking me into an embrace. He sniffed my skin across my face and then licked my cheek. He smiled as the web of spittle hung between us. I was frozen, my legs dangling, and my heart beating so hard in my chest that I feared it might stop.

His teeth flashed forward white and sharp, a mouth full of sharp points. Rows upon rows lined the gums like troops waiting their turn on the battlefield. More animal than man. He dug them into my throat, tearing at the veins, the pain white hot and all-encompassing. My heart thumped and gurgled as the blood rushed out of me. He drank thirstily, and I could feel blood running down my neck to my breast, dizzy and unable to cry out. I was held in thrall, and there was nothing I could do to stop the creature from drinking.

It was like he hadn't eaten in decades, and my blood was ebbing away in a great flood into his open maul. This was different from the way Sabrett drank, and all I wanted to do was escape, but my body would not cooperate.

As the image of the world around me wobbled, and I feared I would faint, I tried one last time to wriggle free. My muscles started to move, but his arms snaked around me further. Tightening his grip and pulling the blood from me faster. I lost consciousness, my head lolling to the side as the darkness fell.

I woke up in a pile like a rag doll at the door to the barn. He was crouched over me, his monstrous visage the first thing I laid eyes on. My heart barely beat in my chest. I feared myself dead.

"Shh," he whispered, his teeth causing a lisp. "Your blood is good." He licked his lips and cleaned his teeth with his tongue until they glowed white again. "You won't be able to move for a long time. It's pointless trying. Has Sabrett warned you about me? Ah, I see by your eyes that he forgot to tell you. And you are having his child?" His tone was mocking. "You know you are as much an abomination as I am. And now you're mine."

At this point, he laughed, something that sounded so alien to him that it was as if he had forgotten how long ago. His face did not change, unlike Sabrett's. He did not become a softer version of himself and stayed forever the monster before me.

"You have Sabrett to thank for this; he should have taken you when he had the chance."

He brushed my hair out of my face so that he could examine me further.

"I heard Sabrett tell you his tale. Do you enjoy stories?"

I wanted to fight back, but the words were caught in my throat.

"I am your maker now; this is the only story you should hear. My name is Nikola Alilovic. I am the Great grandson of the first of my kind, Jure Grando from Kringa." He stood and did a half bow before returning to his crouched position. "The people turned on my grandfather after his death, calling him Strigon. They turned on his family and forced them from their homelands. His wife and two children were brutally rejected, and their property was stolen from them. His family was hounded out of the village they called home. I am the Grandson of Nikola Alilovic Grando, Son of Jure. Nikola took his middle name as a surname when he fled to Italy. It was 1672 when the villagers decapitated the body of my great-grandfather." He puffed his chest as he spoke of his family.

"The family curse followed him, and I was born in 1720. Some say I led a life of sin executed for my crimes, only to rise from the grave as a Strigoi Mort." He pointed at a significant dent in his head. "I say I was taking back what was once mine, and I am more powerful now. I take revenge for the crimes against me and my family. Sabrett was foolish enough to cause me some pain years ago, and now he can have the same pain."

He said this matter-of-factly, like I was a pawn in some game of revenge played out across the decades.

"I have been waiting for the perfect moment, and what better time than a child that shouldn't exist? As you will be mine, so will it. And the years you spend alive will tick down until the moment you join me in the earth. My revenge will have been years in the making. So perfect."

He crooned happily at his plan, almost drooling at his own cleverness. I coughed, choking on my blood.

"Ah yes, let's sort that out; we wouldn't want you to die yet."

He took his finger and bit into it, drawing enough of his blood to rub around my open wounds. It tingled, to begin with, and then a prickling sensation followed until it finally burned. Like fire sealing the wounds, stitching up the veins and skin. Scars formed, and tight white skin told the tale of the torn flesh that existed before it. An ugly reminder forever of this night.

"That's better, isn't it?" Still, I lay prone, unable to move. Now, let's move you into your precious barn."

He picked my limp body up, carrying me, my arms and head swaying at his side. He wasn't rough, but he was far from gentle. Reaching the door, he looked at the protection symbols scratched into the wood.

"Hmm, a good try."

He said as he pushed against the invisible net that strained to keep him out. It gave around me, which caused a tear in the fabric of the spell. It could not keep up the pressure and broke under his force.

Never yours

He flopped me down on the same straw on which Sabrett had lain with me. I managed to turn my head now, letting out a croak through my damaged throat. My voice was unrecognisable to me; shocked at the sound, I pushed myself up to sit. My throat was raw when I went to speak.

"Everything in time, my child. Now, you will look and sound different, but that is not all. As a living vampire witch, you will have new gifts. These can be discovered in time as the hour approaches where I must leave you. I will return in ten years if I choose to complete the curse. When I come, you will drink my blood and join me in the earth for eternity. Settle your affairs and pass on my thanks for a new mate and delicious meal to Sabrett."

A grin spread across his face again, and he went to leave.

CHAPTER TWELVE
Heartsease

When Nikola left, I lay back down on the straw. My body was a lead weight, too heavy to move, and my eyes burned. I stayed put half hoping he would come back and finish the job. My knees curled, and I took the foetal position, facing the barn door with my hands on my stomach. I didn't know if the baby could survive this body now. I looked out into the dark of the woods. My head pounded like I had not drunk enough water on a stifling day. I contemplated the sun and how Sabrett had described how it would feel for him to die that way. Still, I did not move when the first rays touched the mouth of the barn.

My white robes were crimson with my blood, and I wrapped the cloak around me as if to hide it. The sun rose in the sky, and its light touched the fire pit at the centre of the room. An hour passed as I lay there, the straw now poking my skin through the cloth. I started to notice the smell of the barn as if I had never been there before. Layers of oil scents on top of each other. The pungent rosemary and geranium clamouring against each other. Soft rose floating in the background, barely registering. The smell of years of smoke and ash baked into the beams above was warm. The sun touched the bottom of the bale making it sparkle like gold.

The colours of the woods blinded me. I lifted my hand to shield my eyes and slowly allowed them to grow accustomed to the brightness. I had never seen greens this complex. It wasn't one colour, but like a painting. The trees were dark green, viridian, and emerald mixed with blues and browns, and this was all in a single leaf. The whole woods glowed with colour.

I let my eyes wander, taking in all the new sights. Even the rock hues were a mix of blacks, greys, yellows and browns. There were sparkling crystal formations in some that reflected the sunlight. The world outside grew more alive, more real. The sun crept up the side of the bale and was now reaching the edge. I made no move. What would be would be. It tipped over, spilling across the top like liquid amber and brushing the ends of my hair. Soft molten light approached.

I heard crickets, but not their cheerful chirruping. Instead, their slow march through the grass at the barn door was like thunder in my ears. Then the sun crashed over me in waves, and I closed my eyes and waited.

There was heat on my skin, but no more than I had experienced as a child lying in the meadows. I cried, but this time with happiness, I may still survive this. I held my hands to my ears to block the noise and fell asleep like that.

I had heard their approach before they reached the walled gardens. Listened to the happy, fast-paced chatter of Bess and Lenora. I heard Lenora's wheeze worse now than I remember it being, and there was a slight drag of her leg over the pebbles of the lane. Bess's wheeze now almost matched her mother's as the long walk from the village took its toll. I did not open my eyes; instead, I listened.

Their skirts swished as they walked. Little sticks and leaves attached themselves, dragging and then dropping rhythmically. I found it soothing. And then they turned the corner. Taking in the scene like witnesses to a murder, their hearts fluttered as if to stop. I heard their pulse quicken once more with the sight of the pool of blood close to the door, and then their eyes locked on me. I heard Bess's hand grip her mother's old sun-dried skin and then rub free as she made to run to me.

Their skirts swished faster, now flapping against bare legs. Then, knees thumping painfully to the hard ground. They did not touch me at first, fearing the worst as they saw the blood. Lenora was the first to see the new scar tissue, and she touched its raw, white, ragged surface.

And now I breathed. I was aware I had held my breath the entire time. As I gulped air I smelt them. Dirt and sweat assailed my nostrils first. Then grass, the scent of it, soft and freshly ground underfoot, it smelt green.

"Dear God's, what happened?" Bess choked, almost in tears at the sight of me.

"I was bitten," I managed hoarsely.

"Come. We need to get you up to the house. Can you walk?" Lenora asked.

"Not yet, stay," I croaked, but that was all I could manage.

Bess stayed with me while Lenora went to the meadow to find the others. They were back to collect the things from the night before, and all arrived in a rush, panicked at what they had heard. Flora leant over me and stroked my forehead.

"Your stone is missing." Her voice was dark and foreboding.

"Not a surprise," I managed before coughing, my throat raw with effort.

A small smile emerged, and Flora continued, "It's good to see you haven't lost your sense of humour. We will wait here today, and when night falls, we will move you to your bed to rest."

Flora asked other witches in distant villages for knowledge, which was passed down through the generations. None of this was written down. It was usually passed on in stories, but our coven had begun to write a book of what they discovered.

I had been in a fever dream for two weeks, thrashing around and screaming in my sleep. A constant watch was at my bedside; this was not like the comedown from laudanum. That was a walk in the park compared to this. My head burned, and my skin crawled in waves across my body. Nobody was sure I would survive, and if I did, would I lose the child at any moment?

I left claw marks on the headboard, scratching at it in pain. In my calm moments, I would mumble whispers of dreams—visions of the people I loved and of the villagers beyond. I warned of a fire as I watched an ember jump in front of a sleeping shepherd. I spoke in strange languages that no one could translate, and I cursed the daylight. But as I woke from my sickbed, I could remember none of it.

Bess had told James of my mysterious illness and warned him to delay his return in case he got sick. Of course, he obeyed, not wanting to catch whatever it was I had, sending a letter saying he would return after it had passed. I sat in bed surrounded by my friends, and we talked late into the night.

It was November, and Bess was only three months away from delivering her children. The bump was noticeable even through the large skirts. Grace lay across the bottom of the mattress, her feet wiggling in the air lazily as we spoke. The others had pulled up chairs and brought food and water, and I ate tiny morsels while the others dug in. I liked this; I was aware of how natural it was.

"Let's do this every day."

"Ah, that would be lovely, but I think your husband would have something to say," added Lenora.

The others laughed in agreement and nodded.

"No, I mean it." I was determined. I wanted to find a way that we could do this all the time. "If you all lived here, we could protect Bess and her children. We can set up the bakery and the forge in any of the outbuildings. We can protect each other and learn more together to protect others."

They had fallen silent, looking at each other. Their chewing had slowed.

"There's still your husband," Flora said.

"I have considered that, and I have a plan. But I'm afraid you won't like it."

"Tell us, and then we can be the judge," interjected Bess.

"He's not a good man," I started, and this brought a snort from Bess and several rolled eyes, as if I was the last to know. "But I will make him an offer. I will tell him he's free to go and live or do whatever with whoever. I won't complain, and I will always stay in the country. He can pretend this child is his to save face. No one will know any different. All I need is an allowance and to have you all live here."

"I think you are naive if you think he will go along with that when he can get you locked up," Bess looked sad as she said this.

"I know, but I'm not sure he can. Not while I'm pregnant anyway, unless he admits it's another man's child, but that would be too much for his ego to bear. I've also heard that divorce is more available to those with money. I don't care what everyone thinks of me, but he does."

"I still think you are giving him too much credit; look how much he's hurt you before; he might just kill you." It was Tansy's turn to speak her mind.

"Not if you killed him first," Grace spoke almost dreamily.

We all paused at this. She was just a child. Sometimes, she spoke without the weight of the world and consequences in her mind.

"Maybe not kill him, but I might need some protection in case." I hadn't considered killing him or anyone up till now; I wanted to live in peace with my new sisters. That's what they had become to me; we were family.

Lettie cleared her throat, "I've been experimenting a little. After researching in your library, we came across some books on old weapons; there are a few I've been having a go at. I'm unsure how my husband would feel about moving the forge, but I can ask him."

"Well, I know my husband would love to see your kitchen," Tansy laughed.

"I'm old, and a soft bed for me and my husband would be welcome," Lenora said, and Flora nodded enthusiastically.

"Our children could grow up together in more safety than I can offer in our cottage. I'm in. If we can offer protection to sisters from other villages, against the human and the vampire realm," Bess said, bouncing a little in excitement.

I was grinning, happier now than I think I had ever been. "But first, I must deal with James. Bess, can you write to him and tell him it's safe to return in three days? Does that leave you enough time to make me something for protection, Lettie? Preferably something small, so he doesn't suspect anything."

She rubbed her hands together, looking forward to the challenge.

"Everyone else best pack. When he's gone, we can use the farm carts to move all your stuff," I said.

With three days to prepare, we all busied ourselves, making the house look as normal as possible. We had taken over, and research was strewn across the dining room table. Pages of writing were pinned to walls. We took everything down, stuffed it in cupboards, and tidied. But while we did this, we also planned how the house would change when we were in control.

The dining room would become a planning and coordination room, the table was large enough for us all to gather to discuss our goals. The library would need more chairs and the kitchen would be where we would all gather to eat and chat while Tansy and her husband would prepare the meals.

The glasshouses would be utilised better for growing more herbs. The kitchen garden would be enlarged to supply more for the village and stores for the winter. I would keep the formal garden, not wanting to remove all traces of my family from the house. And I would take back my father's study for my own.

We wandered around the stable yard and soon found a corner barn that would work for the forge. Lettie's husband wasn't initially keen, but she talked him around. I think her newfound skills with weapons helped her convince him. That and the fact that more space, with no rent, would be good for the business.

We would keep our barn for distilling, but we would expand. Employing people and knocking through moving the entrance to the inner courtyard of the stable block, no longer hidden from view.

The house and lands would become welcoming for visitors and those who needed shelter. We would use our knowledge to treat the sick and wounded and help those with otherworldly problems. Sister witches had been left to the mercy of the vampire clans for too long, going cap in hand whenever they needed help. Left to the Strigoi when the fancy took them. It was time we were able to protect our own. We would become equals in these worlds and be respected instead of looked down on.

Of course, we would help those vampires who had genuinely helped us—those we had befriended over the generations. But the others would only be welcome when we decided they would be. The taste of freedom and agency was on the tip of my tongue, and I was desperate for more.

James arrived late in the afternoon, looking weary from the journey. His long coat was covered in dust and appeared not to have been washed since his time in the Americas. He had grown stubble in an attempt to grow a beard, but hadn't entirely pulled it off. There were flecks of grey in his hair now, and he looked older. I still looked sallow. Of course, his eyes flicked over me and he immediately gave unwanted comments on my appearance.

"I see my time away hasn't done you any favours."

My eyes had dark rings around them that I had done my best to cover with makeup. My hair was up, meaning every flaw was more visible, including the new scar. I had deliberately chosen not to hide it with one of the many chokers in my collection. This he chose not to ask about as I saw his eyes flicker over the white flesh. His bags were rushed upstairs by Jack, who kept his face on the floor lest he give away our plans by making eye contact.

"Did you employ someone new?"

"It's Bess's husband. She is pregnant and he agreed to help out," I said, thinking on my feet. "You must be hungry." I gestured toward the dining room.

"Yes, we may as well eat." He eyed me up and down.

He shed his dusty coat and slung it over the banister, a small cloud rising into the air. As he sat at the head of the table, I decided to join him at his side instead of at the other end. I didn't feel like shouting our conversations tonight. He side-eyed me as I sat, unsure what to make of the choice.

Bess brought our food, looked me in the eye, and curtsied, her contempt for James crashing like waves over me. I was aware the others were waiting in the kitchen. They were not prepared to leave me alone, knowing what was about to be discussed. I was grateful for their support and could feel the love and concern. It buoyed me, and I acknowledged that tonight would make or break me.

As we ate, the sensation of his eyes on me grew unavoidable, and I turned to catch his gaze.

"The sickness has left you looking like a shell." he put it bluntly, but he was not wrong.

"It has." I agreed.

"Where did you get that scar?" His eyes wandered to the raw place on my neck.

"I will get to that." I dismissed.

"What? How dare you speak to me like that." he leant forward.

"I will speak as I wish."

He looked like he had been slapped, his face a picture of shock at this remark. I decided to stare directly into his eyes now. Holding his gaze before he dropped it to one side, annoyed at my insolence. A small battle had been won, and I had taken back a bit of my soul from him.

"Well, no matter. If you're not pregnant, I will write to the Alienist, and he can take you away." He put his fork down and stared back at me with a huge smile spreading across his face.

I paused, my stomach doing flips. I was aware that now I was in the most danger I had ever been in. Escaping him was always going to be a risk and one that could easily backfire. His anger was going to escalate, and if I didn't back down, it would push him further and further. But I had backed down too much and now was the time to regain the power. I had survived two vampires, and if that didn't give me the strength to continue, nothing would.

"James, I am pregnant."

He sat back in his chair and looked at my stomach. "Well, why can't I see the evidence? A phantom pregnancy, perhaps, some trick of your fractured mind?"

I took a bite of my food, chewing slowly, and when I had finished, I said, "I am not showing because it's only been a month."

I watched his face crease, calculating and failing to add up the time. "What? I've been gone for months. How? Who?" His voice broke with rage, and his fist slammed on the table.

I jumped. The noise and anger brought back into my mind, every fist landing on my skin, every tortured instruction. It nearly crushed my willpower once more.

"That's not important at the moment." this wasn't what I wanted to discuss, and my voice faltered.

I could see by his lips turning up at the corners that he had heard the falter as well. "How dare you!" his chair screeched in a long, painful movement as it turned towards me. This would make it easier for him to get to me if he chose. I put my fork down, and it clinked against the side of the plate.

"I don't think you can have me committed." He clenched his fists. "Now, let me continue." I held my hand up, and his face contorted in anger. "While I am pregnant, a judge may not be so happy to commit me as I am married and from a good family. And before you consider telling him it's not your child, think how that will make you look in front of all your friends. That you could not control your wife?" I let that settle in his mind for a short time before continuing

"I have a proposal. I will live here with my child and my friends, and you will provide a monthly allowance. After a year, we will divorce and you will agree to continue paying the allowance. This way, you get what you want, and I get what I want."

Silence fell as he slumped back in his chair. He appeared both angry and bemused, his face moving from tensed to smirking.

"Where has this wife been the entire marriage?" he mocked

"You killed her," I replied, looking him in the eye once more.

"Friends? You don't have any friends. The child is probably the bastard of some stable hand or farm boy too stupid to turn down a fuck from an ugly old whore."

I stood slowly and walked the few steps towards him. I raised my hand and slapped him across his face so loud it echoed around the room. His hand went to the pink print left there. His shocked expression made it even better. I sensed his rage before I saw it. It flamed from his chest outwards in an explosion. He leapt up and grabbed my hand before I could lower it again. He squashed the fingers together and I could feel each bone crushed against the other. I fell to the side in agony. His blood coursing through him and the pump of his heart as the anger spurred it on.

He bent and whispered in my ear, "Whore."

"Stop!" I said. I wasn't begging. It was a command.

"Why? What's stopping me from beating the child from you?"

Now, my anger was rising, and a protective urge surged through me, a strength I did not know I had, took over. My wrist bent back, and I twisted. He was forced to bend in the other direction as I became the aggressor. To an onlooker, it would now appear he was bent in fear, and my fist was the one coming to land on him. He released it quickly, stepping back, trying to gain face again.

"Try it!" I spat in his face.

We both held our position while he considered his next move. He charged forward, grabbing my throat and throwing me back on the table. The plates and cutlery clattered to the floor as I thudded hard on the wooden surface. He leant over me, his face leering down, and spittle dripped onto my cheek.

A wave of strength pulsed through me again, and I lifted my legs, already heavy with skirts. I kicked him over my head, sending him landing on his back. Then, faster than I expected, I leapt on top of him. His breath had been knocked from his body. We were now in the centre of the long table with the candlesticks lying around us. A strange light cast our shadows on the surrounding walls. As he went to catch his breath, I sat up, and a smile crept across my face. He looked puzzled.

"This is something I could get used to." His remark made me feel sick to my stomach. "Is this how you rode him?"

Recognising that the new defence was to make me feel ashamed. He was going to try every trick in the book.

"What is it you want?" I said.

"Right now, I would settle for finding out what someone

else saw in you," he replied. I wrinkled my nose, and he saw my disgust, which only urged him on. "What did you do for him that you didn't do for me?" leering at my breasts.

I accepted what I had always known; he would never give me what I wanted.

The sensation of him growing hard under my skirts made me realise I had his complete attention. I raised my arms to let my hair down. Making sure to move in a way that best revealed my breasts. Reminding him of the nights he held my wrists above my head.

I pulled my hairpin from its coiled metal clasp. The twin pin made a sharp ringing noise as it slid free, letting my hair fall about my face. He relaxed between my legs. I looked down into his brown eyes and traced the course of his blood through his veins. Pumping and gushing. I raised my hand, stretching up, and in one smooth swing, I drove the pins down.

The pins met flesh. With a brief pause of resistance, the skin relinquished, and it pushed through into his neck. The sharp tips sunk deep into the skin, and blood gushed forth. It squirted out onto the table and up, arcing across my body, face and up across the ceiling. He contorted in pain, and his hands reached up, trying to pull the metal hairpin free, to no avail. He gurgled, unable to scream and choking on his blood.

I licked at the drops near my mouth, tasting the metallic, warm, thick liquid. And then I bent, licking around the wounds and up across his face, spreading the red fluid. I sat up again and laughed at his expression and my freedom. He would never control me again.

I could feel his energy and wanted it. I craved it like many women would crave sweet treats or strange inedible fancies to sate a growing child. Like a sponge, I soaked up his life force as it ebbed from him. I grew stronger now, his energy leaching out of him along with the blood. The child inside grew stronger, and I knew I would not lose this one.

I fed on James, using every last drop of his energy to feed my child, and it grew hungry. I grasped his head on either side, pulling it up by his hair, pouring the last drops out. His face was forever in a screaming, terrified, statue-like grimace. I sensed his fear and anguish as I drained him. Sparks of red and orange light flew from me, illuminating the room, and I screamed like a banshee in blissful release.

The power flowed through me. It pulsed as his heart pulsed, rising in fear and then slowing, calming, fluttering, and gone. Rising off his body, my arms splayed to either side of me, my head tipped back covered in blood, I hovered over him.

Bess and the others stood in the doorway, frozen in fear.

CHAPTER THIRTEEN
Lilies

"Sorry about the mess."

Bess laughed, and the others were caught up in the moment; we all burst out in hysterics. An infectious laugh, full of relief and joy and fear. And then I realised what I looked like and I stopped. Momentarily shocked and concerned at my own behaviour and the realisation of what had taken place. Bess ran forward and embraced me in a hug. Her pregnant belly pushed against my own, and then we were joined by the rest of the coven in a huddle.

Grace squirmed to get into the centre. "I told you, you should kill him."

I embraced Lettie particularly hard. "Thank you for your beautiful hairpin; it did exactly what we needed."

"Well, I was under the impression you were only going to threaten him, so it wasn't quite finished. I suppose now I can see if there are any improvements I can make."

Shaking with adrenaline, I closed the door of the room. I couldn't face it. "What have I done?" Regret and fear were now gnawing at my stomach. "How could I have been so stupid?"

"He attacked you. He always attacked you. What other choice was there?" Bess tried her best to soothe me.

"You and I both know the law doesn't work like that."

We needed time to plan and devise a way to make this right. We decided to clean up the next day and left James' body to rot. Instead, we went to the library, now with a circle of comfortable chairs ready for each of us. We lit a fire and settled each in our own. The cold evening closed in on us as the sun sank low in the grey sky.

Flora was the first to speak. "We had better read you the letters we had from our sisters. It's time you knew everything we do about your condition. It may help you to know how to proceed." Each took turns reading.

Mistress Flora,

It is good to hear from you, sister. I will do my best to answer, but it's been a while since a Strigoi was sighted in these parts. The curse is said to leave the victim alive for ten years. Once the years are up, she will either be bitten again by the creature, or she will lie dead in her grave. Most are bitten again, joining their masters in their graves. I wish you all the best in your troubles. Oh, if you get a moment, could you send me a recipe for your tonic?

Blessed be
Sarah

*

Dear Tansy

Beloved sister, I miss your letters. Why do you not write more? The Emerald Isle misses you. I hope that your husband is looking after you.

The Strigoi have been a curse here. Only last year, we lost Bridget to one. She was bitten seven years previously and had been sickly ever since. She hardly ever left her bed. We had to cover up the reports of her, cursing and draining the other villagers, lest we be hunted again. She was living, if that's what you can call it, until her actual death. We promised her we would behead her and stab her heart with a yew stake, and that's what we did. Preventing her from rising again.

Your loving sister

*

Professor,

Sir, I would be privileged to inform you more about the subject of Dhampir mythology. As you know, this is my speciality, although I'm slightly surprised by your interest.

In mythology, a Dhampir is the child of a vampire and a human. Usually a vampire father and human mother. The conclusion I draw is that the mother has to be alive to support a child to term, or else it will die. It is an extremely rare occurrence that is mentioned a few times in the literature. The mother will usually be sickly, and the child may even rip itself from her body, causing her death. The child itself is said to inherit specific properties from its father. It will either be a vampire or have abilities. Even if they are not full vampires, they are cursed with a hunger, which they may give in at any moment. There is very little information on the mother's past giving birth. I cannot tell you of their fates. The child can be seen as a threat to vampires, as they often hate what they are and go about hunting down others.

As for the second part of your question, Strigoi Mort are dead and rise from the grave to consume the living. They are often related to other Strigoi or just criminals or evil people in life. In literature, they have abilities to turn into bats or wolves. Their powers can be inherited by their progeny. Strigoi vui are living Strigoi, which turn to Strigoi Mort upon death.

As for clans, I have nothing that says such a thing would exist, and I cannot help with that area of research. I have enjoyed our correspondence, but my curiosity is piqued. Please tell me why you

are interested.
Yours
Aldridge Westfield

There were other letters. Piles of them, with little to no information, were compiled with these nonetheless. Most nailed their colours to our flag, swearing to join us in our cause. The little book they had created grew thick with crumpled pages. Rough looking, but a treasure trove of collected information. We would add our experiences as we went to improve the knowledge inside. A whole section had been lovingly put together by Lettie. Glorious drawings in charcoal of weapons. Tricky hidden ones like my beautiful hairpin. Others are more blatant, like the skull crusher hammer she designed or the elegant axe design. Each had its intricate beauty carved into the surface. With incantations wound into the design, giving the weapon more than one way of killing its foe.

I flipped to a page with a chain mail neck brace. Jewellery is perfect for stopping fangs and breaking them off. They were beautiful. I could imagine them on the necks of theatre-goers. Not looking out of place in the most fashionable of establishments. I was in awe of her talents. I put the book to one side, still troubled by the letters.

"I am concerned that the letters seem to imply I will die, whether it be by vampire or sickness or my child."

"Yes, we are also troubled." Lenora took my right hand.

"But the truth is we are no wiser now than we were before about how this pregnancy will progress. We do know you could live for ten years before…" Tansy blushed.

Grace sniggered, amused by Tansy's clumsy attempt at support.

"Grace." Flora snapped at the girl, causing her to sulk.

"No woman knows how childbirth or pregnancy will go.

We all risk our lives for the children we bring into this world. The only certainty is that we will all die one day." Bess added sagely.

"You're right, of course. It's time I make the best of the days and stop looking at the years to make me happy." I considered my next words carefully: "I want something from you all. I need to know that my child will be looked after, no matter what it may be, if I'm not around to look after it."

"I promised our children would grow up together, and that is what they would do. I will love your child as my own, as I would want you to do for mine," Bess comforted me.

Flora proclaimed, "We pledge our lives to this cause and your children. We have been joined forever in a bond stronger than any of us."

We were happily chatting over breakfast in the kitchens. Tansy and George worked well together as they prepared the food. He kept nudging her and gesturing to the rest of us at the table.

Huffing, he turned and said, "Tansy has designed some clothes for you all."

"Do your talents ever cease," I exclaimed.

She blushed, "It's nothing, but our heavy skirts are such a burden at times. Men's trousers were much more practical. I combined a trouser and a bustle with some light skirts to conceal weapons."

"That sounds wonderful." Bess and I exchanged joyful looks.

"I think I'm too old for that, but I think the younger ones would benefit from such amazing work," Flora said.

"Also, some corsets with hidden pockets."

"Now that's something I could wear," Flora nodded.

"See. She was nervous about putting herself forward, thinking you all were more accomplished than she was." George smiled proudly.

"Never think that." I looked at Tansy, who was now beetroot red.

Changing the subject quickly, she asked, "Have you seen your hair this morning?"

"Why?"

"Oh yes, I see you're sporting a new look." Lenora prodded.

I rose and took up a copper pan, buffing it quickly with a cloth until it shone. My red hair flamed even brighter, but on one side, a large streak of white now tumbled onto my shoulder. My skin still looked sickly pale with a green tinge, but I was energised by the previous evening.

And then I remembered that we still had James' body to deal with.

We stood with mops, buckets, and cloth tied around our faces. Even now, the flies had started to gather, and the stink wafted through the room, more pungent than I had expected. It reminded me of rotting chicken breasts left for days in the warm sun.

Flora had gone to the little chapel to make arrangements for the burial with the clergyman. We had come up with the excuse that sickness had befallen him whilst he travelled. He had collapsed and died as soon as he arrived home. We requested a closed coffin and would have to wait a day or two for it to be made. We would store the body in one of the barns until the funeral. He would be placed in the family plot, and I would play my best mourning widow. As I scrubbed the congealed blood from the tabletop, I could see it staining the wood. No matter how hard I scrubbed, I could not draw the pink pool shape from the grain. The blood was dead; no energy or life force remained now.

As Jack and George carried the heavy weight out, wrapped in a white sheet, James' limp arm fell. Hanging loose, his wedding ring glinting in the light. For a moment, I regretted it and wondered again at how I had become capable of such a thing. I paused my scrubbing and followed the procession as they left the room. I vomited; it caught me by surprise, my breakfast now mingling with the fetid red, stinking fluid. The stench reached up into my nostrils, and this time, I aimed for the bucket. Morning sickness and the stench of death did not mix well. I ran for the windows, flinging them open to let in the cool November air. Breathing deeply but failing to remove the smell from my nostrils.

Bess joined me, looking green.

"I think we underestimated this bit," she said, and we both returned to our places.

Once the room had been cleaned, we gathered some of the fragrant oils and polished the table with them. We made sure to include Rosemary for protection and Lavender to cleanse the room.

Lenora burnt Juniper and Mugwort. Walking the boundary of the room, she chanted as she went, not wanting to risk his returning to haunt us. We decided to leave the room vacant until after the funeral to allow the air to clear. Flora wasn't sure the clergyman trusted her, but he agreed to attend the funeral. And when the time came, we moved his body into the wooden box and placed him on the back of one of the carts. The heavy horse pulled it, the same one who drew the plough. The funeral would have angered him; it was not proper, fitting or dignified; I'm sure he wouldn't have wanted it. That thought made a smile curl up from the corners of my mouth. I covered the look quickly with my hand pressed to my lips.

A small congregation of my friends and some villagers gathered in the light rain. I had written to James' friends and told them the sad news of his death. Making sure they understood the funeral would be for the family only. Knowing of his family's fear of sickness, it was easy to keep them away for the day. Claiming we would get together when it had passed.

The clergyman said some words of comfort for all who attended. He talked of the rewards that awaited James in heaven before we lowered him into the dank earth. I raised my black veil at the side of his grave and threw a handful of dirt and some white lilies on top of the coffin.

Weeping into my white handkerchief. I relished the fact that I wore the same black dress as I did when I lost my first child and how angry James had been that I did. The clergyman caught my arm as I went to leave the little chapel. His fingers wrapped around the black lace, holding it so tight that the pattern imprint appeared on my skin.

"It's strange. He sounded well when he wrote to me."

"He wrote to you?" I shook my arm free.

"Yes, he grew concerned about your welfare while he was away. Knowing how you fretted, I agreed to send all of your mail to him so that he could deal with anything that might trouble you."

"It was you?" I said, "What do you mean by knowing how I fret? You don't know me."

"Yes, I make it my job to be of as much help to my lords as I can. Your husband and I became — close." he puffed up his chest, pleased with himself.

"My personal letters. You took them?" My voice grew low, and I clenched my fists.

"Well, yes, but he insisted you must be taken care of." He stumbled.

"I can take care of myself. Do you even know the harm you have caused?"

"Madame, I am a reverent sent here by god to do his work and — "

"God," I laughed, "As if god existed here."

"As long as I am in charge, he will," his voice raised at me.

"I am the only master of this estate now. I am in charge, and as far as you are concerned, I am God."

I clasped his hand as if to shake it, but with madness and vengeance in mind, I sent a stinging shock through his arm. Not enough to kill, but enough to scare him, and I left him standing confused in the rain.

December came with a chill wind, and we prepared the house for a long winter. I requested the help of Lettie and Henry in picking the lock of my husband's office door. The ghost of my father still lay within. His cigar case was open on the desk, and his pen lay as if waiting for his hand once more.

My husband had also made his mark with his papers spread across the wide, polished wooden surface. They included his correspondence to the alienist and a letter from his solicitor. It explained that once I had been committed or, preferably, deceased, James could marry again and sell the estate. There were other letters from S Webb; they held details of parties and meetings in London. I read these letters in the large leather office chair, my back to an oil painting of my family.

I vowed to write to my remaining sisters and reconnect before it was too late. I wanted them to meet my child and know that I never abandoned them. Sweeping up all the papers and stuffing them into the bottom drawer of the desk, I closed the lid of my father's cigar case and straightened his pens. I wiped a hand over the leather writing surface and walked to the far wall, on which hung a map of the estate and surrounding villages.

I traced my fingers across the boundary lines of what was now all mine. I would be free to use my money and my estate as I wished, answering to no man and more than ready to take the reins. But first, I was reclaiming Christmas.

We would bring a Christmas tree into the house for the first year. James had constantly mocked the new traditions of trees and gifts to the poor. We ventured out into the woods, looking for the perfect-sized tree to cut. The snow had been falling for a week and lay thick on the ground.

Our skirts were heavy with ice as the snow melted and refroze attaching itself to the hem. The woods were dark now, the sun and clouds hung lower in the sky, and the treetops were heaving with snow. The woods were a mixed lot, having been thinned and planted with pine by my grandfather. He had reasoned that we would log them for timber selling the crop every few years.

Pine grew straight and tall and made good long planks. A valuable commodity even if it took a few years to get big enough.

The oaks used on the estate, in years gone by, were a long crop, taking hundreds of years to reach maturity. Their grand forms still graced the grounds. Silver birch grew between, and the elegant beech took pride in place. Yew could be found near the chapel and in the formal gardens, and the rowan grew sporadically at the edges. What was left of their feather-like leaves was brown and curled, wafting in the bitter winds.

The wood was sheltered and safe against the winter that swirled outside. The meadow had become impassable, and the hill poked up, only just visible in the white. We found a small pine measuring against Henry, who stood at least six feet tall. It was a little taller than him, and George took the task of cutting it as we all stood around, encouraging him.

Lenora and I went to cut Holly and Ivy. I found some of the bright red berries that stood out against the snow. As we gathered, Lenora started to sing. Her voice did not betray her age, and it lilted through the woods light and sweet.

Nay, my nay, hyt shal not be I wys,
Let holy hafe the maystry, as the maner ys:
Holy stond in the hall, faire to behold,
Ivy stond without the dore, she ys ful sore acold,
Nay, my nay
Holy and hys mery men, they dawnseyn and they syng,
Ivy and hur maydyns, they wepen and they wryng.
Nay, my nay
Holly stands in the hall, fair to behold:
Ivy stands without the door, she is full sore a cold.
Nay, ivy, nay, it shall not be I wis;
Let holly have the mastery, as the manner is.
Holly and his merry men, they dance and they sing,
Ivy and her maidens, they weep and they wring.
Nay, ivy, nay,
Ivy hath chapped fingers, she caught them from the cold,
So might they all have, aye, that with ivy hold.
Nay, ivy, nay,
Holly hath berries red as any rose,
The forester, the hunter, keep them from the does.
Nay, ivy, nay,
Ivy hath berries black as any sloe;
There come the owl and eat him as she go.

Nay, ivy, nay,
Holly hath birds a fair full flock,
The nightingale, the popinjay, the gentle laverock.
Nay, ivy, nay,
Good ivy, what birds hast thou?
None but the owlet that cries how, how.
Nay, ivy, nay,

I did my best to follow the words and joined her in song as we gathered. We came to a clearing and an apple tree. Its wood was old and gnarled, and mistletoe spilt forth in the crook of its branches. Green stems with pearls of white berries, plump and ripe. Seeds long ago discarded by birds have now taken root, and they would become part of our decorations. Although poisonous, we would hang it from ceilings to ward off evil. Some would steal a kiss under it, remembering the old gods.

Our baskets were heavy, and we returned to the others. They had strapped the tree to a stretcher of branches to protect it as we dragged it back to the house. George, Jack, and Joseph would stay in the woods hunting for game while Henry helped to return our harvest.

Our party traipsed back through the snow, Bess trailing behind with the effort. Once back, we left the tree in the courtyard and went inside. We headed for the kitchens, where we all warmed ourselves. Kicking our sodden boots off, we raced upstairs to remove the heavy skirts.

Tansy sat busy sewing at the table in the evenings. Wriggling against the heavy fabric of my skirts, I imagined trying on the less restrictive trousers. Even riding would be much easier; the weight of the material is nothing compared to skirts. But for now, I would have to settle for my less formal attire.

Hearing gunshots in the woods, I grew excited at the

prospect of a celebration meal. But for now, I had work to do. We had promised an exchange of gifts the next day. None of us had much to give, but we each planned as best we could. I stroked the top of my jewellery box, set to raid it for my new sisters. I searched through the green leather-covered mini chest. Each velvet-lined drawer held glittering gems and family heirlooms.

I would keep my emerald as my mother had given it to me, and I wanted to pass it down to my child. I pulled out a gold brooch with delicate leaves entwined around a ruby. It would be perfect for Lettie. Next, I found a silver and amber ring for Tansy and a pair of drop earrings with pearls for Flora. Grace would have my silver bracelet, a simple but elegant piece that had dangled on my own wrist as a child. Bess would have my gold and ruby ring. It was brash and over the top, but she deserved it. I found a silver locket on a long silver chain and imagined it would be perfect for Lenora. It once belonged to my mother, and I could still picture it dangling from her neck as she bent over to pick me up.

Looking for something to conceal the gifts, I picked out my wedding dress. No more special than any other garment, my fingers brushed its surface. There were no precious memories. Not hesitating to tear the cream silk, satisfied, I wrapped each trinket in a piece of material ripped from my wedding dress. I took some small scissors to the lace to make the ribbon.

Next for the gentlemen, not having anything I considered suitable, I went to James' dressing room. I took his two good smoking jackets, a pocket watch, and some silver cuff-links and wrapped them in the same fabric. I would bundle the rest of his clothing and give it to the church to distribute amongst the poor.

We spent the evening decorating the house and then ate the grouse from the woods. The next day, there would be a stag for the Christmas feast.

We walked through the snow, huddled in our thickest cloaks against the winds. I hesitated in the graveyard, laying wreaths of holly on my mother's and father's tombs. Briefly, I passed by James' grave, more for the onlooker's benefit than my own. Not wanting to become the source of gossip, I made it look like the part. Bowing my head and moving my shoulders as if weeping, like a good little widow. I looked up, brushing my cheek as if wiping tears to catch the eye of the clergyman who had been watching me closely.

The chapel was so full it was fit to burst; every pew was occupied, and there was standing room only. The farmers are all praying for a good year to come. Mothers prayed for sick children and children for food and fun. The people all glowed with hope and wishes. I could feel the vibrations of their prayers as they moved through the air. The little whispers of energy escaped every person present. Even the clergyman shimmered with his prayers. The energy coming from him moved like waves that crashed against me. My hunger grew, and my body swayed with each fresh wave. I could feel the life inside me craving sustenance.

I deliberated on how I could harness this energy, unlike James, whose blood was spilt as I drained his life force. But if I took a little from everyone here, I could be rejuvenated while leaving them all alive.

I would not take from the coven's energy, as that would be taking the liberty of my friends, and it would be needed for our work. A little from each of the others in the congregation would suffice. I started by visualising all the threads of emotions and prayer that were circling the room. Rising into the vaulted ceiling. I reached out with my mind twirling the different colours around my will. Tangling them and pulling them towards me. I faced the ceiling and closed my eyes tight. I could see each one slither, wraiths writhing against me as if caught on a fishing line.

I reeled them in, twisting and turning my will with them. As they drew close, they resisted, but I yanked on them, hungry now, my will stronger than theirs. They were pulled into my chest, and as they were absorbed, I glowed. A thin white light started in my hands. I bunched them into fists to cover the light in my palms. Eventually, when the glow became fierce, I sat on them until every last prayer had been taken.

I looked towards Lenora, who was watching me. *Would she be ready to cover my actions if needed or to stop me?* My eyes were fiery red embers, which faded when I met hers. I smiled at her. We watched the others leave before we stood to go. Every person left as if in a daydream, but they all had peaceful looks on their faces as if they imagined their prayers were heard. Even the clergyman drifted by us.

Christmas morning, I woke late, and the others had left me to sleep. I had drifted so deep that I dreamed that I floated above the clouds. I tied myself with an imaginary cord to my bed, preventing me from drifting too far. There came a sensation of lightness, leaving all my cares with my body.

The house had Flora's aura. Her mark glowed in the timber window frames. Someone moved from within. I could not see who, but they were moving as if injured. I drifted to another window, hoping to catch a glimpse of a face, but it was too late; they were gone. I tried to resist the tug of my body, but I returned to it in time to wake. I brushed the sinking feeling away, thinking it was only a dream, and went to join the others.

My basket, laden with parcels, swung on my arm as we all gathered in the kitchen. The tantalising aromas of roasting meat and vegetables filled the air, heightening our anticipation. We greeted each other with warm hugs and settled around the table, our laughter echoing in the room. The table soon became a colourful mound of parcels, each one a promise of joy and surprise.

Tansy went first, handing out large brown paper gifts tied with string. Inside were the trousers she had been working on. Buttoned up each side of the front with short legs, finishing at the height of riding boots. The parcels also contained modified skirts with an opening at the front easily drawn across to conceal the trousers.

" They are able to be push to the sides to stride forward or ride unencumbered. Inside the skirts were sewn lots of pockets of different sizes. That would easily conceal any number of objects," she said.

We thanked her profusely, but I could see that Flora and Lenora would be harder to win over. Lettie and Henry begged forgiveness. Their presents were taking a little longer to make.

Bess, Lenora, Joseph, and Jack presented each of us with candles made with beeswax from the hives and scented with oils from our stores. Flora and Grace clutched pots of jam made from the fruit that filled the hedgerows. George gave each of us a small pie he had baked for our breakfast, decorated with a sugary crust in different patterns for each of us.

Finally, it was my turn to hand out my gifts. Everyone unwrapped the silk parcels and thanked me in turn. Seeing my friends wearing the presents made me happy as we sat down to eat a Christmas meal. The house breathed a long, slow, imperceptible sigh, full of love and light. The dining table set with all the finest plates on a tinge of pink stained wood had never looked better.

Lenora appeared at the library's door. It was New Year's Day, and I had spent all morning huddled up with the books. She looked concerned. Her forehead creased.

"I didn't want to give this to you while we were celebrating Yule," she said, handing me a creased envelope.

"Another letter came?" I quizzed her.

"Yes, but this is one you will want to read," I moved to stand. "No, stay seated. You will need to be."

This worried me. "Stay while I do, won't you?"

"Of course."

She laid her hand on my shoulder before sitting next to me on a footstool so that she could draw in close. I opened the pale blue paper and pulled the letter out. In matching pale blue, the black letters curled over in perfect calligraphy.

My Dear Adio,

He had been helping as well? I looked towards Lenora, who nodded her head.

My Dear Adio,

I thought you memorised all there was to know of the prophecy. Did your friend Sabrett not tell you of his last encounter with a pretender?

No matter. As one of the keepers of knowledge, I will, of course, impart that which you wish to know. I am not fond of having this in writing, though I understand you need to continue your work. I request that you burn this once you have read it.

It is written that a child will be born to a vampire and a witch who can hold the sun. The Dhampir will have abilities we have not seen, and a new reign of the vampire witch will rise. They will bring with them a deity who will destroy Lilith, Sekhmet and the clans. They will destroy all who try to kill the child.

What I know is that it cannot be a simple Dhampir. Something else needs to intervene to make the prophecy come true. Many have tried to sire with a witch, and even fewer have managed. Only one other was able to hold the sun, and that union failed to produce the witch vampire we fear. The clans dealt with that child once we had tested its abilities.

We don't know what triggers the new breed; pages are missing from the old books. It could simply be the babbling of lunatics. The clans have considered it serious enough to make sure no one succeeds.

Yours forever
Huda

CHAPTER FOURTEEN
Snowdrops

Our commune's new freedoms allowed us all to practise our craft, free from the gaze of villagers or other onlookers. Every day became a day to learn and improve our talents.

As January came, Bess was struggling with the weight of her twins. Their kicks were now visible beneath her clothes. They wriggled, fighting each other for space to grow, and as they moved, they sapped her energy.

My sleep was fitful and filled with dreams. I often felt light as air leaving my body and rising above to look down on my sleeping form. I drifted out through the open window, past the swaying curtain. I perceived the sharp winter breeze as it moved over me, but I didn't feel the cold. The landscape below is laid out as if in a painting, perfect and sleeping. Only the animals moved, leaving tracks in the deep snow. I had spent nights floating over the little hill. Our rock seats in their circle were now mounds of snow, almost unrecognisable. The fire pit had long since been buried. I floated on, not wanting this feeling to end, and I came to a village I didn't recognise and a house that had echoes of Flora. A figure moved inside, but it was alien to this place, and its energy did not fit. The house pushed against the intruder. I moved around it, searching for a gap in the defences to get a better look, but the house snapped and sent me reeling back to my body awake once more in my own bed.

Lenora rushed about preparing everything for the birth. She sat with Bess daily, talking and practising breathing through the pain. I sat in on the lessons, hoping to feel more in control of my situation. Now, roughly five months along, I was showing, my belly now rounded, and my hips and back ached. My body struggled to support the new weight, and my feet and ankles swelled each evening. I had taken to soaking them in warm water in front of the fire.

As my child grew, so did my need for energy. I ate still like any living being, but it did not fulfil me as it once had. Food tasted the same, at least those I could stand to eat, but I craved more. A thirst grew with the child, a need for something greater that would sustain me more. The idea of consuming blood no longer disgusted me, but neither did I feel that I should. I only needed the energy it contained, and blood was the ultimate source. I knew, though, that my cravings were growing and my control slipping. If killing became the only way, then my willpower would crumble. For now, I needed to take a little energy at a time, helping me to resist the urge for more.

Lenora had become my midwife, and she had seen me struggling. With any other craving, she would have found food or drinks to sate the appetite. This was different, and we decided to tackle it as if she were teaching a witch how to use a power. After all, it was a power; tapping into it would help me control it.

Safer in the gardens than close to others, ensuring that no one in the house would be affected by my clumsy attempts. We left the warmth and headed out into the chill air. I would hate to have caused any harm to my friends; I recognised my first try in the chapel as luck, not judgement. We sat in the cold, our breath forming clouds in the air, wrapped in blankets to keep out the chill. Lenora insisted I start slowly, and it maddened me; I was all consumed with the need.

"Centre yourself," she would say, her eyes closed, cross-legged on the big rug Jack had carried out.

I sat and tried to focus.

"No. I can hear your breathing. It's short." She demonstrated breathing in and out in quick bursts. "Slow down, breathe in deep until you can feel it in the pit of your stomach." she jabbed me roughly below my ribs.

"Ouch, you've got bony fingers," I complained.

"Ah, quit your moaning and get on with it. That's better. In through the nose, hold a little, and out through the mouth."

I could feel how my body changed with my breathing. Almost light-headed, as if I had been starving myself of oxygen before. My muscles fizzed.

"This is useful in birth as well, remember it."

I nodded as I continued to breathe in and out, in and out.

"Practise that every day." she moved swiftly for someone her age as she got to her feet.

"What? Aren't we practising?"

"We are; I will return in a few days to see how your breathing is going."

I was flabbergasted as she strode off into the warmth of the house, leaving me to sit on a rug on the frost-covered grass. I spent the rest of the afternoon huddled in my blankets. Even then, my toes were frozen. I held myself as I shivered, chilled to the bone by the time I hobbled indoors, my feet uncooperative. Food waited for me, but Lenora was nowhere to be seen. Good job, too, as I may have let her know how angry I had grown. Cold and annoyed, I ate and headed to bed, glad to be wrapped up in my covers.

I headed out to my rug again. This time, I took extra thick socks to layer on my feet, fearing I would lose my toes to frostbite otherwise. I looked around the bare garden, my gaze falling on the dead leaves and decay. Usually, the garden's abundance grew full of hope and food for the house. But in these months, it seemed like nothing was alive. Nothing moved to be harmed or to provide me with the energy I sought, either. Thinking we could move on once I had my breathing under control, I closed my eyes and practised. *How hard could it be?*

My attention dropped with each noise, and I was frustrated that I had to start again. My mind wandered with thoughts I could not control. They would pop into my head, disrupting my progress, and all I could do was start again. I grew impatient with myself as my anxiety grew. I berated myself for my lack of focus and willpower. *If I couldn't even control my breathing, how would I ever control my thirst?*

Trying once again, I started to notice my heartbeat in the now all-but-silent garden. I breathed in, hearing the slow thump, thump, thump in my ears. I concentrated on the rhythm of breathing: thump, thump, and hold, thump, thump, and out, thump, thump. As I did, I tapped my chest with my fingers as if drumming to the beat. The pace soothed me, and my heartbeat slowed. Separating it from the bird chatter and crickets helped me to hear these noises clearer. I could hear the faint crack of a branch in the woods and the breeze through the leaves. Our lives are busy and full of noise. By using the pace of my heartbeat, I started to judge the direction and speed things were going. Having my eyes closed helped to focus my mind. I was pulled from my meditation by a hand on my shoulder. Lenora, holding a lit lamp, had come to find me.

"You were missing at dinner. I see you're starting to appreciate the breathing."

The tip of my nose was cold as ice, and a wave of exhaustion crashed over me. I skipped food and went straight to bed. The next day, I rose before dawn, this time excited to see what I could do.

I snuck out to the garden, although it took a while to settle my mind, clearing the notions that danced and the voices that chattered excitedly within it. The excitement of what might be possible clouded my ability to clear my mind. I focused on the breeze that tugged at my hair.

I used the feeling to draw deep into myself. The dark behind my eyelids grew darker still, and I was weightless as I had been in my dream. Although I rooted to the spot with the rug soft on my legs, I breathed in thump, thump, thump and held it thump, thump, thump and out thump, thump, thump. I heard movement in the dead leaves that lay across the woodland floor. Concentrating on the spot, images began to appear to me.

The smallest of feelings were pushed from the corners of my mind, wriggling and jostling for position. My mind was separate and yet one at the same time. An image came, white and small but warm inside my food. I was wriggling next to my brothers and sisters, skin against skin and bone. Piles of us were wriggling and writhing around, consuming. I could not make out what it was we were all so excited about, so desperate to be within, all the other little bodies and me.

Then Soft paws, pit patting through the crunchy leaves. Fear as our dinner was threatened. Red fur covering a bushy tail that swung lightly as it stepped. Whiskers on a black nose, twitching, looking for scents. I moved from separate feelings to one strong, inquisitive one. Paws pushed against dead flesh, now unrecognisable, where maggots fell onto the ground. A nose wrinkled in disgust at the rotting smell and sought out something new instead. Padding on through, soft, light and hidden under brambles.

A flapping pulled me up into the treetops. Black eyes scanned the fox below. Head tilting to one side and then the next. A long beak grooming black feathers which turn green blue in the rising sun.

Terracotta clinked against Terracotta as a mouse scurried between a stack of pots. My mind was now drawn to the glasshouse, and then a familiar shape moved through the walls of the garden.

Old and slow-burning energy filled the garden like a smouldering fire, moving towards me until it was pulled from my grasp. My skin stung like I had been slapped, and my eyes springing open as Lenora came into view.

"Now, now, keep your hands off," she laughed as she sat. You're getting the hang of this, aren't you? Now, let's go deeper. Hold my hand, and I will follow, seeing what you see."

We sat opposite each other, holding hands and eyes closed.

We breathed together in thump, thump, thump, two hearts as one. Thump, thump, thump, primal drumming. I could hear a crackling stretching noise underneath the rug. I listened closer and recognised the sound to be the grass thawing in our combined warmth.

Then, earth moving, a grain at a time, as a worm slipped and tunnelled. Louder now as a mole caught it up, its teeth ripping and slurping it down.

"Try to use their energy," Lenora's voice cut through my mind, although she did not utter a word.

I focused first on the dying worm, feeling its life force fading. I grabbed hold of it with my mind. Like a piece of ribbon, I pulled on it, dragging it from the mangled body. It was tiny, no bigger than my thumbnail, and didn't represent much of a boost, but it wriggled and was warm. Energy is never-ending; death means it passes from one thing into another. An animal would consume another, and the energy from its prey would become part of it.

The energy was like tasting strawberries. Sweet and juicy. But if you concentrate on the parts of the flavour, there is an almost imperceptible acidity at the end. Without it, the strawberry wouldn't taste the same. All its components combine to make the fruit what it is. Energy has this kick that only comes at the very end. Using a little will leave you feeling as though something is missing. It leaves you wanting more, only in death that the acid kick comes, bringing with it the full glory of life. It made stopping like an ache that moved through your body, an addiction that held sway and fought you.

It was different in the chapel. There, so much energy flowed and was held in prayer and wishes. My appetite sated before the need for the kick at the end. In James' blood, I had tasted the acid kick. It was the end of life in full flow, making it harder to resist.

"Try to control the hunger," Lenora communicated again. "Look to the mole."

I found the mole tunnelling away, looking for its next prey. I held it with my mind, and it stopped tunnelling, sniffing the earth. I pulled at it, looking for a gap in its defences. No wound existed, and it did not pray or wish, making it hard to grasp its energy. It started to move off and I held it firmer, and it squeaked as if feeling the squeeze.

"Softly," Lenora commanded.

I pushed deeper, searching for an opening, jabbing at it as it squeaked, furious now at being stopped in its journey. There, anger. That's what I needed. I grabbed it, yanking on it, pulling hard. As I pulled, the angrier it got, feeding the ribbon of red out as if from a ball. I prodded again, pulling until the little creature flailed and screeched. As it grew fearful, the energy grew stronger, and the hunger took control. I pulled and jabbed and grinned as the creature came to the end of its fight. Its energy ebbed away, and with every kick or twist as it tried to break free, more energy escaped. It collapsed, exhausted, but I did not stop. I was within reach of that kick, that little acid taste on the tip of my tongue.

I could vaguely feel Lenora trying to get me to stop. She pulled at the side of my mind, a small voice, but I could not make out the words. Then a louder voice grabbed me and shook.

"Sekham!"

Sabrett stood over me. It was dark, and the moon glowed behind him, making it difficult to make out his face. I had dropped the mole, ripped from my trance. I sensed it was still alive, but only just.

"Your back," I said, through gritted teeth.

"I see you are greatly changed," he said, and I wasn't sure if this was good or bad.

"Come, let's go to the house!" Lenora broke the tension.

As we lifted the rug, a large circle of soft green grass appeared surrounding it. Where once there had been frost, there now bloomed snowdrops. Hundreds of little white flowers popped up and the ground was warm, as if the sun still shone.

My hands shook as I clasped them together to steady them. Sabrett sat opposite me in one of the high-backed dining chairs, the long wooden table and its pink-stained wood between us. I had, on purpose, chosen to sit with my husband's death in his view. I was unsure which direction my mood would take.

"Sekham, I did not know you would fall pregnant," He tried to assure me.

"But you were aware it was possible?"

"Yes, but it rarely happens. I wanted you to join me." He shifted his position.

"Become yours? And what about what I wanted?" I sat tall, my back straight and my hands clasped on the table in front of me.

"Don't you remember? You wanted to die." He pleaded, reaching for my hand.

He was correct, of course, I had "And now?"

"Now, I do not know what to do. In all honesty, I have only returned to you for one purpose," his eyes cast down to the floor.

"To kill me. This time forever?" I asked.

"Yes," The silence hung between us for longer than I was comfortable with.

"I won't let you," I stated.

His eyes widened, and he sat back, startled.

"You see this stain?" I let my fingers follow the grain of the wood. "This is what is left of the last man who tried." I smiled at him.

It was his turn to smile. "I like this new you. Your husband?" He leant forward and pointed at the stain. "Good. But that's not all that's different about you. Your abilities are growing. I saw that in the garden."

"I've been practising." I did not move; I did not want him

to think I was backing down.

"No. That's not it," he stood, moving around the table towards me, looking at me as if he expected the answer to present itself. Once he reached me, he leant and stared into my eyes.

"There's a glimmer of something else inside you. I can feel the child; it's strong, but so are you."

I stood, nearly knocking him backwards. I didn't want him to have the upper hand. I moved my hair to one side, revealing the scar.

"I had a visit from a friend of yours."

He stepped back. Staring at the scar in the candlelight. His teeth appeared from his lips, larger and angrier than I had ever seen them.

"What happened?" His voice was guttural and low.

"Nikola Alilovic. I believe the message was that you should have taken me when you had the chance." I crossed my arms, sarcasm dripping from my words.

Sabrett moved so fast that I didn't know his position had changed until he had me by the hair.

He bent me backwards over the table, his teeth moments from ripping my throat out. But he hesitated.

"You're his?"

"So he thinks." I managed. "That's not my plan, though." He released me. "I know about the prophecy."

"It's the only reason I was sent back," he said.

I struggled up onto my elbows and pushed myself into a sitting position. "If I have this right, I'm a living vampire with a Dhampir inside me. Correct? I have new abilities and hunger, but I don't need to survive on blood. Yet. Nikola will return to turn me on my deathbed in roughly ten years." he nodded. "This gives me ten years to raise our child. And, in that time, we can find a cure for me?"

"None is known."

"As far as I can tell, this is all new to everyone. We don't know anything. What if you turned me before then?" I suggested.

"We have no idea if that would kill you. No one has mixed Strigoi Vui and Morio blood. The clans will kill the child and you the night it is born, if I do not before then."

I stepped back. "Are you going to try?"

"The child is prophesied to destroy all I am and all my kind."

"What if the prophecy is not true? We need to give our child a chance to grow. Parents can influence what a child becomes." I held my stomach, feeling the flutter of tiny movements.

"I have killed others for less."

"But you did not want to go through eternity with them." I stepped forward. "And I have never wanted to give my life to anyone else."

I brushed his hair away from his face and kissed his cheek. "Together, we could be strong enough."

He wrapped his arms around me and held my head as he kissed me. His teeth scratched my lips, drawing a little blood. He licked at it.

"Witch," he said, smiling at me.

Sabrett spent the days in the tower room, its windows now permanently boarded up. The sun was barred from entering whilst he rested. I spent my days practising my craft, but as February drew to a close, Bess's labour started, and the house became busy. We had set up a birthing bed in her room, and Lenora ordered Tansy to supply plenty of hot water. Jack paced about the house, going from chewing at his fingers to barking orders. Flora assisted Lenora in fetching towels and clean clothes for Bess.

The labour was long; her first child and twins added danger to her life, and we acknowledged this could all end in disaster. A day passed as her pains came and went. On day two, we heard her cries echo around the house, and Grace prayed to any god who would listen. But it was when her cries grew less that I worried most. I had avoided going to her, scared about seeing what was in store for myself. She had been my friend, and she needed me. I opened the door to find Lenora listening to her stomach. Flora dashed past. Bess lay covered in sweat, her nightdress soaked through.

"Here, Jane!" Lenora commanded me, "I need you to push hard when I say."

"Where? I don't know what I'm doing."

"We need to turn the child; it's a breach. Bottom first. Haven't you been listening?"

I flung myself down at the side of the bed, placing my hands on Bess's stomach. The skin was tight and stretched as though it might burst.

"Now, when I say you push. You need to push down and round, and I will push up and round."

"I'm ready," I gulped.

"Now." Lenora started to move her hand in strokes as if spinning the baby. Bess screamed in pain. "Don't stop!" Lenora yelled over her.

We kept pushing, and I could feel limbs moving beneath the thin skin. Blood pooled on the bed. Finally, Lenora commanded us to stop. She listened again.

"Now, Bess, push."

Bess bore down, and at first, there was no noise, then a low guttural moan started rising into a grunt as she pushed hard. She stopped and panted, and I mopped her forehead.

"Again, push!" Lenora yelled.

Bess pushed again. Lenora pulled, and together, they brought a screaming bundle into the world. She handed it to Flora, who took it to one side and cleaned it up.

"It's a girl," she shouted.

"No time to stop now. There's another that needs to be born."

"I can't," Bess sounded exhausted.

"There is no choice in this. Push," Lenora held her hand. "Use my strength."

Bess lifted herself, using Lenora's hand, and pushed with all her strength.

"I see it," I shouted.

Another two pushes, and Bess collapsed, but her child was wriggling on the bedclothes. Once Lenora cut it free, I picked it up and took it to Flora for her to clean. She handed me the baby girl, and I took her to Bess. Flora joined me at my side and handed over another clean baby. "It's a boy," she said. Tears streamed down Lenora's face as she wept with joy. Her child had survived the birth, and she had two grandchildren to love.

CHAPTER FIFTEEN
Destroying Angel

Jack and Bess were the proudest parents I had ever seen. He would say the children favoured their mother's black hair and his own strength. Bess needed to recover for weeks and didn't leave her bed for the first two. Childbirth had been hard. She had been lucky that her mother was knowledgeable and able to get her through the worst of it. Many others have not been so lucky, and their graves sat as a testament to that. Once recovered, we took them to the chapel to be baptised. Their names would appear in the parish records this way, as well as doing much to keep our secrets. Death could come at any time for infants as much as their mothers.

The clergyman eyed our gathering with suspicion and reluctantly completed the service. Later, we held our own ceremony, blessing the new lives. Bess and Jack chose Gabriel, or Gabe for short, for their son. The girl's name was Phoebe.

Sabrett had stayed away for the chapel service, but joined us in our celebration. We held the naming ceremony on our hill. As the wriggling children mewed and cooed, birds flew overhead. Cawing as the last of the sun disappeared.

Jack lit the fire, and we all gathered around. Flora offered the names of the children to the sacred place and the ancestors. She affirmed the parents' union and their commitment to the children. Bess beamed with pride, and Jack's face set, his jaw tight with concentration. He took his responsibility seriously. Sabrett appeared next to me and took my hand in his.

I smiled up at him, and the heat started. It was a warm glow in my palm. I mistook it for the heat between us as his palm pressed against mine. Of course, his hand held no heat. Once the ceremony had finished, we headed down the hill towards the house.

Chatting amongst ourselves, but the heat was growing. Sabrett's hand twitched. Then, the uncontrollable urge, as I saw swirling energy around our gathered crowd. This many people and the new life was a chaotic spin of colours and hope. My hunger grew, and my growing child stirred. It hadn't hurt the congregation at the church. *A little from each, nothing more.* I tried to resist, but the urge gnawed at me.

I held Sabrett's hand tighter, trying to refrain. But as I did, the urgent hunger reached out and took me. It wrapped a little of the hope around and pulled it into me. I could feel the energy again. *My lessons would have to pay off this time?* I let it happen; a warm feeling of pure joy seeped through the cold night air. It warmed my heart, and my hand glowed. My fingers tightened as I concentrated on taking small amounts. Trying not to give myself away. Lenora's head tilted as if she could sense something, and I held my breath.

I could feel Sabrett's fingers crushed into mine, but it did not distract me from the task. The sudden burst of light lit up the night, and Sabrett screeched like an animal.

I jumped to the side, releasing his hand; shaken from my meditation by the noise, I saw him clasping his hand. A thin wisp of grey smoke rose from it. His dead flesh burnt, and a hole appeared in the centre of his palm. His teeth barred, and he crouched as if trying to escape me. The rest of our merry band stood watching, horrified at the scene. The flash of light and cry brought their attention to my mistake.

"I'm sorry." I held my hands to my face, covering my mouth and drawing up my shoulders.

I was mortified that I would betray my friends in their special moments. But I had lost a little of everyone's trust. I could see it in their eyes.

Sabrett spent every night helping us secure the house against the oncoming attack. His hand healed in time, with the help of his own blood as medicine. It grew back, but the ragged edges betrayed my unintentional damage. My hunger had grown unbearable, and I grew desperate to find a way to be sated. My sanity was slipping, and part of me considered which friend would have the biggest supply.

I began to distance myself from the rest of the group; isolation was the only safety I could provide them. My anger at my weakness grew as well. I would stalk the woods, pacing back and forth. I clawed at my own hands and arms; the pain helping me to control the urges. My blood dripped down them, falling to the floor in a gory path. One night, Sabrett found me this way. He followed the trail of red drips and discovered me sitting on a tree trunk, rocking back and forth.

"Sekham," he called to warn me of his approach.

I was wild-eyed, driven mad by hunger. I could not be satisfied with food alone anymore.

"Help me," I begged. "How can I live amongst my

friends when all I want to do is consume their power?"

"There is only one way, but I'm not sure you're ready."

"I'm ready. I need to feed before I regret my actions." I leapt up and grabbed his coat.

"You don't know what you ask." he took one step back.

"It's killing me. I'm afraid of what I will do."

He sighed, "Then follow me."

We walked for miles until I grew fearful I would drop. Heavy now and slow, it took me longer than it would have before. Only my hunger kept me going. Sabrett came to a stop at the gate to a farm. A little light flickered in the window of the farmhouse. We crept closer, peering through the windows. Two children were inside, with backs towards us, heads bowed. They then moved to climb the stairs. The two men sat at the table. We stepped away from the light, and Sabrett caught me by the chin, his hand holding my gaze on him.

"I know this is going to be hard, but I've been keeping a few choices of victims for you."

"Victims?"

"You're a hunter now; if you don't feed, you will destroy your friends."

"But I don't need blood." My forehead furrowed.

"No, but you need life. Energy from others, especially while you support the child."

"I was convinced I could control it until I became like you."

"No, your curse is different. I want you to know it's possible to do good. It will make it easier. These men hurt the children. Their mother is long dead, and the father and uncle abuse them. You could help the children. Follow my lead."

He took my hand and returned to the house, knocking on the door.

A large man with a huge beard answered, "What time do you call this?"

Sabrett stood at his full height and caught the man's eyes. They followed his every move. "My wife needs to rest; let us in," he crooned.

The man caught in his gaze, muttered a greeting and bid us enter. The second man stood up from the table.

"What are you doing, brother?" he watched as his brother returned to his seat, not answering.

The second man turned to Sabrett, who reached him in seconds, wrenching his neck. I heard it snap. Then he bit and watched me as he drank, draining the farmer as his brother sat paralysed. His face turned from the man I knew to a creature of hunger and base instinct. His cheeks were hollow as if in death, and his eyes rolled to reveal them pooled in black. His wide mouth was now crammed full of pointed white teeth. Now covered in a red viscous liquid that hung in great lines of spittle between them. I was rooted to the spot, unsure what to do, filled with horror, but too hungry to fight the urge. I watched as the first man's limp corpse dropped to the floor. My whole body began to shake, and my teeth chattered against each other. Sabrett's eyes flashed, and he grinned, blood dripping from his lips.

"This time, you will feed." he held his hand out to me.

"I can't do what you did." I couldn't imagine my own mouth ripping into another's skin. The idea was sickening.

We heard a shuffle upstairs, and Sabrett turned to the seated man.

"Tell them to stay in their rooms." His black eyes focused on the man's brown ones.

"Children," the man called. "Stay upstairs until morning; do not come down."

He walked behind the man, who sat with the palms of his

hands resting in well-worn grooves. His fingers gripped the wooden arms as if he wanted to leap up. The man went to speak, but was silenced by a look from Sabrett. Sabrett bid me come closer, and with a fingernail, he sliced the throat of the man. His blood bubbled up and spilt out from the wound.

"Remember, this man has done unspeakable things," he said, standing behind the man.

I could hold back no longer. The call of the blood rang in my ears, and my skin crawled and twisted, urging me forward. I circled him, pulling the threads of life force from his body. Relishing every angry and fearful slip of energy. As the threads grew thin, I understood there was only one source left, and riding a wave of euphoria, I sat on the man's lap.

As if in an embrace, I licked at the wound and sensed the kick of death on the tip of my tongue. I reached out with my mind and pulled with all my strength at every last inch of life. I locked eyes with Sabrett as I drained the man, enjoying every moment of his death. I licked at the wound again, hoping to find drops of his essence in the fluid, but it was extinguished. I stood and kissed Sabrett, both of us red and bloody, but our senses heightened.

"Come, I want to show you the night." He took my hand but pulled his back again, hesitating, before returning it once more to mine.

Lighter now, butterflies of excitement built in my chest as we made our way across the fields. The moon shone silver and drenched us in a cool light. The heat started again; the glow rising inside, but I held it back for fear of hurting Sabrett. My soul and his were connected as never before, and we were joined now in death. I could feel people sleeping in their beds. Miles from where we stood. Visions of animals as they tripped along, hidden from the view of ordinary humans. Concealing this was no longer possible, nor would it be to pretend it wasn't happening anymore. It was part of me. I knew I had to tell the rest to give them a choice.

We met at the dining table. Papers were now strewn across the walls— designs for weapons and traps, along with plans of the estate. I called everyone there to let them know the full extent of what they had signed up for.

"You know, I love you all like sisters and brothers, of course. I know you know of the prophecy. Well, are you sure you want to risk your lives?" The others shifted their weight but said nothing.

"Sekham wants you all to know that she has changed, and she has killed." Sabrett put it bluntly, his arms crossed as he stood behind me.

"I can't control the hunger. I killed. But only so that I wouldn't hurt you," I reassured them as much as possible, toying with the steaming cup of tea before me.

"She will need to kill again," he butted in once more.

"No. I'm not sure I will. I need to learn to do this without killing."

"We sensed you would eventually," Tansy said.

"We have been preparing ourselves. We have considered what would happen if you turned against us," Bess added.

My eyes grew wide, and my heart broke, shocked and saddened, but if I had been in their position, I knew I would have done the same.

"We have been thinking about how we can allow you to live without the need for other people to die," Flora said, leaning heavily on the table.

"We haven't found a way yet, though," Tansy gave a short laugh. She sounded like she didn't think it was possible.

"You know that the clans are coming for my child. Are

you sure you want to get in the middle of this?" I decided to lay all the problems on the table.

"You forget, you're going to be giving birth to a vampire and a witch; it's as much one of us as them. It is our prophecy as well, and we claim it. We aren't going to be told who decides a witch's fate," Lenora spoke up.

"I'm old. I have nothing to lose, but I may send Grace away with the babies." Flora joined in.

Bess had a tear in her eye. "Jack will go with them, but I will stay here with my sisters."

"Have you thought this through?" I asked her, my eyebrows raised in questioning concern.

"Yes, It's our job to ensure we have a coven for them to return to. They are not going to tell me where they are going, ensuring I cannot give them up."

I went to her, hugging her close. "I'm so sorry," I said. She hugged me in return.

Tansy stepped forward. "The rest of us will stay. We have already drawn up plans for the defence of the house and grounds. You will be unable to defend yourself."

It had not occurred to me that I wouldn't be in a position to fight. They would attack me when I would be weakest whilst I gave birth, ready to take the child as soon as it came into the world.

"I will be your midwife, as I was with Bess." Lenora held my arm, her touch soft and comforting.

I couldn't help but feel both privileged and selfish all at once. Tansy held out another hot cup of tea to me. I breathed in the potent herbs, soothing my senses.

"Thank you".

Jack and Grace prepared to leave despite having a couple of months before the child was due. They wanted to put a considerable distance between the house and their place of safety. There was a network of witches who understood the situation. They would communicate between the parties to keep them safe. They would travel under aliases and crisscross their paths to throw the scent off.

Bess paced back and forth, packing and repacking their belongings. Clutching at her husband and bursting into tears at random moments. Inconsolable at the separation of her children and her husband. Lenora soothed her, reminding her she had been through tough times before. She was strong and would come out fighting.

Grace grew distraught at the separation from the only mother she had known. Begging to be allowed to fight, but to no avail, Flora stood firm, strong-willed, and resolute. All parted with tears flowing.

Bess's struggles did not end there; unable to feed her children, her breasts grew tender and hot with milk. I collected cabbage leaves and ran around after her, trying to make up for her sacrifices.

My stomach now grew so large I found moving difficult. I rubbed my belly as aches and pains ate at me before fetching and carrying water for Lettie. She was hard at work building ingenious contraptions. Her forge had become a hive of industry, employing the stable hands to help. Her husband put them to work on the various changes she had designed for the house while he worked on weapons. She had made her duties on the defences each of us would wear. Much needed to be done in the couple of months we had left.

As the days grew longer and the nights shorter, our time together dwindled. Sabrett, his voice filled with concern, tended to my wounds from the day's work, scolding me for pushing myself too hard. The hunger gnawed at us, forcing us to hunt together. Exhaustion weighed heavily on me. My eyelids drooped with weariness as I struggled to stay awake during the precious hours we had together.

Books of medieval weapons and tomes of spells mingled on the dining table. They sat amongst half-consumed cups of herbal tea. Everyone's clothes were grimy from work, and we lacked time to clean them. We sent messages to people we knew and trusted in the village to prepare to stay in their homes and ignore anything that happened at the estate. Instruction had been sent: if there was fire, let it burn. If there was noise, pretend as though you were deaf, or risk their own lives.

The horses were sent to temporary stables in other villages. The stable hands eventually left with them. I sent the other staff away, instructing one to take the dogs to safety. This left our estate manned only by us.

Our defences started one day in late April. Flora had sensed him, and warning signs had sprung up in her readings. Then she spotted him on her nighttime patrols of the boundary. We had planned a huge protection circle to surround the house and gardens as a first line of defence. We were spaced equally along the line of the circle, each with a quartz crystal point in our hands.

The crystals were begged and borrowed from local witches. The professor had provided many of them, which he had collected on his travels. Although he had wanted to join us, I did not want another life on my hands and refused him. We turned as one, well-practised in this spell. Calling to each of the elements and calling on the spirits to hold the line.

Usually, a salt line would be drawn, but we needed this to last. Fearing it would be washed away, we had to devise another solution. Metal bell shapes were placed where each of us stood. As we blessed the circle and imbued the crystals with our energy. We placed them beneath the bells. Lettie then hammered nails through prepared holes deep into the earth. Afterwards, we covered the bells with earth and twigs to disguise their existence.

When I had consumed enough energy, I could make out a faint light where the circle lay. I feared the force to come would be able to see it as well. We understood these were only going to last until one of the clans found the hiding places. We certainly couldn't rely on the circle completely. But if nothing else, it would provide an early warning system. We decided to taunt the spy further and held our Beltane celebration out in the gardens, in the open air. We danced and cavorted as if no threat existed. Our fire burnt bright, wine and food flowed, and we celebrated.

We wore elaborate headdresses of twigs, flowers, and jewels. Cobbled together and glinting in the firelight. Mother held daughter, husband held wife, and all the sisters held and empowered each other.

When our revelry had finished, Sabrett took me to our barn and presented me with a gift. I had been unable to leave the grounds again, my home becoming a prison once more. My hunger had been growing, and I knew that to save my friends, I would need to eat. He had brought me a meal, which was currently tied up against the brick wall. The man squirmed, as weak as a newborn, when we entered, his eyes never shifting from Sabrett.

"This time, you will draw the life force alone. I have already eaten."

Without hesitation, I took a knife from the shelves. Walking towards the man whose eyes locked on me. His feet scuffed against the floor as he pushed himself against the wall. He watched fearfully from his position. His hands were bound above his head, and his mouth gagged with cloth. I took the knife and nicked his neck next to two puncture marks. The blood trickled down. I gestured to Sabrett to join me, but he bade me eat. The acid tang came faster than I expected. His life was extinguished before I was satisfied.

"What had this one done?" I turned to face Sabrett.

"He was a thief."

"Are we punishing petty crimes now?" I stood, my eyes wide and fastened on him.

"We are doing what we must to survive, as any animal does."

This left a bitter taste in my mouth. "I like to think we were better than that."

He held me close. "If you want to survive, you will have to do worse. I can promise you that."

"Have you?" I asked.

"Many times, it's been my life or someone else. It's a choice you have to make."

"Nothing about that feels right." I pulled away from him.

"Right or wrong, it's going to happen. You don't understand the foe you stand against. They are ancient and have been hunting for longer than you have existed. They know what they want and how to get it. If you don't have the same belief, you won't get through this, and neither will your friends or your child."

I leaned on his chest, my head against him, and sighed as hope slipped from me. I sensed the man's life within him, his energy feeding my lover's ability to exist as it did mine. We were not so different now.

CHAPTER SIXTEEN
Snapdragon

Both clans were coming for us. The Strigoi didn't get involved in politics or prophecies. Preferring chaos, they allowed things to take their course. But the Lilith and Sekhmet clans made it their business. Sabrett explained how the clans worked, allowing us to plan our defence strategies.

A large piece of paper was hung on the wall, and he wrote the hierarchies in charcoal. The black burnt wood made clear the sheer scale of the force we were to expect.

"The descendants of Lilith are a cult-like following. Once turned, you are connected and part of a larger network. Men and women are equal, as Lilith would not have it otherwise." He explained as he drew. "It is maintained Lilith still lives, or all of us would be dead. A maker's dying causes the loss of his progeny. Within the sects are extremist zealots who are dedicated to finding Lilith. They call themselves Lilith's Chosen Children." He scrawled this on the paper. "The Chosen Children tended to keep their hands clean. They had sworn an oath not to partake of blood, but to keep themselves pure. This has driven most of them mad. The ones that weren't rambling lunatics were focused on finding the mother. They stay within the great library."

"The council is made up of the oldest or wisest leaders and representatives of each group within the clan." He wrote, council below 'chosen children.' "The clan's leader is Luther; he is what's known as a First. First, of his kind, he was created by Lilith and was loyal to her alone. Most have never met him, and if they do, it's most likely they have incurred his wrath." He wrote 'First' in large letters above 'chosen children.' "Other jobs exist within the clan, such as the Map makers. Their job is to discover new lands. They do the grunt work of the Chosen Children, finding clues or locations to investigate." He wrote Mapmakers and then Cleaners under them.

Sabrett explained that, as a mapmaker, he used wars and explorers to cover his identity. The Seven Years' War involved all the great powers of Europe: France, Austria, Saxony, Sweden, and Russia. They all aligned against their common enemies: Prussia, Hanover, and Great Britain. This allowed him to jump from one army to another, exploring and killing with ease.

The War of Independence was another opportunity to explore vast areas. The wars meant hunting in the open went relatively unnoticed. While exploring with people like the professor proved a little more complicated. But he wasn't the only map maker, and these would be formidable enemies. They were the cannon fodder, and most accepted their fate. He was unsure how many would be close enough to travel here.

"Enforcers, like the twins, keep clan law and will be ruthless in carrying out their duties. Smaller in number, but no less dangerous. All have the ability to turn people, but in this, the outcome would be only death." He squeezed Enforcers between the Chosen Children and Mapmakers. "The Cleaners would come in after the action and make sure the secret of their existence is kept." He turned back to the group. "Adio's clan believes the mother is Sekhmet, daughter of Ra, and a vengeful mother to her children. Members of both clans can be killed," he continued. "It's important to remember that as they come at you. Aim for the heart."

"I'm not sure I can," I said as Tansy handed me a bowl of soup. I stirred it as he talked.

"If nothing else, we can do enough damage that they will think twice," he said these words to reassure me. I looked around, and nobody was convinced. Their eyebrows raised and arms crossed.

"Start with small weapons, like holy water."

"Does that actually work?" Flora asked.

"It's not so much the water as the belief in it. Like spells, the belief will make things happen. Tell someone they are going to die enough times, and it has a powerful effect. It's better to get it from a large church with a lot of worshippers, but we will use what we can. If you believe that helps, then it will."

These were all things I never imagined I would need to know, and now I was writing little notes like a schoolchild.

"Crosses are the same. It's all about belief, if you have an amulet or symbol you treasure, use it. But the only surefire way is to put a stake through the heart and burn the body to ash."

Lettie stepped forward, "I have the perfect present for all of you."

Henry joined her with a black velvet curtain draped over outstretched arms. Lettie pulled the cover away dramatically. Flinging her arms in the air as if she were a magician revealing a trick. A pile of leather and metal clinked. She started to hand out the contraptions, strapping one on Bess to show us how it worked. The leather gauntlet covered the back of her forearm and hand, pulled tight by leather straps. I turned it over to reveal a heavy mechanism of gears and arms that grew out to the sides like a metal bird. Loading it with a bolt, tipped with a pointed metal arrowhead, no longer than a kitchen knife.

She pulled the mechanism back, using the cord that wound its way through the cogs. The cord was taut. She held Bess's arm straight. Holding her shoulders against her chest, she took Bess's finger to a hidden trigger and pulled. The little bolt flew straight and true, burying itself in the wall opposite, shattering plaster. We all caught our breath and then, as one, turned to Lettie, patting her on the back and excitedly pulling on our leather gauntlets.

"There's more, but I need time to finish it all," she said, her cheeks rosy and breathless with pride.

"We are going to need to practise," I said.

"Let's take them to the walled garden; at least we can't lose them there," Lenora added.

We spent the afternoon shooting at hay bales we had managed to drag from the stables. It was the perfect thing to distract Bess. We all fell about laughing at the countless missed targets and jumping for joy when we hit our goal. Piling Potatoes on top of each other, we aimed for smaller and smaller targets. Over the coming days, we will continue to practise. Eventually, even the worst of us could hit our target, for the most part.

Our attention turned to the house. Sabrett told us that, unless invited, they would not be able to enter, and none of us would invite them. We had to fortify each room. The first-floor rooms were left gloomy, with little to no light getting through the heavy boards. For the larger windows downstairs, we used cannibalised metal for the shutters. They would drop from the ceilings above at the touch of a button and cut off any entry. Henry had left arrow slits in each panel to allow us to shoot through them. The library, dining room and study had shutters and so still had daylight until the time came.

Smaller windows were roughly boarded up, leaving most of the house in the dark. This made Sabrett's days easier. Choosing where he spent his time instead of being captive in the tower. I hadn't been used to his company for a long time; we spent it talking as we prepared. I learned more about his family. Sabrett had been born on 19 March 1709 in Baltimore, Maryland, USA. His father, Moses, was 41; his mother, Florence, was 33, and they had five children before him. He had been turned at twenty-eight, and he had been married once before the twist of fate had separated him from his wife forever. This news made me jealous, and it took me back to James and his blonde in bed together. It surprised me that his past life would make me more angry at him than I wanted to admit.

His first wife had died in childbirth, and the child with her. It had come too early, and the doctor had been too far from the farm to save her. His death had not been unwelcome, as mine wouldn't have been when we first met. This is why he had decided to return to me, and the bet had been his way of giving me what he never had a choice.

I asked about his relationship with Nikola, perhaps to evoke the same jealousy I had for his dead wife. "Why am I caught up in his revenge?"

"I am truly sorry you got involved in that," he said, as he removed a large painting from the wall and handed it to me.

"Never mind that it's too late; I want to know what you

did?" I stood the painting against the staircase.

"Ah yes, did he tell you how innocent he was and how everything was my fault?" He feigned a sad face as he climbed down the ladder.

"He didn't say much, only that you caused him pain."

"That surprises me; he usually likes to wax lyrical on the story. Ah, well, then I will tell you. In life, he was criminally insane. His family history meant that he was already doomed to take his place with the Strigoi. His great-great-great-grandfather was the first of their kind, destroyed by his own neighbours. His great aunt is now acting as the first. Nikola robbed ten people over five years.

"After he held them at knifepoint, he would steal their belongings. Then, as they were confident they would be released, he would stab them to death, putting them down the town well. He decided this would be a clever way of hiding the bodies. But as the townsfolk started to get sick, his body count grew.

"The poisoned water spread the sickness. In the townsfolk's investigations, the bodies were discovered. They searched every house, and he had been sloppy in keeping tokens from each of them.

"One of those was a gold token with engravings. It was something I needed, as it held clues to Lilith's resting place in the engravings. As a relative of the Strigoi First, I couldn't directly access it. I may have left a few clues for the townsfolk, which led them to him. After he was arrested, I could take it from the jail with no problems. Well, that's where Nikola's troubles started. The Mazzatello was an execution used by the Papal States for the most loathsome crimes. It involved the infliction of head trauma using a poll axe.

"It was one of the most brutal methods of execution and

needed minimal skill by the executioner. They led him to a scaffold in the public square, accompanied by a priest, and on the platform stood a coffin.

"He pissed himself on seeing that coffin, but still refused the priest as his confessor. The priest prayed over him despite his profanity. The executioner swung the poll axe through the air several times. The wind created a parting of his hair as it passed. The momentum built, and it was brought down on his head with such force that it bounced up. The blood splattered the crowd. But still, he lived unconscious. Two more swings would be needed to finish the job. Each sounded more like wet washing bashed against the rocks. His skull is broken and dented, but as we know, unless you put a stake through the heart, there are no guarantees." He puffed his chest, standing with hands on hips, surprisingly pleased with himself.

"I understand now; he blames you for his execution. That's where his head wound came from. Doesn't that heal after you turn?"

"No. Only wounds inflicted after death will heal. Scars or wounds in life will stay, only things the blood doesn't recognise as part of you".

"What will happen when I die?"

"Either you will choose that we kill you before Nikola can return to claim you, or you will become Strigoi like him."

"But I don't want to look like him; they all look grotesque?"

"That is part of the Strigoi curse. They turn into the creatures that lurk at the corners of your eyes and in your nightmares. For them, the imperfections of life become exaggerated, becoming deformities." He saw my face. 'There is no point in lying to you."

The tears had started to flow, and I struck him on the

chest with one clenched fist. "Why didn't you turn me?"

"I was going to." He held his hands up.

"Well, you should have done it sooner," I shouted.

We had word from Jack as soon as they were boarding a ship, but he kept the destination from Bess. It would be weeks before she heard anything more from him, and she missed her family terribly. She had thrown herself into helping Lettie with the preparations. Tansy and George had been stocking the cupboards with as much food as they could find.

As it approached May, the gardens were not ready to produce summer vegetables. Only the winter crops were ready. They concentrated on storing smoked meats, cheese, flour, and preserves so we wouldn't go hungry in the battle.

The clergyman had grown impatient with me. He had stormed up to the house one day to demand I attend the services and encourage the village folk. As it was my duty to protect their souls. He showed his disdain for me and did not attempt courtesy by pointing his gnarled finger in my face. I sent him on his way with a flea in his ear. Something I'm sure only added to his hatred, but with no lord of the manor to complain to, he had no choice but to leave. Part of me acknowledged that it would not end there.

Tired from the encounter, I walked to the library and slumped in one of the chairs. The sun beat down outside, but a chill passed over me. I pulled a blanket from the chair beside me and curled up, falling asleep like that. As the sun hung heavy, moving towards the horizon, I woke, a pain tearing through me. I screamed out, not expecting the sharpness in my stomach. The muscles tightened across my belly, causing it to harden, and pain ripped through me again. I heard a crash outside. Hammering started at the door.

"Sekham, are you alright?"

It was Sabrett, but I couldn't figure out how he knew to come help. He had been in his tower at the far end of the house; there would be no way he could have heard me from there.

"I can't move; something's wrong," I yelled from the chair. The sun was low but not set.

"I'm coming in," Sabrett yelled

"No, you can't!"

He was next to me in a flash and lifted me from the chair as I screamed again. He carried me from the room; the skin bubbling and blistering on his face by the time we reached the door. He carried me upstairs and laid me on the bed. The sun was now down, and he went to fetch Lenora and Bess.

CHAPTER SEVENTEEN
Clary Sage

Lenora came racing in, breathless, closely followed by Bess.

"It's too early." I cried

"They have their own schedule, my dear try not to worry."

She moved her hands, feeling my stomach and listening. "Ah, we are progressing nicely." She picked up the teacup next to me, now only a few dregs remained, and sniffed at it. She whispered something to Bess, who ran out of the room.

"What's wrong? I demanded."

"Nothing with you, my dear, but if your child is coming, then so are they."

Flora joined us, carrying bottles and herbs ready for any eventuality. I contemplated what was to come, growing more afraid now. Before, foolishly, I imagined I could hold the child back or wield a weapon. But now I understood there would be no way I could defend myself while the pains were coming. Another started, and my panic rose. I tried to get to my feet.

"This can't happen, I won't let it."

"Don't be silly; what are you going to do to stop it? Put a cork in there. It's going to happen whether you like it or not."

The pain brought me back onto the bed again. The women went behind the bed, and in a long screech, it slid slowly across the floor to the middle of the room. Flora was circling me, spreading salt, whispering oaths, and casting a protection circle around the bed.

Lettie burst in wearing scale mail over her usual leather tunic. It Glittered in the candlelight, and she waited until the pain had passed.

"Here, I have something for you, and I know you won't want to wear it."

She began to wrap a chain mail choker around my neck. The metal wrapped around me was held heavy and unyielding; I fought her, and she won easily. I grew convinced it could drag me down, any extra weight too restrictive. As I rolled on the bed, clutching at the covers for support.

I heard the slide of metal as the heavy shutters fell downstairs. The others were following the plan and making the house secure. Lenora was the only one who would stay with me; everyone else had their own positions. We had been practising for weeks, but now I was unprepared.

George and Henry were stationed on the roof. They were armed with the two larger versions of the crossbow and large branches of the Ash tree sharpened into points.

Flora was positioned at the front door, ready to stop any assault. Bess was waiting at the top of the stairs in case they got that far. Lettie and Tansy occupied the towers, ready to shoot anything that came towards the house.

Sabrett had gone out into the grounds. He wanted to try to reason with the vampires of both clans, hoping to stop the attack.

The pain took hold again, and the world vanished around me, leaving me in the dark hole of my mind.

My stomach tightened, and the muscles moved in waves downward. I gritted my teeth and gripped the bed head as it passed. It was like a hot fork scraping my insides out.

"I don't think I can do this," I turned to Lenora in a lucid moment. "Make it stop, please." I was crying now, "I want Sabrett."

"He's no good to you here. He needs to try to stop them, you know that."

"But I'm not strong enough."

"You're stronger than you think."

I was not convinced by her words. The pain was too much to bear.

I heard it first, and my senses set on edge. It was like someone running a wet finger around a glass. A thin noise, shrill and threatening to shatter. Lenora peaked through the boards.

"What do you see?" I asked,

"They must be at the protection circle."

"Will it hold?"

"For a while," her voice trailed off. "Come on, let's see when this little one is joining us." She returned to my side and listened at my belly, "We have some time yet. It's on its way but on its own schedule."

"I want to see what's happening."

"You should stay here, it's safer."

"No, I want to see; I will come back here when I need to."

I was resolute, and she knew it, so taking my weight, she helped me to the window seat. I peered through the boards, across the roofs and gardens towards the far edge of the estate.

A thin glow had appeared. Following the line of the protection circle. Now and again, a burst of light shot across the dome as someone tried their luck. Little pings of light like fireflies hitting a wall. I could make out Sabrett's voice in a shout over the pings. Someone was answering him, but I could not hear their conversation. Pings of light began to move further from the voices and started to circle the house. Each failed in its task to enter, they tested the circle, looking for weakness.

The other voice grew angry, and I could hear a male shouting at Sabrett. They cursed his disloyalty and promised to make him suffer for the insolence. I recognised something familiar about the pitch and tone of the voice, but I couldn't place it. Another mass of light pings against the circle started on the opposite side. I guessed that the other clan had joined the fight. The pings had turned to lightning bolts as more and more force was applied. Then they spread out, moving around the circle, barely touching it to find its edges. Evenly spread out, they began hammering on the wall of protection. In rhythmic drumming, the circle wobbled as the tone increased. But still, it held. I could see Sabrett leap up a stable wall and head across the roofs towards George and Henry. His negotiations must have failed.

A pain increased in me again, but I was determined to know how this played out. I stayed put, much to Lenora's annoyance. I shrieked and clasped the window ledge; the pain running its course. One of the enemy below found a chink in our armour. Metal rang out as they threw themselves on the bell. Ripping it from the ground and revealing the crystal hidden below. As if taking their time, moments passed before shattering was heard. The circle faltered, cracking and falling. Allowing the unseen enemies to access the grounds.

The pain passed, and I looked again to see shadows moving. There were more than I had imagined, and I counted at least twenty in my view alone.

Another pain came like fire. This time, my waters spilt over the wooden window sill and trickled down the wall.

"Now, you must move to the bed," Lenora yelled.

I spotted a shape below as I stood, relying on Lenora's arm. I paused to squint into the dark, letting my eyes adjust until the blur became sharp. It was a man in a suit, his clothing slightly shabby, as if dragged through dirt. He was tall, and his thin skin hung from his bones, shining through the flesh.

"Lenora," my voice quivered. "It's James."

"That's not possible. He's dead," she replied.

"No, it's definitely him."

Behind him stood a pale, dark-haired vampire. Whose fingers pulled at invisible strings attached to James.

"I don't know how, but I would bet he has something to do with it."

As we walked to the bed, I heard the crossbows above firing their bolts and thuds as their targets fell. The bodies crashed against the roof with shrieks and curses, and the vampires did not die quietly. More shuddering and crashes told us that more vampires were there. Ready to take over from their fallen comrades.

Downstairs, metal clanged as the foe crashed at the shutters. Screeching and trying to reach through the arrow slits. Arrows, made from yew, hurtled through at the bodies beyond, and screeches threw up as they hit their mark. There was noise and death in every direction, and I prayed under my breath that we would all come out of this alive.

I made it to the bed in time for another pain; this time, the waves of muscle cramped so hard I had the urge to push. It was something I had meditated on; *how would I know when or how to push?* It came more naturally and instinctively than expected.

When Lenora told me to stop, the urge was so strong that I grew angry with her.

"What do you mean, stop? This is what I'm meant to do, isn't it?" I shouted.

"One moment," she sounded patient. I regretted being short with her, but the pains had a grip on me. "Hurry up, I shouted again."

"Now," she said, as calmly as ever.

"Aarrgghh," an animal sound broke free from me, and the noise in the house paused and continued once I stopped.

Panting between the pains, irrational, and out of control. The urge came again, and I pushed with all my might, but nothing was happening. Again, it came, and I pushed, this time a hard feeling pressed solidly against my pelvis. My bones creaked as if they would break and the skin would split. I panted, and this time, I resisted the urge.

"NO." I looked at Lenora. "It's going to tear its way out; I can't." Fear had taken over again.

"Now, listen to me, girl. You've faced worse. I've seen you battle your demons and win; this baby will be yours, and it will love you as you deserve. I'm proud of how far you've come, from the snivelling scared child to the warrior I see now."

She held me close, and I remembered my mother's hugs; these were as good a tonic as I needed. I braced myself once more and pushed with all my might.

The force of the push moved the solid object out into the world. I screamed. The pain of it breaking free from my body was worse than anything so far. I lay back, panting for breath, the echoes of the pain still reverberating around my body.

Each nerve stood to attention. Lenora swaddled the child as its lungs broke and it screamed at its arrival. I laughed at hearing the power in its cry. Relieved I no longer had to endure the birth. Sweat pouring from my brow and hair drenched, my face red with the effort.

The collar I wore had pressed marks on my skin as I had thrashed around. Lenora brought me the bundle, and I held it close. My breathing stopped, and my heartbeat thumped hard as I looked into the face of my newborn daughter. I couldn't help the smile that spread.

"Hello," I greeted her. "You don't know the trouble you've caused". Her nose wrinkled, and her wisps of wet red hair betrayed her lineage.

Screams sounded around the house. This time, I could hear them above my own as the battle raged around me. I heard a shout from the roof and clattering as one of the crossbows fell, shattering tiles as it went. It slipped past my window and crashed to the floor below. As it did, a scream fell with it, and then silence for a moment. Lenora opened the door a fraction to see what was happening.

Downstairs, I could hear Flora, "You." she yelled.

"I'm home," came the answer. I recognised James' voice immediately, even after the worms had their way. "Come in, lord and master and all of your friends," he shouted as if from a script.

"They are in." Lenora relayed from Bess as she stood guard at the top of the stairs.

Then Lenora screamed and ran from the room, "Bess".

I lost sight of everyone, alone now with a quietly sleeping baby in my arms. She didn't seem bothered at all by the surrounding chaos. I could hear metal clanking and crossbows firing. Something rolled down the stairs, falling heavily.

Never yours

The door to the bedroom was flung wide open. James stood facing the bed, his dead eyes misted over but still seeing.

"How?" I asked.

"Because of you, it's always because of you," he spat. Liquefying flesh dripping down his chin. "I should never have married you. Look what you've done." He lurched toward the bed.

Behind him appeared the vampire, still firmly at the controls.

"It was you. That's how they got in," I said.

"Well, look at you figuring it out. The clergyman was very helpful. He imagined something evil was happening here. Didn't he get a surprise when vampires showed up at his door?"

"You didn't have to like helping," I replied.

"Why wouldn't I? You killed me, you bitch!"

"I will kill you again before the night is over."

"This time, I welcome it. Look at me!" he looked over his decrepit body.

Behind the vampire appeared a tall shape, silhouetted against the light. His long hair hung past his shoulders. His voice sounded like gravel as he asked the first vampire to move aside.

As soon as he entered the light, I recognised him. My memory sent back what felt like forever: to the ball and hiding behind a curtain, listening to a conversation—a stolen moment I had not thought of since.

"You? You are the one they call first? You must be Luther," I said, pulling myself up my back as straight as I could in my bed.

"I see my reputation precedes me," he replied, moving closer.

His long black coat reminded me of pictures of death as he circled the bed.

"You're not what I expected," he said from behind me.

"You will have to excuse me. I've been a little too busy to dress for visitors," I said.

I was vulnerable, dressed only in a white shift covered with my blood and my neck armour.

"Well, your friends put up a good show for you."

"Are they safe?" I asked, afraid of the answer.

"Some are, for now."

"What have you done with them?"

"Let's not worry ourselves about that for now. We have more important things to discuss," he replied.

I could see the twins standing in the corridor behind, acting as bodyguards. Their clothes were blood-spattered, and my stomach wrenched at the sight.

"Hand me the child." he reached a bone white hand out towards me.

"Why would I do that?" I clung on a little tighter.

"Why, to protect what's left of your friends, of course."

I looked at my daughter, her pink skin still shiny, and my heart filled. I didn't take my eyes from her in case my resolve faltered.

"No, I can't." My voice was filled with sadness.

"So be it. Xanthe, Trillion, bring the prisoners."

I could see the twins moving in the dark beyond. Xanthe appeared first, dragging a bleeding Bess and throwing her into the corner of the room. She slumped against a wall. Trillion walked in, holding Lenora by the neck. Lenora's feet were dangling, and the toes barely touched the ground like a condemned woman. She made gurgling noises.

"We will start by killing this one," Luther spoke again.

He walked towards Lenora.

"No," I screamed, holding back the tears. "Please don't hurt them."

"The child." He held his hand out towards the bed, unfurling his fingers while the other one was clasped around Lenora's neck.

"No, don't give him your daughter. I'm old; I've lived my life," Lenora whispered.

"But…" I snivelled; the words would not come

Luther took Lenora from Trillion and turned her to face me. He stood behind her and looked me in the eye. Holding my stare, he moved her hair to one side.

"Please," I looked at Lenora, and she smiled at me.

Luther's teeth were sharp; the points made dents in the wrinkles on her neck while he paused. Then, pushed deep, the blood flowed freely, and he ripped into her throat. Her scream woke Bess, whose scream joined hers. Bess scrambled forward to save her mother, but Xanthe grabbed her by the hair. Flinging her back into the corner, where she curled into a ball consumed with pain.

I did not scream. I gritted my teeth and turned my eyes to Lenora's. I tried to hold on to her, looking into her eyes and holding her gaze as if I were holding her hand through the ordeal.

She only smiled at me. When he was done, he threw her body towards the bed. It landed, skidding through the circle of salt. Sensing the lowering of the protection ring, Luther was at my shoulder faster than I could react.

He whispered in my ear, "You should have saved your friends; we were always going to take the child."

He reached over and pulled my baby from my arms and was back by Trillion, who cackled. He held my daughter by her feet, holding her high enough to look at her eyes and hair.

"She looks like you, but she will never know you. If she

passes the tests, we will let her live; let that give you some comfort in what remains of your life. I smell the Strigoi in you. Once you are one of them, you won't care about her anymore."

My daughter started to cry as she dangled, her blanket falling from her naked body. Xanthe moved to her master's side as he handed her the baby, she took it in her arms.

Luther walked towards Bess.

"Shall we take her to care for the child?" He pointed at her prone body and asked me this question. "I will need to turn her. Of course, we can't have her trying to escape."

"Leave her alone!" I commanded.

There was a sensation of something on my hand, and while Luther looked over at Bess, I tried to see what it was. Lenora's fingers crept over the side of the bed into mine, reaching from the floor where she had landed.

"Take what's left of my energy." Her words were faint.

"You're alive," I whispered.

"No. I'm dead already, but you can save my daughter and yours. Take it," she pleaded.

"But I will kill you."

"Do it." She sounded desperate. "Before it's too late."

I recognised I had no choice, and I reached for her life force. It was easy to find, seeping out through the holes in her neck along with the blood. I let the hunger take over, absorbing me completely. Reaching further into Lenora and pulling and pulling harder than I had ever done before. Sucking all I could from her, I let my hand run through her blood and searched for any energy still there.

I gripped her hand as she slipped further to the floor. The acid kick of her death hit me full force. Lenora had a powerful life force. It had kept her going this long and was imbued with her magic. Given freely at this moment, it contained more power than any criminal. The heat rose. The glow in my hands had started, but this time, my eyes shone as well. I lifted from the bed, shedding blankets in my wake. Xanthe and Trillion called to Luther.

"Something's happening."

He stood holding Bess by the arm, wrenching her off the ground.

I could feel the power surging through me, clawing to break free. Lenora's life force urged me forward to protect her daughter. It was my turn to smile as it took hold of my mind.

A single thought.

"You took my child," came from my lips in an otherworldly voice I did not recognise.

He stood, his shoulder shook in laughter, confident in his own immortality. I moved towards him, drifting like a ghost, my hair flowing free like a fire's flames.

I could feel the presence of my ancestors. The lost sisters down the line who had been burnt for their powers. I heard the call of every woman who had died in childbirth, and power coursed through me as if from Hekate herself.

The souls gave me yet more strength, and I finally knew that this was what I had always been. James' corpse shifted nervously in the other corner, a meat puppet for his vampire master.

I looked at Bess, who was awake now and staring at me in disbelief. She nodded as I moved to stand in front of them. I rose slowly into the air, my toes dangling gently, brushing the carpet as I floated, looking him in the eye.

"Let her go!" I commanded.

His smile faded as doubt slipped across his face before he regained control once more.

"Girl, you don't know what you're messing around with."

"No, you're right. Shall we find out?" I tilted my head to one side, and my voice was filled with menace.

He threw Bess hard against the wall and started to run to Xanthe, who still cradled my daughter. As he ran, I screamed with rage and grabbed his arm. He stopped running and spun; the momentum sending him toppling to one side. He let a loud howl escape as he grabbed at his hand, which had burst into flame. My hand now glowed white hot, so bright I couldn't see my fingers.

My attention now turned to Xanthe, my eyes on her, and I released his arm.

"Give the child to Bess, or your sister is next." I was afraid I might burn my own daughter if I took her. She looked at her master, far more powerful than herself, lying howling on the floor.

She stepped around him, and I could see her fear of what might happen if she did as I asked. Changing her mind, she started to turn back to her sister.

I ran to Trillion and reached her before Xanthe's foot touched the ground. I held a hand close to her face. I could hear her skin sizzling as it started to dry out from the heat. A wisp of smoke curled up into the air.

"Stop." Xanthe pleaded, wincing, her eyes closing as if she, too, experienced the pain inflicted on her sister. "I will do it."

I moved my hand further from her face, but kept it close enough to take action if needed. Xanthe placed my child in Bess's arms as she lay on the floor and stepped back towards the door.

"Leave and take all your kind with you!"

Trillion and Xanthe took each of Luther's arms and dragged him through the door. As they went, Trillion stumbled, and Luther slumped, his arm crumbling to ash in her hands.

I went to Bess, still on fire, the flames flickering across the skin of my hands.

"I'm going to find the others; you stay here!"

She could only nod as the baby cried and snivelled in her arms. I ran from the room to find Flora. I stood at the top of the stairs and could see her in the middle of the hall floor. I heard movement behind me and turned to face James. I had forgotten he even existed as he hid in the shadows of the room. His face was creased with fear, but his master sent him hurtling towards me. His arms were outstretched as if to catch me up. In his desperation to escape, the vampire had acted rashly, and I stepped easily to one side.

I grabbed his flailing arms and threw him off the balcony. He gurgled as he flew through the air. As he fell, his face relaxed, as if pleased he would no longer have to participate. He hit the ground with a wet thud, his bones splitting apart and his organs spinning free from their skin cage.

I looked down at him, seeing the mess. I wrinkled my nose in disgust as the smell filled the air.

I turned to face the vampire necromancer, who had been in control. He must have been a weasel of a man in life, but now holding power, he used it to exact revenge on a world he never fit into. His shoulders were hunched around his ears, and his face was creased in wrinkles.

From below, we both heard, "Oh, come on." James had discovered he would know no rest.

With nothing left to control, the vampire ran down the stairs and out of the building. Flora coughed and sputtered below. Knowing she was alive, I turned to the stairs that led to the rooftop.

Pain seared through my thighs and stomach, but I could not stop until the danger had passed. My feet thudded up the wooden stairs, and at the top, the door was jammed. A sizeable wooden stake had been driven through the bottom, and blood ran down it, dripping onto the top step. Opening only enough to see that a body lay in front of it. I couldn't move it, no matter how much I pushed.

I stepped back, out of breath, unsure how to reach my friends. I looked at my hands, still glowing furiously in the dark. I pressed them against the top of the door. Two wooden panels made up the door, surrounded by a frame. If I could burn the top panel out, I could climb through. I concentrated on the door. It was harder and less instinctual than when I burnt Luther. It smouldered under my palms, and then the fire started. I controlled where it moved, making sure not to let it spread too far until I had a hole big enough to climb through.

I lifted the blood-stained shift and scrambled through. Scraping my thighs on rough, hot timber, though no marks were left on my skin. The body, pinned to the bottom of the door, was not one I recognised. In death, he looked like a teenager, his skin smooth and pale, like innocence lost.

I stepped over his corpse and moved across the slippery lead path. It glistened with blood. A red rain had fallen in the attack.

I found Henry slumped against his crossbow; no bolts were left for the weapon, and his legs were broken. A large tree stake lay next to them. Blood ran from the corner of his mouth.

"Lettie?" He asked.

"I haven't found her yet," I replied. "Where's George?"

He weakly lifted his hand and pointed to the edge of the roof. I stood and carefully made my way to peer over. Down in the stable yard below lay his cold body. My heart tore for Tansy.

Never yours

I promised to return for Henry, knowing he would be too heavy for me to move alone. Making my way back into the house, I headed for the closest tower room. Lettie burst forward as I approached the top of the stairs, aiming her crossbow at my head.

"It's me, stop," I said, holding my hands up to protect myself.

"Your hands are on fire!" She shrieked.

"It's alright. I'm controlling it. We have to find Tansy."

Lettie's tower room wall held evidence of the melee that had occurred, and bodies lay in a small pile behind her. She grabbed an axe that lay at her side. It was almost as tall as her, and the head was ornate, decorated in silver with intricate magical symbols. It dripped with blood, proving a formidable weapon.

Lettie followed me down the stairs, and we quickly found the door to the second tower room. Climbing the stairs, we could hear movement above—the scrape of feet on wood and gurgling. We exploded through the opening, finding Tansy pinned to a table by a huge vampire.

He was bigger still than Luther and made us pause while we considered how to tackle him. Tansy's face slipped from pale pink to blue as his hands kept the oxygen from her lungs. His teeth bared, ready to strike.

Lettie moved behind me; stepping out, she swung the axe in a perfect arc. It sang as it flew through the air; the wind rushing past its sharp blade. Finding its target and burying itself in the back of the vampire's neck, it beheaded him in one easy movement. The head rolled slowly off the shoulders and crashed to the floor. His jet-black hair and dark skin revealed him as one of the Egyptians. The body went limp and fell, releasing Tansy, who leapt to her feet, taking Lettie in a huge hug.

"Thank you, thank you," she cried.

I put my hand on her shoulder. She turned to look at me. I held back, ensuring the heat in my hands did not touch her, controlling the energy flow between us.

"I have bad news," I said.

"No, not George?" She must have seen it in my expression.

"I'm sorry," I held her, trying to find more words of comfort, but none came. Her body convulsed as the tears soaked my shoulder.

We escorted Tansy to find George's body, collecting a wounded Flora as we went. Lettie had gone to find her husband. I still hadn't found Sabrett, and I worried the vampires had taken him with them. George lay in a heap, his arms and legs twisted in a gory pose that caused Tansy to faint. Flora caught her and sat, with Tansy's head cradled in her lap, while I rearranged his body for when she woke. I found a horse blanket from the stables and covered him.

Flora bade me go to find Sabrett, and she sat on the hard ground. I was unsure how much longer Lenora's life force would keep me standing; the birth pains were taking their toll.

Vampire wounded were making their way away from the house, disappearing as fast as I saw them arrive. I was convinced I had seen Adio and followed where he had fled to. Finding my way through the stables in the dark with my palms, which still glowed enough to light my way.

Nothing moved, so I went to the walled gardens, which lay empty and still in the night air. I turned to leave, but a faint noise made me turn back towards the glasshouse. No light came from within, and I opened the door slowly in case another clan member came at me. Blood covered the floor, and I slipped on it. Catching the door frame for support and then following the drag marks further inside. I picked my way over the blood to follow the marks in the gravel. Long lines of blood moved towards the dark benches at the back.

I held my hands up using the magic Lenora gifted for light and made out a shape on the wooden surface. It did not move, and so I went faster towards it. I took a short intake of breath before it left my body. Sabrett lay on the wood. He was still, his hands and legs pinned with wooden stakes, hammered, sharp edges splintered through his limbs. He lay spreadeagled. From his throat to his stomach, he had been cut, a ragged edge made with a rusty garden scythe that lay at his side. Then, across the bottom of his soft belly, they had worked. Spreading his skin towards his hands, leaving his rib cage revealed, white shiny bone covered in liquid red. Blood dripped from the table in slow, congealing globules, and his face was turned toward the wall.

I felt my knees buckle, threatening to give up altogether. My heart broke; this final death took from me my hope. My friends lay broken and dead, and all because I had wanted to live. The light in me faded. And I grabbed the side of the bench to steady myself.

Sharp talons gripped my arm and spun me. I twisted as I fell and landed hard on top of Sabrett's body. Moisture coated my back as his blood began to soak through the shift's light material. I screamed, in part from the horror of lying inside the corpse of my lover and in part from the shock of the attack.

Standing over me was a beautiful woman. Her skin glowed like quartz in the moonlight, and her eyes were like daggers piercing my soul. Her short, ebony hair swept back from her face with clasps decorated with black feathers. Her sharp metal-tipped nails dug further into my arm, letting the blood spill.

"What is special about you?" She hissed.

"Nothing," I said. "In truth, I am nothing."

"Ugh, you are pathetic. Why Adio decided we should keep you alive, I don't know, but for some reason, he thinks you will fulfil the prophecy. He seems to think we have all misread it." She examined every inch of me.

A wet feeling brought my attention back to where my head lay. A faint flutter of movement startled me but I lay still. His heart still beat, although very weak. I wriggled, pulling at the arm caught up by her pointed fingers. Shaking as if to free it, her grip tightened again. The cold metal dug deeper, and the pain seared through my arm. The blood ran down it, trickling into a pool within Sabrett's chest. It ran across his ribs below me and out of sight of the woman. I wriggled one time too many, and she dragged me up and off his body. I could only hope it was enough. She pulled me up, my back and hair now caked in Sabrett's blood, as Adio burst through the door.

"My Queen," he stopped before her, kneeling. He lifted his head enough to take in the scene. "Dusana, Luther has fled."

"From this?" she shoved me forward.

"The sun witch burnt his arm, and it crumbled away. The twins left with him."

"Cowards. This is why Sekhmet will be victorious."

"Please, I believe this is Ra's doing. The prophecy needs to come to fruition. I can't tell you why yet, but I'm working on it. And it's a baby. There's plenty of time to finish what we started here tonight."

"What would stop this one trying to exact revenge?" She shook me again.

"She has been taken by Strigoi. She doesn't have long. Let that be her punishment." He took her other hand.

"I will hold you personally responsible." She dropped me and lifted Adio to a standing position with ease. "You may be my favourite, my pragma, but if you are wrong, you will cost us everything."

Her finger was beneath his chin, and the talon dragged, scratching, as it went. His blood glistened in the moonlight. Behind me, I heard faint sounds of movement.

"I promise, my love." Adio lifted his hand to her face and held her.

"I will give you until this one's death to find the proof that we should let the child live. If you do not, I will kill you with them," Dusana's voice cracked, but she was resolved in this matter.

"I know you will. I have accepted my fate and lived long enough to know that now is the time to stand by my convictions."

Then Sabrett shifted behind us. His hands were free of the stakes. The skin of his chest was now pulled back over his ribs, and the jagged edge of the cut was slowly sealing. My small amount of blood dripping from my arm had helped enough to get him this far.

"What have you done?" Dusana screamed at me as Adio pushed me away from Sabrett.

The glasshouse door flew open, and Luther and the twins came rushing in. Luther reached Sabrett and took his hand, pulling him up from the bench. Once Sabrett was standing, Luther bent his knee and fell onto the ground in front of him.

His head lolled forward. "I failed," he sputtered.

"You have sacrificed much," Sabrett said, "but all is not lost."

The twins glared at me, Trillion's face still smouldering, tiny wisps of smoke rising up. "Let us kill the witch."

"Not yet!" Sabrett commanded, holding his bloody hand,

palm out, in the air. The hole in it now healing.

Tansy appeared at the door holding a bundle of rags in her arms. At the sight of us all standing there, she stopped dead in her tracks. Her face grew pale and her eyes wide as they darted between me, Dusana, and Sabrett.

"Run!" I yelled.

But instead of running, she calmly walked to Sabrett and held out the rags. As he took the bundle, I heard small cries from within, which built into the wails of a newborn.

"Tansy, what have you done?" I asked, my heart skipping a beat. "Why did you bring her here?"

She smiled at me as she kissed Sabrett's face and then stepped behind him. The familiar shape of the silver lady pin, arms outstretched and wings spread, glinted on her shirt as she did.

"Sabrett, give me my daughter," I asked, holding out my hands towards him.

"Sekham, she is my daughter."

"What are you doing? Why?" my voice shook.

"I'm taking control of the prophecy. My daughter will not destroy all the clans, only the ones I command. All vampires will be loyal to me."

"I don't understand." My eyes stung with tears.

"I have been searching for a way to control the direction the prophecy took. Others tried before me. Through their failures, I learnt that not only did I need to sire a Dhampir with a witch—one that could harness the power of the sun—but she would also need to be willing."

"You did all of this for a child."

"Yes, a very special child. But little did I know that Nikola would be the key to taking a simple Dhampir to a child of prophecy."

"Tansy, you were my friend." I stepped forward, raising

my hand as if to strike her.

She took a step back. "You all looked down on me. Poor Tansy, her husband, is a cheat, and all she can do is cook. I want more. Stuck in this shitty village. I'm going to be a vampire witch." She stood taller than I had seen her, confident in her new future at Sabrett's side.

I turned to Adio, "Isn't Luther the First?"

"We have long suspected that Sabrett swapped places with Luther to protect his own identity. I'm only sorry I didn't find out about you sooner."

"Sabrett, you will not threaten my clan. I will not let you leave this place." Dusana commanded.

Sabrett laughed maniacally. "My Sekham saved me. That was your only chance to stop me. Come, we are leaving."

"You heard your master." Tansy aimed her disapproval at the twins.

They looked at each other. "Do you hear our mistress, sister?"

"I remember no mistress sister. We have lived longer than she has existed."

"You are right, of course, sister. She is but an insignificant insect. We will make her wish her father had cast her on the floorboards with the rest of his self-pollution."

The twins appeared on either side of Tansy. As she turned to leave, still smiling, they each fell upon her neck, ripping from either side. Her hands shot up, trying to staunch the flow of blood, but to no avail. She dropped to her knees next to Luther, who stood to escape the blood which flooded the ground beneath her.

Luther and the twins went to leave, but Adio darted forward. He charged Luther and slammed him against the wall. He fought against Adio, pummelling him with one fist while the stump of the other arm flailed; useless. Luther could not defend himself. Adio ripped a plank from the bench and slammed it through Luther's chest. Luther used his one arm, trying to pull the timber free. It was embedded too deep, and he screamed and thrashed as death took him.

The twins stood in the doorway, waiting for Sabrett, who stepped over Tansy to join them. Her face drained of all hope, and tears fell from the corners of her eyes, rolling down her milky white cheeks. Dusana ran at him, but he swerved to the side, and she fell headlong into the twins, knocking them through the door. Adio ran from the glasshouse to help Dusana, and I was left facing Sabrett.

"You could still come with me, you know. Ever since I saw you in London, I could tell you would be the one to fulfil the prophecy." He held out his hand to me.

"London? I looked at Sabrett and at the pin now on Tansy's body., realisation dawning. It was you. You walked straight into me and left me against the window while you spoke with the peeler."

"My darling, I have done far more than that. Your husband was cruel even without me, but he did not have the intelligence to seek out an alienist or to conjure screaming women in the dark. I whispered ideas in his ear while I entertained him in the city. Then I followed you here because you are special. I was angry that Nikola had tainted what was mine, but now I see he was another cog in the machine. Just a mosquito, needed for the prophecy and nothing more. You have always been special, and I want you. I need the child, but you, I want."

"I want my daughter."

"There's only one way that's going to happen," he said, holding his hand out towards me.

I hesitated before my hand reached out, and my feet dragged as I reluctantly started the walk towards him. As I reached his fingertips, the memories of their soft touch in an embrace broke my heart. I took them, and they curled my hand towards his palm. I stood in front of him, his green eyes sparkling. With my free hand, I brushed the hair from his face.

"I would have been yours forever," I said.

"You still can."

"I can't come with you," I said. "I have survived a cruel husband. I have survived your games, I have survived Nikola, and now I'm taking my daughter with me."

My hand let his hair fall again as I lay my palm stroking across his green eyes, blindfolding him. I screamed and dug deep for the remaining energy Lenora had gifted. Pulling everything I had from the depths, my hands burnt deeply. I harnessed every part of the sun holder's power, and the hand I held was now on fire at his side. He yanked at it, trying to break free and trying to keep hold of the child with his other arm. My other hand was still clasped over his face while his eyes, boiling and molten beneath my fingers, popped like an egg frying in the heat. I looked at my daughter's face as he held her still, and I did not relent. He screamed and writhed beneath the fire. His face contorted and sprang between the hollow-cheeked, gaping maul to man. And everything in between.

Releasing his ashen hand, I wrapped my arm around the bundle and pulled her quickly from his grasp. My hand was still across his face as it bubbled and cracked. The screaming stopped, and silence fell as his body crumpled to the floor. My daughter slept, and her face was peaceful and smooth.

Adio and Dusana appeared at the door.

"The twins escaped," Adio informed me.

"I'm tired," I said.

I held my daughter close, but my knees wobbled; the full

force of physical exertion hit my body like a hammer blow. I looked down at Sabrett's body as it lay on the gravel. It lay in the same spot where he had knocked me to the ground on the first night we met.

CHAPTER EIGHTEEN
Sundew

Lettie burst through the door, her breathing fast and her whole body trembling. She clapped her hands together, her cheeks flushed, as she beckoned us all to come see. It had been a month since the terrible night, and we were all taking time to heal.

We stood and dutifully marched behind her to find Henry in his chair in the hall. His legs had been broken and twisted in the fight. Since then, he had been in a crude wheelchair woven from wicker. It was high at the back, with a long base and a small wheel at the front. It was steered with a handlebar but pushed from behind, and he hated it. She went to his side, glowing with pride.

"Ready?" she said, making sure we were all gathered and could see.

She nodded at Henry, who turned in the chair, placing his feet on the floor one by one. He then rested his hands, one on the handlebar and the other on the high back of the chair, trusting his weight to them. Pushing himself into a standing position, Adio moved to help but was shooed away by Lettie.

He shook, moved one foot in front of the other, and walked. As he moved, metal clinked, strapped to the sides of his legs, hinged at the knee and attached to a plate under his shoe.

The contraption helped him to stay upright, and as he walked, it supported him.

"This is brilliant, Lettie." I gushed.

We had never imagined we would see him walk again, and confined to his bed or wheelchair, he had sunk into a depression. Without being able to walk, he could not see how he would make anything again. Working with his hands was what his life was about.

He moved cautiously into the sitting room from where we had all come. In the middle of the room sat a table full of baked goods. Little cakes topped with cherries. Scones are golden, filled with butter, and dripping with jam. Pastries that steamed sat next to tiny sandwiches. A teapot stewed next to the heap of food. Adio had been helping me learn how to add herbs and spices, and my cooking has improved dramatically.

Ever since the funerals, we have sat on large couches and armchairs and lounged. Eating and drinking, celebrating being alive.

Five funerals were held. Henry could not attend and stayed in bed, too broken to move. The bodies were stored in the old icehouse on the grounds until we could give them proper burials. Funerals were usually held as fast as possible to stop the stink of rot from affecting the loved ones. But we had no one to perform the service.

The day after the battle, Bess had gone to find the clergyman and organise the arrangements. Not finding him at his home, they had gone to the chapel. I only guess that he had interrupted James when he rose from the grave. They found him slumped against the door, his throat ripped open. We had written to the church for a new religious leader for the village.

We decided to conduct the funerals before he arrived in case he questioned the means of death. Flora held the service, still nursing the bump on her head. Tansy's parting gift, as she lay cradled in Flora's arms on the stable yard cobbles. We dug the graves by day, but the funerals were held under cover of darkness. Poor Lenora's death would be easy to explain. She was an old woman, but she was beloved by the village. Despite the rumours that surrounded her, everyone who needed help knew she was the one to turn to.

Bess and I had hugged tight to each other. Our hearts broke for the woman who was her mother and could easily have been mistaken for mine. Tears rolled down our cheeks and mingled with the mud and effort of digging her grave. We helped to lower her body, which was wrapped in white cloth. The shape of her face could be made out against the soft material. Lenora had taught me much and she had been there when I needed her. She had given her life for both our daughters, and I had taken it.

I had kept a little of the energy back from her death. Not wanting to part with that last part of her. Knowing I could never ask her advice or seek a warm shoulder when I needed one. Memories of my anger at her, leaving me in the walled garden. Now, regrets and wishes to change the past were pointless. Why hadn't I been more grateful, more affectionate, to a true friend? But regrets were too late now; there was no going back and no way to make it up to her. Bess' shoulders heaved with sobs. My shoulder was soaked with tears by the time we joined the others at Georges's graveside.

We threw Tansy's body in with him, no longer caring for

her as we once would have. We buried the clergyman with equal disregard. A rough hole in the ground and headstone was all that showed for his life.

And then James. We had gathered all the pieces and shovelled them into a horse blanket. He had grumbled the entire time; the necromancer had left in a hurry and forgotten to remove his spell. Or he had left him to torture me on purpose. I had been tempted to keep his head around; it was the most amusing he had ever been. But the idea of his rotting flesh oozing everywhere solidified the reasons to rebury my dead husband. Muffled moans and protests came from within the blanket, but we let the dirt fall, anyway.

Four fresh graves were all that was left of our friends and enemies. A sad procession started for home. I was glad of all the company, and the house was fit to burst now that Adio had joined our throng. Flora wrote to Jack to come home. Bess would have to wait as the letter would have to find him, and then a ship journey later, he would land on home soil.

We had walked in silence. Each reflected on our memories and did not attempt conversation. The only sound was the occasional burble made by the tiny girl wrapped in white. Being near the chapel had brought to mind a formal ceremony to welcome her here. Her birth had been blighted by the prophecy and deaths, and I had not yet decided on a suitable name. Maybe a joyful event was needed to help us all move on. When we returned to the house, I suggested this to a muted response. The days would pass before anyone was ready to celebrate anything.

Weeks passed, and there was news that Jack, Grace, and the children were headed home. Bess was frantic, preparing their room and trying to keep busy; the rest of us stayed out of her way. At last, the day came when the carriage and plodding horse came up the drive. It was piled high with more boxes than they had left with; Grace was barely hanging on. We went out to greet them in the morning sun. Grace ran to Flora, wrapping her arms around her, sobbing. The only mother she had was safe, and that's what kept her up at night. Jack enveloped Bess, and they stayed like that for an age before separating and going to the children.

Now sitting up by themselves in a box strapped to the cart. They gurgled and sucked at chubby fingers while their mother burst into tears at the sight of them. It turned out that Jack had travelled to Ireland with the professor. His ancestral home had provided them all with shelter and safety. The professor was very old now, and his health had deteriorated. Not wanting to travel, he had sent back half his library with Jack. Jack's sadness at leaving the professor alone at such a time was evident. But the professor had insisted, saying he would follow on when he was on the mend.

We hauled the boxes into the entrance and left them stacked where they landed. I took one book from the top of the pile and turned its dusty covers over in my hands. The dirt from travel had all but covered its title and I brushed it off onto the floor.

Divine Flora (Gods & Plants)
by
Professor Merryweather

Another of the professor's books has made it into my collection. I gladly held on to it, planning on filling my days between its covers. The book was thick, as if used as a scrapbook, and its pages were filled with added items of interest. Jack and Bess took the children to their room, but we didn't see them until the following afternoon.

I made piles of food, which we left outside their door before digging in ourselves. The dining room still held blood-splattered plans pinned to the walls alongside maps. The metal shutters are still in use at night in case of fresh attacks. New holes in the plaster, where arrows that missed their targets had lodged, were yet to be repaired. The blood-stained table now had new patches of pink wood grain. The stains from the bodies of the vampires that had died there. A huge scorch mark blackened the grass outside the window. Where we piled the vampire bodies and allowed the sun to finish our work.

It was Grace who mentioned a naming ceremony again, and this time, everyone had more of a stomach for it. She asked me where we would hold it.

"What about the glasshouse? That's where you met, isn't it?" We hadn't told her the whole story yet.

"A lot has happened in those glass walls, but no. I think our library will be perfect," I suggested.

"I bet I could make it look pretty." The now sixteen-year-old girl had a twinkle in her eye.

"Yes, you can decorate it if you like," I agreed.

Changing the subject, I told Adio about the professor, and his concern was evident. He decided that once the ceremony was over, he would go to Ireland and help. The old man had been such a help to us. Adio was older than Sabrett by 103 years, but there was no way you could have known. He brought spices with him that he had started to teach me about.

Grace volunteered to help him. They locked themselves away in the kitchen for the next three nights, preparing for a feast. Grace would briefly appear to run about. Taking items from the house and disappearing into the garden with them.

Jack and Bess were inseparable. Flora rested weary bones in front of fires that warmed the days and nights. Lettie and Henry practised walking, and eventually, he made it to his forge. Clumsily attempting some basic thatch hooks. The house was calm. I started the professor's book, which it turned out was not one he had published but a journal of his early travels. It had been a draft of a book. With sections about gods from different countries. Listing the plants they were associated with. But for the most part, it was a surprisingly exciting tale. Describing adventures and mysteries he had encountered along the way. It included a section on Sabrett, but I couldn't face it. Putting it to one side I kept it to read when I was ready to.

The days and nights passed, and Grace and Adio were eventually ready for us. As soon as we entered the library, the twinkling lights became a flood of candlelight. Lit by a myriad of chandeliers and candelabra, it shone like stars. She had made garlands of flowers and strung them in long arcs around the room. In the centre was a long table with flowers adorning the run down the middle. Petals were scattered at our feet, pushing them aside as we walked through a carpet of them to take our seats. The table was laid with pastries, cakes, strongly scented couscous, and roasted vegetables with herbs.

The smell made our mouths water, but the spices were unusual to our taste buds. We dipped in and out, trying all the different flavours. We loaded our plates high and celebrated in style. We toasted Grace's beautiful work and Adio for the food. Grace sat on the floor playing with Bess' son and daughter, and my little girl lay bundled next to them. The future of our little coven, all sitting together on a rug on the floor of our home.

And then, at last, we came to name my daughter. Joining Flora at the head of the table, I cradled her and then handed her over. Flora looked down at my little girl. She mumbled blessings before launching into a speech.

"All who are gathered here know of the difficult journey this little one has had in life. We know the sacrifices given by loved ones so that she could be with us. We honour their memory and look to the future and all it may hold. I have ruminated on this, and I see blood. But I also see light. The prophecy may be true or a part of the truth, but all here will play a part. This little one holds both the light and the dark. Her name will be Celeste. For the heavens, which hold both the sun and the moon, and Lena for Lenora, lost protecting her. Harris will be her surname, although she will be known as Bell to protect her further. Like her mother's late husband."

We all cheered, and little Celeste started to cry. I cradled her and took her back and went to sit in a wooden chair to feed her. I lifted my top as I had done many times now, and she latched on, sucking furiously. I looked down into her green eyes, her hair as bright as fire. I was conscious of love and a deep connection that grabbed hold of me the moment I saw her. The night had brought horror, loss and deception, but it had brought love and need with it, too.

It was easier than I imagined risking my own life and that of my friends for her. It was too easy and scared me, but I would do it all again in a heartbeat. If the prophecy was true, I may have to do it many times more. I grieved the loss of Sabrett. His love was a selfish one, a lie to get what he wanted.

Adio explained that although both had started as clans, the Lilith clan had become a cult. Sabrett was the leader, and he used the rest of the cult for his own ends and had hidden his identity. He had used the others to collect riches for him and to kill for him. Sabrett used the zealots. They were cover for finding treasures and assimilating new cultures and technologies. Once bound to the clan, vampires cannot leave, or they are hunted down and killed by the twins. Some had tried. They were made examples of in front of the clan. Luther and the twins were the only ones who were aware of Sabrett's true nature. Luther was the one who had grown up in Maryland and was killed by Sabrett. Sabrett had used Luther's story as his own, covering his true identity.

Adio had explained that Zane had tried to assassinate Luther. Zane had escaped and had taken with him a sun holder to try to bring about the prophecy. Sabrett thwarted his efforts. His plan was hatched to gain total control over all vampires. He decided he would be the one to make the prophecy real. Sabrett's body had disappeared, and we presumed the sun had burnt him to dust.

My future was uncertain. I had not known whether I would be strong enough to resist the lure of the Strigoi. Knowing that if I did, I would not care, leaving my friends and daughter without a backward glance. If I didn't, I would die just as my child still needed me to protect her. Would I shrivel with sickness, a burden to all around me? At a mere ten years old, Celeste would not be ready for what this life had to hand her.

Two vampire clans baying for blood and a coven who were all old or dead. How could she hope to survive into adulthood, and what would await her there? I spoke to Bess, who was sitting next to me, feeding her little girl. Two sharp points latched around my nipple. I winced with the pain as they stabbed into my breast, blood mixing with milk.

Addendum Tansy

A common bitter herb found across the British Isles, it has button-yellow flowers clustered on stems of ferny foliage. It can be used to treat parasitic and worm infestations of the gut. However, it is highly toxic, hallucinogenic, and damaging to the liver and kidneys. Pregnant women should steer clear, as it may bring about early contractions or the loss of a child.

Author Notes:

The official bit, S. Hall-Wood spent 18 years as a landscaper and garden designer, building her business from the ground up, starting at the kitchen table of a council house. Her passion for plants and design was deeply influenced by her mother, a Western herbalist, and her father, a Chinese herbalist, fostering a unique understanding of both horticulture and natural healing.

As a mother of five (two grown and flown), she skilfully balances her family life with her creative pursuits. While her writing experience has primarily focused on gardening articles and client briefs, she is now enthusiastically expanding into fiction, embracing the craft with dedication and passion.

Now the unofficial bit:

Hi thank you for reading my book and I genuinely hope you enjoy it. If you want to find me to interact I'm on social media as Shadowkraft or Shadowkraftbooks. I hope to see you there.

I am not a writer that grew up dreaming of publishing a book. These stories came to me while I was working and would not be quiet until I got them on paper. I have long adored periods dramas, historical fiction, and myths and legends. I thoroughly enjoyed mixing these up to give you my new Prophecy series, starting with book 1 Never Yours.

Book 2, Divine Flora, is now in editing and will be a prequel.

Trigger warnings:
Miscarriage
Grief and loss
Pregnancy
Domestic abuse
SA
Suicidal ideation and depression
Adult scenes
Death and violence

Printed in Great Britain
by Amazon